Half-Price Homicide

A DEAD-END JOB MYSTERY

Elaine Viets

AN OBSIDIAN MYSTERY

OBSIDIAN
Published by New American Library, a division of
Penguin Group (USA) Inc., 375 Hudson Street,
New York, New York 10014, USA
Penguin Group (Canada), 90 Eglinton Avenue East, Suite 700, Toronto,
Ontario M4P 2Y3, Canada (a division of Pearson Penguin Canada Inc.)
Penguin Books Ltd., 80 Strand, London WC2R 0RL, England
Penguin Ireland, 25 St. Stephen's Green, Dublin 2,
Ireland (a division of Penguin Books Ltd.)
Penguin Group (Australia), 250 Camberwell Road, Camberwell, Victoria 3124,
Australia (a division of Pearson Australia Group Pty. Ltd.)
Penguin Books India Pvt. Ltd., 11 Community Centre, Panchsheel Park,
New Delhi - 110 017, India
Penguin Group (NZ), 67 Apollo Drive, Rosedale, North Shore 0632,
New Zealand (a division of Pearson New Zealand Ltd.)
Penguin Books (South Africa) (Pty.) Ltd., 24 Sturdee Avenue,
Rosebank, Johannesburg 2196, South Africa

Penguin Books Ltd., Registered Offices:
80 Strand, London WC2R 0RL, England

First published by Obsidian, an imprint of New American Library,
a division of Penguin Group (USA) Inc.

First Printing, May 2010
10 9 8 7 6 5 4 3 2 1

OBSIDIAN and logo are trademarks of Penguin Group (USA) Inc.

LIBRARY OF CONGRESS CATALOGING-IN-PUBLICATION DATA:

Viets, Elaine, 1950–
    Half-price homicide: a dead-end job mystery/Elaine Viets.
        p. cm.
    "An Obsidian mystery."
    ISBN 978-0-451-22989-2
    1. Hawthorne, Helen (Fictitious character)—Fiction. 2. Fugitives from justice—Fiction. 3. Women
detectives—Florida—Fort Lauderdale—Fiction. 4. Consignment sale shops—Missouri—Saint Louis—
Fiction. 5. Saint Louis (Mo.)—Fiction. I. Title.
    PS3572.I325H35   2010
    813'.6—dc22   2009053835

Set in Bembo
Designed by Ginger Legato

Printed in the United States of America

For Sherry Schreiber, who said I would be amazed by what happens at designer consignment shops. You were right.

ACKNOWLEDGMENTS

There is no Snapdragon's Second Thoughts. It doesn't exist, nor does its clientele. Fort Lauderdale has lots of designer consignment shops. My personal favorite is Hibiscus Place Emporium, 1406 East Las Olas Boulevard. Special thanks to former owner Manny Lopez, Laurie Hooper, Chris Lopez and Josefina Rivas, who does the finest alterations in Fort Lauderdale. I did button shirts at Hibiscus Place, and dusted the stock, including those pineapples. Why those pineapples are so popular is a mystery I will never solve.

Special thanks to D. P. Lyle, MD, for helping me determine signs of death. His Writer's Forensics Blog (writersforensicsblog.wordpress. com) is recommended for all your forensic needs. Fred Powers of Powers Bowersox Associates, Inc., told me how to bury a body in a basement.

If you follow my account of body disposal and get caught, those mistakes are mine, not theirs.

Librarian Doris Ann Norris helped me plan a traditional Catholic funeral.

Steven Toth, of Mr. Entertainment and the Pookiesmackers, answered my questions about punk/indie bands, even after I admitted to liking the Dandy Warhols.

Thanks to the tax experts and lawyers who advised me on Helen's tangled financial and legal affairs, including M. Susan Carlson of Chackes, Carlson & Spritzer.

A special thank-you to editor Sandra Harding at NAL, her assistant Elizabeth Bistrow, Kara Cesare and Lindsay Nouis, and the NAL production staff. Thanks also to my long-suffering husband, Don Crinklaw, who eats the orange chips and butter-and-onion sandwiches like Phil does, and to my agent, David Hendin, who is always there when I need him.

Many other people helped me with this book, including Detective R. C. White, Fort Lauderdale Police Department (retired), Synae White and Rick McMahan, ATF special agent.

Special thanks to Valerie Cannata, Colby Cox, Jinny Gender, Karen Grace, Kay Gordy, Jack Klobnak, Kevin Lane, Robert Levine, Janet Smith and Carole Wantz, who could sell fur coats at a PETA convention.

Les Steinberg of Steinberg & Steinberg, LLC, is my expert on boys' toys, not to be confused with boy toys. Tom Barclay and Mary Lynn Reed told me how to get fired from radio.

Librarian Anne Watts lent me her cat, Thumbs, for the Dead-End Job series. Thanks again to the librarians at the St. Louis Public Library and Broward County Library. Yes, I could get information from the Internet, but I'm not smart enough to know what's solid and what's misleading. I need librarians for that.

Thanks also to my sister bloggers on The Lipstick Chronicles, for their advice and encouragement—Nancy Martin, Harley Jane Kozak, Sarah Strohmeyer, Lisa Daily and Kathy Sweeney. Read us at http://thelipstickchronicles.typepad.com/.

I'm also grateful to the many booksellers who hand-sell my work and encourage me.

Finally, any errors are my own. If you want to complain or, better yet, tell me what you like about the novel, please e-mail me at eviets@aol.com.

CHAPTER 1

"I need to see Vera right away," the pocket-sized blonde said. Her voice was a sweet whisper.

Helen Hawthorne could barely see the woman's curly head over the counter. She reminded Helen of a cream pie with her high-piled sugar white hair and lush curves. A size two, Helen estimated, based on her years in retail.

Cutie-pie was no tourist vacationing in Fort Lauderdale. She belonged on fashionable Las Olas Boulevard. But Helen figured Cutie-pie would pay full price for her skimpy white dress, not hunt used bargains at Snapdragon's Second Thoughts, the high-end clothing consignment store where Helen worked.

Cutie-pie dropped a stack of soiled men's shirts on the counter. They landed with a thud that told Helen extra starch wasn't what weighed them down. She hoped the dark red stain on the white shirt was ketchup.

"Do you have any dry cleaning for pickup?" Helen asked.

Cutie-pie looked around as though checking for spies, then said, "Tell Vera it's Angelina Jolie. It's urgent."

This Angelina wasn't bringing up babies with Brad Pitt. Vera gave all her prime clothing sources celebrity code names. She had to make sure the up-and-coming lawyers, businesswomen and social butterflies who bought her designer consignment didn't travel in the same circles as the sellers. Selling your barely worn clothes was a worse faux pas than sleeping with your friend's husband. As with adultery, the real sin was getting caught.

But Vera cleverly provided Cutie-pie and her selling sisters good excuses to come into the store. Snapdragon's also did first-rate dry cleaning and sold expensive knickknacks. Cutie-pie could say she was at Snapdragon's doing her wifely duty and dropping off hubby's shirts.

"She's in the back room," Helen said. "I'll get her."

"Hurry," the blonde said. "He can't know I'm here."

The sellers were always in a hurry. What if a friend came in to sell her castoffs? The shame would set off seismic shudders in their circle.

Helen didn't run through the narrow store, packed with high-priced clutter. But her long, loping stride covered several yards at a time. She cut through bins of dirty laundry, dodged a display of designer purses, tiptoed past the Waterford and powered through the consignment clothes racks. Versace, Gucci, True Religion and other designer names flashed by.

After booking nearly a block through this pricey obstacle course, Helen stopped at the print curtains leading to the office of Vera Salinda, Snapdragon's owner.

She could hear a man's voice say, "What do you think of me now? Do you love me?" His voice was the sort of whisper that made good women do naughty things.

Vera's was light and teasing. "Love you? Keep performing like this and I'll marry you."

Oops, Helen thought. I'm interrupting a private moment.

"Please, hurry!" Cutie-pie pleaded. Helen could hear her all the way in the back of the store.

Helen knocked on the doorjamb, and Vera said, "Come in."

Helen tried not to stare at the man next to Vera, but he was a fallen angel with a narrow waist, broad shoulders and artfully tousled golden hair. He seemed surrounded by sunshine. Or maybe it was a halo.

"This is Roger," Vera said.

"Who should be leaving," Roger said.

"No, don't go," Vera said. "I still need you. I'll be right back. Wait here." She pulled the print curtains shut. Helen and Vera stepped into a dressing room. Vera's sleek dark hair was like an ax blade. Her plump red lips looked like fresh blood. Her pearl white skin had an otherworldly glow in the underlit room.

"What?" she asked Helen.

"Angelina Jolie is here," Helen said. "She wants to see you. She says it's urgent."

"Hell's bells," Vera said. "Not her. The only thing worse would be Kate Winslet."

Vera hurried toward the front, adjusting her bloodred mouth into a scary smile. Tight black Versace jeans and a pink tank top showed off her gym-toned body.

Helen picked up the Windex and started cleaning the costume-jewelry case, where she could watch and listen, but not be noticed. Snapdragon's odd acoustics amplified voices.

"Chrissy Martlet, how are you?" Vera asked. She swung her cutting-edge hairstyle and leaned on the counter. Muscles rippled under her hot pink top.

"In a hurry," Chrissy said. Her sweet breathy voice was a breeze through a bakery. "I have something to show you."

She moved the soiled shirts to reveal a brown leopard-print purse with a Prada logo. "It's a pony-hair purse. Still has the original tags and the certificate of authenticity."

Pony hair, Helen thought. A purse made from a baby horse? She decided the material wasn't any creepier than calfskin.

Vera ran her fingers over the gold Prada logo, prodded the hairy purse with her long, bone white fingers and unzipped it. Helen saw the brown signature lining.

"It's the real deal," Vera said. "I can sell it for four ninety-five."

Chrissy went even whiter. "What? That means I'll only get half. Two hundred fifty dollars."

"Two forty-seven fifty," Vera corrected. "And that's if I sell it."

"I can't do anything with that kind of money," Chrissy said. Her sweet whisper changed to a thin vinegar whine. "That purse was three thousand dollars."

"It's like a car, Chrissy. Once you drive it off the lot, it loses its value. Leopard print is so last year." Vera's voice was harder than her fake nails.

"What about Tansey? Call her. She'll take it." Chrissy couldn't hide her desperation.

Chrissy must be a regular, Helen thought, if she knows the names of the women who buy her clothes.

"Tansey hasn't been buying," Vera said. "Her ad agency is laying off staff."

"Couldn't you give me a little more money? I have the tags *and* the receipt. Unlike some of your sources, I don't steal."

"Nobody cares about your receipt," Vera said.

"The police would." Chrissy returned to sweet-talking. "Please, Vera. You know me. My code name is—"

"I know your real identity, Angelina," Vera said, quickly cutting her off. "Hush. You never know who could walk in."

With a screech of brakes, a black BMW with a grille like a hungry mouth slid into the loading zone in front of the shop. The driver's door slammed. A man filled the shop door, blocking out the harsh August sun.

Chrissy looked frightened. "It's Danny," she whispered. "I think my husband followed me here. He's getting suspicious. That's why I asked your girl to hurry." Chrissy hastily dropped the soiled shirts back on top of the pony-hair purse.

Big didn't begin to describe Danny Martlet. He was dark and threatening as a thunderstorm. His black eyebrows were like low-hanging clouds. His eyes flashed with barely controlled anger. He wore a navy suit, but didn't sweat in the sweltering August heat.

"Chrissy, pumpkin, you're up early," he said. "It's not even noon." His smile showed sharp teeth that made Helen shudder.

"I'm taking your shirts in for laundering." Chrissy's voice trembled slightly. "Vera is the best dry cleaner in town. I want only the best for my hardworking man."

"Be sure and show her that ketchup stain on my white shirt," Danny said. He grabbed the Hugo Boss shirt, exposing the pony-hair purse.

"What's that?" he said.

"It's a purse," Chrissy said.

"I can see it's a purse. I also see that Gucci bag on your shoulder. Since when do you carry two purses? Are you trying to spend twice as much of my money?"

Helen heard him accent that "my."

"No. I must have picked it up by accident."

"Unless you were trying to sell it. This is a designer consignment shop. Was she bringing in that purse to sell, Vera?"

"I told her leopard print is so last season," Vera said.

"You didn't answer my question, Vera," Danny said. "You sell designer clothes on consignment and my wife is addicted to logos."

"So what if I am?" Chrissy exploded. "You want me to look better than all the other wives, but you won't give me any money."

"I don't trust you around cash, sweetie," Danny said. "It disappears at the touch of your little white fingers. But I let you shop as much as you want. You have unlimited credit at Neiman Marcus, Gucci, Prada and every other major shop from here to Miami."

"Did it ever occur to you I might want my own money?" Little Chrissy looked like a Chihuahua yapping at a Doberman.

"Then get off your lazy ass and make some," Danny said.

"I can't! I gave up my acting career when I married you."

"I hardly think a mattress commercial and a straight-to-DVD movie counts as an acting career," Danny said.

"I didn't have a chance to develop my art," Chrissy said.

Danny snorted. "The only acting you do is in the sack." He meanly mimicked a woman in the throes of pretend passion: " 'Oh, Danny, more. More. More.' More sex or more shopping, dear heart?"

Helen kept her head down and scrubbed the already-clean display case. This was way too much information. They were talking so loud, she felt like she was inside their argument.

Danny's diatribe was interrupted by the clip-clop of high heels. A jingle of bells signaled Snapdragon's door was opening. Vera slipped between the warring couple and said, "Continue your conversation elsewhere, please."

Danny dragged his wife by the arm to the back of the store.

There was a tiny tinkling sound in their wake. Helen found a woman's diamond Rolex wristwatch on the floor. Was it Chrissy's?

She heard a dressing room door slam. She waited, then knocked on the door. Chrissy and Danny were facing each other in the cramped space. Her face was bright red.

"Sorry to interrupt," Helen said. "Is this your watch, Chrissy?"

"Yes, thank you. The clasp is loose. That's my next errand." She absently fastened it on her wrist as her husband shut the door in Helen's face. She caught snatches of their argument over the store's low background music.

"What do you mean, am I cheating on you?" Danny said.

"I saw the way you stared at her last night!" Chrissy said.

"I wasn't looking at her designer dress, that's for sure."

"No, you were looking at her fake tits," Chrissy said. "Mine are real. So are my designer dresses. She wore a knockoff and everyone knew it."

"And none of the men cared," her husband taunted.

"You don't love me anymore," Chrissy said. "You want rid of me. That's why you're following me around. You want a divorce."

"Cut the melodrama," Danny said. "If I wanted you gone, your ass would be out the door. Gone. Over and out. Understand?"

CHAPTER 2

Helen didn't want to hear another ugly word. She moved toward the front to wipe down the sunglasses rack and tried to block out Danny and Chrissy's argument.

Vera turned up the background music a notch, then loudly welcomed her new customer. "Loretta Stranahan. How nice to see the best-dressed woman on the county board of commissioners."

Helen nearly dropped the spray bottle. Loretta could have been Chrissy's twin sister. Her blond hair was a shade or two yellower, but she was as small, creamy and curvy as Danny's wife. And as well dressed in black Moschino and polka-dot heels. She looked about thirty and dangerous. No one would ever call her "little Loretta."

"Broward County has lots of women commissioners," Loretta said. "But I like the competition. I came by to see if you got in more suits from Glenn Close."

"Sorry," Vera said. "Glenn hasn't made a delivery lately."

"Is she hanging on to her suits longer now?" Loretta asked.

"Even the rich have money problems," Vera said. "Men who

never noticed the price of laundry now want their shirts on hangers instead of in boxes. You know why? Shirts are seventy-five cents cheaper on hangers. Seventy-five cents! These are the same men who used to leave their change on the counter because it made holes in their pants pockets. Now they count every freaking penny."

"Please, let's not go there," Loretta said. "I've had endless meetings about budget cuts. With the picketers, postcard campaigns and petitions, I'm about to snap."

"Let me show you my new arrivals in the back," Vera said.

"Watch the store, Helen," Vera whispered. "I have to make sure Loretta doesn't run into Danny."

Loretta trailed Vera through the store. Helen could hear Vera say, "I have a Chanel suit in your size."

"Too expensive-looking," Loretta said. "My constituents will think I'm on the take."

"A black Ferragamo, then," Vera said. "That's rich-looking but not rich."

"Vera, honey, I have a hundred black suits. They all look alike."

"I'll find you a new blouse," Vera said. "A touch of color would freshen a suit. I have some hand-painted scarves. They'd look good on television."

"Well, I could look. That wouldn't cost anything." Loretta was weakening.

Helen heard a small surprised shriek. "Why, Danny," Loretta said. "You're the last person I expected to see here."

"I'm shopping with my wife," Danny the bully said. Helen saw no sign the couple had been arguing, except maybe Chrissy's slightly strained smile.

Helen watched the drama unfold in the overhead security mirror. Chrissy and Loretta had squared off. Chrissy's back was arched like an angry cat's. Danny loomed above the blondes like a dark mountain.

"That's right," Chrissy said. "He has a wife. I'm Mrs. Danny Martlet." She wrapped her arm protectively around Danny's.

"Trust me, honey, I'm not interested in your husband," Loretta said.

"Then why do you call him a hundred times a day?"

"It's business," Loretta said.

"Until midnight?" Chrissy asked.

"Important business. A little cream puff like you wouldn't understand."

"I'm not stupid!" Chrissy said. "I know about those three thousand new jobs Danny's project will bring to the city. And the house with the seven toilets. It's not exactly the House of the Seven Gables, is it?"

"Shut up!" Danny said, his voice dangerously low.

"Danny can't afford to get rid of me, can you?" Chrissy said. "He tells me everything."

"If he told you everything, he'd tell you why he spends so much time with me," Loretta said. "I can't see why you shop here, Chrissy. With all Danny's money, he could buy this store."

"Hey!" Danny said, stepping toward her. "I'll barely break even on the Orchid House project."

"Right," Loretta said. "That's why you're fighting so hard for that height variance. For nothing."

This fight was too good to watch from a distance, Helen thought. She slid behind a clothes rack near the dressing room and started buttoning shirts.

Vera, the shop owner, broke up the discussion. She took Danny's arm and dragged him to a rack of men's shoes. "I have some wonderful Bruno Maglis," she said.

"I don't wear used shoes," Danny said. "They're disgusting."

"They're new," Vera said. "These are four hundred dollars, Danny, and I'm selling them for less than a hundred. I think they'll fit you." She slid shoes the size of sleds into Danny's hands.

Next, Vera steered Chrissy toward the dresses. "Try on this pretty cotton dress. It's cool, but simple."

"Perfect for a simple person," Loretta said.

"Ladies!" Vera sounded like a disapproving schoolteacher. "Chrissy, you are the wife of a major developer caught in a controversy. You can't be seen fighting." She handed her the dress and pushed her toward the back dressing room next to her office.

"But—," Chrissy began.

"It doesn't hurt to try it on," Vera interrupted.

"Wait!" Chrissy grabbed Vera's arm and dropped her voice. Helen leaned closer and heard Chrissy say, "Don't tell him about our deal, please. You can keep the Prada purse. I don't care if I get any money for it. But he can't find out."

"I know how to keep secrets or I wouldn't be in this business," Vera said. She shut the dressing room door on the desperate Chrissy, then dashed back to Loretta.

"You, dear, are an elected official who must behave as well as she dresses," Vera said. "Come see my new things. I haven't put them out yet. Perhaps I can find you a little extra tact."

Loretta docilely followed Vera into her office.

Vera stopped at the curtain to the back room and said, "Helen, forget those shirts. I see dust on those shelves next to the dressing room. Clean them now."

More dusting. Helen tried not to sigh. She picked up a Limoges pineapple lightly coated with gray fur and wiped it down. Why did rich people think this junk was ornamental? she thought sourly.

She'd dusted a graceful Blue Willow bowl and shined six Venetian wineglasses when the doorbells jingled.

Helen recognized this new customer. Jordan lived in Helen's apartment complex. She practically haunted Snapdragon's. Jordan had straight dark hair, slanted green eyes and a long nose that made her look rather like an anteater. A stylish anteater. She shimmied in, wearing a summer dress tight as a tourniquet.

"Helen!" she said. "Any new cocktail dresses from Paris Hilton?"

"Going someplace special?" Helen asked.

Jordan dropped her voice and said, "I've found a man, a special man. He wants to take me clubbing in South Beach. Paris's clothes would be perfect."

"But what about—?" Helen said, then stopped. Jordan was living with Mark. But that was Mark's problem, not hers.

"What?" Jordan asked.

"The price," Helen finished. "Paris left two dresses, but they're three hundred each."

"Don't worry. I can get the money from Mark. A girl has to move up in the world, doesn't she? Let me see the dresses. Are they slutty?"

"Slightly," Helen said.

"Good. I want raw sex. My new man has to pop the question. I'm not getting any younger." Jordan should have sounded hard, but her frank remarks were refreshing.

"Then try them on," Helen said. "But I'd better warn you, you could walk into a domestic argument back there."

"Oooh, free entertainment." Jordan gave an extra swish to her hips as she followed Helen to the back. Danny the real estate developer was pushing through the designer racks, and Jordan ran straight into him. Helen watched Jordan's face light up and her eyes soften. "Why, Danny," she said.

Danny surveyed her as if she were a virus under a microscope. "Do I know you?"

Jordan stepped back as though she'd been slapped. "Danny, how can you say that? After—"

She never finished. Danny dropped the monster Maglis on the floor with a clatter. "You!" He pointed to Helen. "Tell Vera I'm not interested in castoffs." He stormed out.

Jordan, Helen's neighbor, was still as a stone. Maybe the skintight dress had cut off her circulation.

"Prick!" Jordan wiped away tears and smeared her mascara.

"He's not worth crying over," Helen whispered. "And his wife is in the back dressing room. Come look at these dresses." She steered Jordan to the cocktail-dress rack. "The pink and the red dresses were both Paris's."

"What about that yellow?" Jordan asked.

"That's a hand-painted silk scarf." Helen picked it off a hanger. "Feel it."

"I'm not interested in covering anything up," Jordan said. "It's showtime."

Helen settled Jordan and the two dresses in the other dressing room, then picked up the shoes Danny had dropped on the floor and put them back on the shelf.

Vera came out of her office, took a deep breath and said, "I need a break." She settled wearily behind the front counter. "Is it really only eleven fifteen?" Vera took a long drink of bottled water and popped two aspirin. "Anyone still here?"

"I have Jordan in the dressing room," Helen said. "She's trying on dresses."

"I got rid of Roger," Vera said.

"Sorry I interrupted," Helen said.

"Why?" Vera stopped. "Wait. You thought I do the wild thing with Roger?"

"I thought you had a relationship," Helen said.

"A relationship!" Vera laughed. Helen felt her face redden.

"Roger is dumber than a box of rocks," Vera said. "Stupid men make bad lovers, in my experience. They're not inventive. I'm not some man with a midlife crisis who needs my ego stroked by a Gucci geisha.

"You want to know my relationship with Roger? He brings me clothes and shoes. First-rate names—True Religion, Jimmy Choo, Moschino. I sell them."

Helen made a clumsy effort to switch the subject. "Is Loretta, the best-dressed county commissioner, still here?"

"I let her out the back entrance after I got rid of Roger," Vera said. "Loretta didn't like anything I showed her. I couldn't risk having her run into Danny and Chrissy again."

"You handled their fight well," Helen said.

"Thanks," Vera said. "I used to do live radio in the nineties. I learned to think on my feet. It was just a little college station that played punk music, but I loved working there."

"So that's why you listen to such cool music," Helen said. "But it doesn't sound like the punk bands I remember."

"I hope you're not talking about this background music," Vera said. "It's like syrup pouring in my ear."

"No, the music you were playing in your office when I came to work this morning."

"That's punk," Vera said. "The Pixies."

"They sound too soft and inventive to be connected to that monotonous seventies sound," Helen said.

"That's what punk evolved into," Vera said. "The term 'indie' is better. The bands I like all have that do-it-yourself attitude."

"Do the Dandy Warhols count?" Helen said. "They did the theme for *Veronica Mars*, 'We Used to Be Friends.' "

"Maybe in the beginning, before they became a crappy pop band. They're sellouts now, like me. I hustle old clothes."

"You're recycling," Helen said. "Why did you leave radio, if you loved it?"

"I got fired," Vera said. "I played music and read the news on the hour. At two o'clock one morning, I decided to tell the truth about a staff resignation. I can still recite it."

Vera switched to a newsreader's voice: "And in news you won't hear on this campus station, the dean of students was caught banging a freshman in his office. He was allowed to resign with a full pension. The dean said they were deeply in love. She said his love wasn't that deep. Maybe two inches on his best day."

"You said that on the air?" Helen said.

"Oh, yeah," Vera said. "You'd be surprised who listens to a nowhere campus station at two a.m. The GM came in and personally fired me. I was out of the business.

"It's my own damn fault. My mom lent me the money to buy this place and I joined the wonderful world of retail."

"Is it always this crazy here at Snapdragon's?" Helen asked.

"You ain't seen nothing yet," Vera said. "This is an emotional business. Everyone wants to look richer than they are. Loretta is the easiest type to deal with, a professional who has to look good.

"Your neighbor Jordan is hunting for a man. She's convinced if she finds the right dress, she'll get a rich guy and be happy."

"It didn't help Chrissy," Helen said.

"Poor Chrissy. Her husband, Danny, is a control freak."

"I couldn't imagine my fiancé, Phil, caring how many purses I have," Helen said.

Vera took another long drink and said, "Phil doesn't need to control you. I doubt if he could. Danny is a developer. Until his Orchid House hotel complex is approved, he's in the spotlight. He doesn't like it."

"Then why do it?"

"Despite the way Danny was poor-mouthing, he stands to make millions," Vera said. "Developers are like riverboat gamblers. One year they're rich—the next they're busted. He can't help that. The only thing Danny can control is his wife. He won't give her a dime, but she has unlimited shopping at all the major stores. Chrissy out-foxed him. She buys superexpensive merchandise, keeps it until she can't return it to the store, then brings it to me for consignment. I sell it and we split the money. She's hauled off about four thousand dollars so far this year. Danny never tumbled to her scheme until today. He's usually too smart to blow up in public, but right now he's playing a dangerous game."

"How?" Helen asked.

"He needs the approval of the county commission to tear down the old Orchid House and build a new project. That's why he's cozying up to Loretta. He's after her vote, not her ass. She's one of two holdouts."

"Danny doesn't play around?" Helen asked.

"Of course he does. Chrissy is his third wife. He has at least one sweetie on the side. I've seen him having dinner with pretty ladies in the restaurants along Las Olas. I don't think he was asking them for loans."

"Too bad for Chrissy," Helen said.

"She's no angel," Vera said. "She's a customer of the Exceptional Pool Service."

Helen looked at her blankly. "What's that mean? Our pool is cleaned by my landlady with a long-handled net."

"Exceptional Service lives up to its name. Their ads promise, 'We get into places you never consider.' The joke is they're exceptionally good at getting in bed with unhappy wives. Check out their ads online. Their employees look like Chippendales and their service uniform is tight white shorts and a tan. Almost makes me wish I had a pool.

"I've been up here yakking too long," Vera said. "I'd better go check on Chrissy."

"I'll see about Jordan."

Helen was almost at the dressing room when she heard Vera scream.

CHAPTER 3

Chrissy was bizarrely beautiful in death. Her head drooped and her spun-sugar hair fell forward to hide the horrors of her hanged face. Her noose was a brilliant blue scarf.

Chrissy hung on a wall hook meant for dresses. The flowered summer dress she was supposed to try on was draped on a white chair.

"She hung herself with a designer scarf," Vera said. Her voice trembled. All trace of the cool, hip Vera was gone. Live radio didn't prepare her for a dead customer.

"It's Gucci," Jordan said, her voice flat with shock. "Why would she commit suicide?"

Vera said some words the FCC still wouldn't allow on the air. "Why the hell did Chrissy commit suicide in my store? Why couldn't she use her car? Or her home?"

Then she stopped suddenly. "What's wrong with me? I'm a total bitch," Vera said. "Poor little Chrissy was afraid to go home to that bully. She killed herself to avoid him."

"I don't get it," Jordan said in that strange, flat voice. "How could she commit suicide? Chrissy didn't jump off the chair. It's not turned over or anything."

"Didn't have to," Vera said. "A girl in my dorm hung herself in a closet. She sort of bent her knees until she strangled."

"Ew," Jordan said. She started to cry.

"Maybe Chrissy didn't commit suicide," Helen said. "That's blood on the dressing room floor."

"Since when did you become Miss CSI?" Vera asked.

"Why would there be blood if she hung herself?" Helen asked. "See this?" She pointed to three dark dime-sized drops on the scuffed tile. One was slightly smudged. "Look at her head. There's blood in her blond hair. Somebody could have hit Chrissy on the head and then hung her with the scarf. You can see more blood drips on the wall."

"Maybe you'd better let the experts figure out what happened instead of shooting off your mouth," Vera said. "Personally, suicide would be better for me than murder. If my customers think a mad strangler is lurking in the clothes racks, they'll be afraid to try on dresses in this store. I guess that sounds cold."

It did, but Vera had an excuse. "Shock makes your mind work funny," Helen said. Her head felt like it had been kicked in a soccer match.

"Is that a diamond Rolex watch on the floor?" Jordan asked. She spotted the designer watch in the corner below the corpse. "Where did that come from?"

"The watch is Chrissy's," Helen said. "The clasp broke and she dropped it when Danny dragged her back to the dressing room. I found it on the floor and gave it to her when she was arguing with him."

"Looks like the glass face is broken," Jordan said. "The hands don't seem to be moving."

"Let me check," Vera said. She bent to pick it up.

"Don't!" Helen said. "That's evidence for the police. We should call 911. Right now. Otherwise, the homicide detectives will wonder why we waited."

"How do you know about homicide detectives?" Vera asked.

"I was at a wedding where the groom was killed earlier this summer."

"Oh, right," Jordan said. "Was that the gossip dude on Hendin Island? King What's His Name?"

"Kingman Oden," Helen said. "I was at the wedding. I met a Hendin Island homicide detective after Oden's murder."

"That's good," Vera said. "The east end of Las Olas is technically part of Hendin Island. You'll get to see your detective friend again."

That's what Helen feared. "He wasn't exactly my friend." She remembered handsome Detective Richard McNally with a shiver, and it wasn't of delight. The last time she'd seen him, Helen had been in the hospital emergency room. McNally had threatened to arrest her if he ever ran across her again. Now here she was, mixed up in another murder in his territory.

"You weren't a suspect, were you?" Vera said.

"No, the detective thought my boss killed King Oden." She had to stop this conversation now, before it got too personal. "I know Lauderdale's fancy shops are on Las Olas. As the boulevard goes east toward the beach, there are a bunch of man-made islands with high-priced homes and yacht docks—Nurmi, Isle of Venice, Isle of Palms and Hendin Island. I didn't think Hendin Island's jurisdiction went this far west on Las Olas."

"Probably political rejiggering to get another crook elected," Vera said. She'd kept her alternative view of politics.

"Maybe we'd better call the police now," Helen said. "What if a customer walks in? We can't put her in a dressing room."

"You're right." Vera punched in three numbers.

"If you're calling 911, I'd better change," Jordan said. She had run barefoot out of the front dressing room and was wearing a half-zipped pink satin strapless dress.

"Your dress is smashing for a police interrogation," Helen said. "That shade of pink will set off the officers' dark blue uniforms."

"Why are you so sarcastic, Helen?" Jordan looked hurt and ready to start weeping again.

Helen felt like she'd kicked a puppy. "I'm sorry. That was out of line."

"Apology accepted." Jordan managed a smile through her tears.

"Thanks," Helen said. "That dress looks nice on you, even when you're upset."

Helen heard Vera tell the 911 operator, "I think the woman committed suicide. Unless she was murdered. I'm not sure what happened, except she's dead. No, I can't stay on the phone. Just send someone, quick."

Vera slammed down the phone and said, "The 911 operator gave us our orders. We're not supposed to touch anything, sell anything or change anything. We're not supposed to change our clothes or wash our hands. I'm not supposed to admit any customers or let anyone leave."

"Can I at least get out of this dress and into my own clothes?" Jordan asked.

"I don't think you'd better," Vera said.

"The police might want to take the dress and check it for hair and fibers," Helen said.

"Why?" Jordan said. "I didn't kill Chrissy." More fat tears slid down her cheeks.

"But you were in the store when Chrissy was murdered," Helen said. "Of course, so was the developer Daniel Martlet, Roger, and Loretta, the county commissioner. But Loretta wouldn't hurt a voter. She's a rising star."

"Danny wouldn't kill anyone, either. He's too gentle," Jordan said, her voice suddenly fierce. The tears dried up like a summer rain shower.

Danny? Helen wondered. Did Jordan know him?

"Gentle?" Helen said. "You weren't here when 'gentle' Danny dragged his wife back to this dressing room. His fingers bruised Chrissy's arm. The cops will see his finger marks when they investigate this murder."

"She wasn't murdered. She committed suicide," Vera said.

"Maybe," Helen said. "I still say she was murdered."

"I can't believe Danny would kill his wife," Jordan said.

"That's for the police to decide," Helen said.

"Can I put ten dollars down on this dress so no one else takes it? I really like it," she said.

"Why are you buying a dress when we have a dead woman in the store?" Helen asked. "What's wrong with you?"

"I don't know how to react," Jordan said. "The only dead person I ever saw was my grandma. She was old and sick. We knew she was going to die. I saw her at the funeral parlor. I didn't find her hanging in a store. I've never seen someone who died unplanned. I'm twenty-one."

I'm twenty years older, Helen thought. She opened her mouth to say something when Vera interrupted—or erupted. "Helen, you told me you've been under a lot of strain. I've made allowances for the fact that your wedding was canceled at the altar and your mother is in a nursing home. But I won't have you attacking my customers."

She's right, Helen thought. I've been behaving badly. "I'm sorry," she said. "Chrissy's death was an awful shock to all three of us. I shouldn't have said anything. There is no normal way to behave when someone is murdered."

"Commits suicide," Vera corrected.

Helen gave Jordan a hug, and accidentally pulled her long hair.

"Ow," Jordan said. "You hurt me."

The sirens interrupted Helen's clumsy attempted reconciliation. Police cars parked every which way, blocking Las Olas Boulevard. The long, narrow shop was overrun by an army of blue uniforms, until a sergeant sorted things out. Yellow crime-scene tape was strung to block off the store from the cash register on back. White jumpsuited crime-scene technicians arrived. Helen heard one say, "Do you know how many fingerprints there are in this place?"

"We're about to find out," her partner said.

Snapdragon's was near the Floridian, a venerable grease spot that defied the trendy look of Las Olas. Patrons poured out of the restaurant and gawked in the shop window as if it were an exhibit at the fair. Helen recognized Johnny, a Floridian regular who held court daily at the restaurant's outdoor tables with his little yellow Lab, Buster. Pretty women loved to pet Buster. Tourists liked to be photographed with him.

Johnny lifted the pup so it could see inside Snapdragon's. A blonde in shorts and a red bikini top reached up to pat Buster on his soft, furry head and gave Johnny a view that made his eyes widen. Buster was born to be a chick magnet.

A few folks tried the shop's door handle until a uniform was posted there. Then the morbidly curious were turned away. Another officer put out the store's freshly fingerprinted CLOSED sign.

Vera, Jordan and Helen were separated and interviewed by uniformed officers. Vera was taken to her back office. Jordan sat in a sale chair by the ginger jars, and Helen perched on a tall chair at the counter up front.

Helen was going over her account of the fatal morning for the second time when the front doorbells jingled merrily.

In walked the last man Helen wanted to see.

CHAPTER 4

Detective Richard McNally wore a suit the color of iron bars. His shirt was bone white, his tie a blood slash. His handcuff tie tack was a warning, at least to Helen. The man had been trouble for her before and he was going to be a problem now.

A dark suit and tie in Fort Lauderdale in August was an invitation to heatstroke. Detective McNally looked cool as a Canadian winter.

Helen did not. She felt queasy when the man walked through the door. She felt sicker when he put on protective booties and went back to see Chrissy's body. She felt even worse when he returned with that knowing smile.

"Miss Hawthorne," he said. "Or is it 'Mrs.' now?"

"Ms.," Helen said. She meant to sound defiant, but couldn't quite hide the quaver in her voice.

"I gave you a wedding present three months ago when I let you walk," he said. "Now there's another dead body and here you are."

"I didn't kill Chrissy," Helen said.

"But you just happened to be here when she died. And you just happened to be at the scene when that gossip King died. Imagine my surprise when I found you were also working at a Fort Lauderdale hotel when a maid just happened to be murdered there."

"I didn't have anything to do with Rhonda's death," Helen said.

"You weren't arrested for it. But you are what we call a link in three murders."

At least he doesn't know about the others, Helen thought.

As if he'd read her mind, Detective McNally said, "If I put together those links, I bet I'll find a long chain. If I yanked that chain, I'm sure I'd find something you've been hiding, Ms. Hawthorne. Something you don't want the police to know."

Helen knew he would. McNally was smart. It wouldn't take him long to figure out Helen had been on the run for more than two years. So far, no Florida cop had tumbled to her secret. But McNally would. He only seemed handsome and harmless. With his blue eyes and white hair, he looked like those older men in the drug commercials. But Helen knew he wasn't a smiley male model pushing pricey prescription pills. His eyes were blue steel and his heart was hard.

"How was your wedding?" he asked.

"It wasn't," Helen said.

"Did the groom wise up?" he asked.

She winced. "It was more complicated than that."

"With you, there are always complications, Ms. Hawthorne." McNally said "Ms." with a buzz like an angry insect. "Why aren't you working at that hair salon anymore? Was there a falling-out among thieves?"

"Miguel Angel and I are still friends," she said. "My mother had a heart attack when she came here for my wedding and I have to be with her. She's too sick to go home to St. Louis. She's in a nursing home now. I couldn't bear to go back to the salon where I'd been a happy bride-to-be. Miguel understood. He told me Vera had an opening at Snapdragon's Second Thoughts, and I started working here about a month ago."

"How well did you know the victim?" he asked.

"Hardly at all," Helen said. "Vera knew her. Chrissy Martlet was a regular customer."

"Martlet. Is she the big developer's wife?" Helen was sure McNally already knew that.

"That's what I heard," Helen said. She was sitting on the tall chair at the register, behind a barricade of shell jewelry and battery-powered toys. Tourist lures.

McNally stood next to the counter. The detective didn't lean on it. The man stayed alert and focused.

"Why would a rich lady buy used clothes?" McNally asked. "Danny Martlet has a multimillion-dollar project in the works."

"Chrissy didn't buy our clothes, as I understand it," Helen said. "She sold her designer clothes here. She said her husband let her shop all she wanted, but he wouldn't give her any spending money."

"That's strange," Detective McNally said.

"He was a control freak," Helen said. "That's how Vera explained him. It happens more than you'd think. Rich wives bring in their barely worn designer clothes all the time."

"So when did the victim come to the store?" Detective McNally asked.

"Just after we opened at ten this morning. Chrissy had her husband's dirty shirts. We do laundry and dry cleaning, too. She tried to sell Vera a pony-hair purse. Then Danny the developer came in and she hid the pony purse in the pile of shirts. But he—"

"Whoa, slow down," McNally said. "Now we've got ponies."

"Just their hair," Helen said. "Chrissy had a Prada purse made out of pony hair that cost three thousand dollars."

"Three grand for a purse? Did it have wheels and a motor?" The cop looked shocked. "I owe my wife an apology. I bitched when she spent eighty bucks for a Couch bag."

"It was probably a Coach bag, not a Couch," Helen said. "They're good, too. Chrissy's purse was a Prada, which is extremely expensive. It still had the tags on it."

"Did she shoplift it?"

"No," Helen said. "She had the store sales receipt and the authenticity documents to prove it wasn't a counterfeit. Vera said she could sell the purse for about five hundred dollars. Chrissy's cut would have been about two hundred fifty. Chrissy said that wasn't enough.

"They were still bargaining when Danny's BMW roared up out front. Chrissy panicked when she saw her husband in the doorway. She tried to hide the purse in his shirts, but he saw it and they started arguing."

"Tell me everything you remember about this argument," McNally said. "Every detail."

Helen tried. But she was woozy from a long morning, the shock of seeing the dead woman and her fear of Detective McNally. Breakfast was a distant memory and there was no lunch in sight. She was sure she forgot something.

"Danny was making fun of Chrissy, saying she faked sex to get what she wanted from him. That's when Loretta Stranahan walked in."

"The county commissioner?" Detective McNally said. "She was here, too?"

Helen nodded.

"What a cluster fu—mess this is," he said.

"Vera wanted Danny and Chrissy to leave. Instead Danny hauled Chrissy to the back dressing room to continue their argument. He gripped her arm hard. I saw the bruises. Those are his fingerprints on her arm."

"What were you doing while they were fighting?" McNally asked.

"I was working. I wiped down that display case," Helen said.

"Where you could hear every word," McNally said.

"It would be hard to miss what they were saying." Helen said. "Danny and Chrissy were yelling loud enough you could hear them all over the store."

"Were they still arguing about money?" McNally said.

"No. Chrissy accused Danny of being unfaithful, of staring at another woman's uh . . . chest. Then Commissioner Loretta Stranahan walked back and saw Danny and his wife. The women seemed to know each other, but I don't think Chrissy liked the commissioner. Chrissy made a remark about Loretta calling her husband too often. Loretta said Chrissy was too stupid to understand they were discussing business.

"That's when Vera stepped in. She showed Danny some Bruno Magli shoes, sent Chrissy to the back dressing room to try on a summer dress and took Loretta to her office to see some blouses she hadn't put on the racks yet."

"Those Bruno Maglis, is that the brand O. J. wore?" McNally asked.

"I think so. O. J. called the shoes cheap, but they weren't. Anyway, Vera separated everyone and the store was quiet. That's when Jordan came in, wanting some of Paris Hilton's cocktail dresses."

"Paris Hilton sells her used clothes here?" McNally asked.

"No, Vera gives her regular sellers code names that sort of match their personalities. They all have regular buyers. Vera's Paris Hilton is a rich, young woman who likes to party, sort of like the real celebrity. Loretta likes Glenn Close's suits."

"Does this seller woman look like Glenn Close?" McNally asked.

"No, she's a brunette businesswoman who likes married men," Helen said. "Vera knows she can't sell clothes to women who run in the same circles. They would be embarrassed to be seen in a friend's cast-off dress. She shows them to people they'll never meet. Jordan lives at my apartment complex. She's safe to sell to because there aren't any rich party girls hanging around the Coronado Tropic Apartments. Jordan wanted to try on two Paris Hilton cocktail dresses. She ran into Danny and he was rude to her. He was rude to me, too. He threw the shoes on the floor and walked out."

"What time was that?" McNally said.

"Around eleven fifteen."

He raised an eyebrow. "And how do you know that?"

"Vera and I took a breather and she looked at the clock. Then she went back to the dressing room to ask Chrissy about the pony-hair purse and found her dead."

Helen stopped. This was the bad part. The cheerful clutter of the store seemed to close in on her. She gulped, afraid she might cry, and grabbed the edge of the counter. She didn't want to show any weakness around McNally.

"Do you want some water, Ms. Hawthorne?" Detective Mc-Nally asked.

"I have a bottle here under the counter," she said. She took a sip of water and felt a little better. The relentless questioning had stopped for a moment.

"You said Vera found the body," McNally prompted.

"I heard Vera screaming and I ran to the back," Helen said. She felt calmer now. "Jordan was in the front dressing room trying on a cocktail dress. She came out of the room in a half-zipped pink satin dress. Vera called 911. That's all I remember."

She left out their debate about whether Chrissy's death was murder or suicide.

Helen stared out the window. Heat waves rose from the sidewalks. The relentless sun was bleaching the brightly painted shops and colorful canvas awnings. Sensible locals were inside, except for the uniformed cop on duty outside the shop door. He was dripping sweat. Only the window-shopping tourists were on the sidewalks, determined to enjoy their vacations. They were as wilted as week-old bouquets.

"We found something," a crime-scene tech announced. She showed Detective McNally the warty porcelain pineapple. On the bottom edge was a thick dark smear and what Helen thought was a couple of hairs clinging to it. Her stomach turned.

"It was on the top shelf," the tech said. "We've photographed it."

"Which top shelf?" he asked.

"Under the fan, next to the armoire," the tech said.

"So a tall person could reach it easily?" McNally said.

"So could a short one," Helen said. "There's a chair next to it."

"We didn't find any footprints or shoe prints on the chair seat," the tech said.

"Can you get any fingerprints off the pineapple?" McNally asked.

"With that surface, probably not," the tech said. "Maybe some smears. We can take it back and fume it."

"I've dusted everything in this store," Helen said. "I dusted that pineapple this morning. My prints will be on it."

"I think you'd better come back to the station with me, Ms. Hawthorne," McNally said.

"Why? Am I under arrest?"

"No, I want you to give your statement again and sign it. Then I want to take your prints. Just for elimination."

"Do I need a lawyer?" Helen asked.

"Only if you're guilty," McNally said.

CHAPTER 5

Helen staggered out of the Hendin Island police station and squinted into the scalding sun. She felt like a drunk who'd left a bar after hours of carousing. She was surprised that it was only six o'clock and still daylight. Detective McNally's interrogation seemed to last for days.

Steam rose from the wet pavement, and puddles soaked her shoes. Fort Lauderdale had already had its afternoon monsoon. The brief, hard summer rain drenched everything and cooled nothing.

Helen hoped the troubled citizens of Hendin Island never needed to find their police station in a hurry. The sign was so small and discreet, it could have been a private clinic behind that high ficus hedge. The nasty business of police work was hidden by a pretty facade, the way people once hid outhouses in fragrant gardens. The rich Hendin Islanders wanted no reminder of life's ugly necessities.

Helen sloshed through lukewarm puddles until her shoes squished. She felt battered by Detective McNally's relentless questions. She was too tired to walk home through this sauna. Besides, Helen had a new cell phone. She could call her fiancé.

Phil answered the phone after two rings. "Helen, where are you? What's the matter? You got off work two hours ago and you aren't home. Did I forget that you were going somewhere?"

"There's been a problem," Helen said. "A Snapdragon customer was murdered. Chrissy Martlet."

"The developer's wife?" Phil asked.

"That's her."

Phil whistled, then said, "Are you all right? Were you hurt?"

"I'm fine. I couldn't call. I had to go to the Hendin Island police station and give a statement. They took my fingerprints and palm prints, but didn't arrest me."

"That's good," Phil said. "How did the woman die? Was she shot?"

"I don't know how she died, but she wasn't shot. We didn't want to touch anything and mess up the investigation. Vera swears Chrissy committed suicide. I think she was hit on the head and hanged."

"Where are you?" Phil asked.

"On Las Olas, walking toward home."

"Did you get any lunch?" Phil asked.

"I haven't eaten since breakfast," Helen said, and suddenly realized she was hungry as well as tired. She hadn't eaten for ten hours. No wonder she felt dizzy.

"It's too hot to walk home," Phil said. "Can you make it to the Floridian? We could have dinner there. It's cool inside."

"Deal," Helen said. "I'll be there in five minutes and get us a table."

"The Flo," as the locals called it, stubbornly refused to change. While other Las Olas restaurants served teeny portions and picked pockets for two-hundred-dollar dinners, the Flo had generous food and small prices. This was diner food, with sassy servers and a lit dessert display case. Meals for serious grease abusers.

If you were in the right mood, the Flo was friendly, funky and affordable. If you weren't, then you could turn up your nose and decide the place needed a good scrubbing. In that case, the Flo hoped you'd order braised quail with kumquats elsewhere. It didn't need your business.

Phil turned heads as he walked into the dark diner. His long hair was pulled back into a silver white ponytail. He wore jeans and a soft blue shirt that matched his eyes. Phil was a private eye. Helen knew he'd want the seat at their table that kept his back to the wall. He was more comfortable when he could watch the room. Sitting nearby was a young man, pale as a boiled egg, shoveling a chef salad into his mouth.

Phil kissed Helen and pulled out his chrome chair. The low light softened his laugh lines and eye crinkles. Helen was a sucker for eye crinkles. She couldn't understand how she'd found such a good man. She'd had a lot of bad luck in her life. Maybe it was time for a change.

Phil ordered a beer and a ham-and-cheese omelet with a side of chopped onions. Helen asked for a turkey wrap and coffee. When his omelet arrived, Phil smothered it in ketchup until Helen couldn't see any egg, then topped it with onions and hot sauce. Helen picked at her turkey wrap, drank coffee and told Phil about her day.

"Vera found Chrissy dead in the back dressing room," Helen said. "She thinks Chrissy committed suicide. The crime-scene techs found a white porcelain pineapple with blood and hair on it. I think it could be the murder weapon. The police won't say. I'm guessing the killer knocked Chrissy out with the pineapple, then tried to make it look like suicide by hanging her with a scarf. When

I said Chrissy had been murdered, Vera got mad and reminded me I wasn't a crime-scene expert. She wants Chrissy's death to be suicide. Murder might scare away her customers."

"Suicide or murder, it's a nasty way to go," Phil said. "I hope Chrissy was unconscious."

"I always thought that pineapple was a stupid ornament," Helen said. "It's as useless as the people who like it."

"Any ideas on the killer?" Phil asked.

"I'm betting it's the husband," Helen said. "Chrissy was afraid of Danny Martlet. He's a bully and Vera said he fools around. He'd want his little wife out of the way."

"That makes sense if she didn't sign a prenup," Phil said. "But the last thing Danny would want was a murder trial while he's negotiating the Orchid House deal. Bad publicity could scare off the board votes he needs for his project."

"Maybe," Helen said. "I'll tell you what's scaring me. Snapdragon's is in Hendin Island, and Detective McNally has the case. He made my life miserable after King Oden was killed. He's looking for any excuse to arrest me."

"But he didn't, did he?" Phil asked.

They didn't stop talking when the waitress refilled Helen's coffee cup. The waitress didn't react. It was that kind of place.

"No, but I don't know why," Helen said. "My fingerprints were all over the Limoges pineapple that bashed Chrissy."

"But you work at the shop," Phil said. "Your prints are supposed to be on things. Any good defense lawyer would point that out. When fingerprints are someplace they're not supposed to be, then there's trouble."

"Still, the detective took me back to the station for elimination prints," Helen said. "The cops took Vera's and Jordan's prints at the scene. McNally is out to get me."

Phil took a long swallow of beer, then said, "Helen, we've had this conversation before and you've always refused to listen to me. But there's been a murder at your store. The wife of an important developer was killed. A county commissioner was present."

Helen knew where this conversation was heading.

"I have no connection to Chrissy," Helen said. "I didn't know her. Today was the first time I ever saw her. I certainly didn't fight with her."

"It doesn't matter," Phil said. "Law enforcement will be all over your store like a cheap suit. Sooner or later, McNally is going to find out you're wanted in St. Louis. You defied the court and refused to pay half of your future income to your ex-husband, Rob."

"But Rob disappeared. Nobody's seen him in months," Helen said.

"Which makes you look even more suspicious," Phil said.

"But he disappeared because his second wife—or whatever Marcella was—gave him a million dollars to go away. Everyone in law enforcement knows the Black Widow has had five or six husbands who conveniently died."

"They also know she's never been arrested or convicted of murder," Phil said. "Marcella can afford the best lawyers in the world. You can't. You've made yourself an easy target."

"But the divorce judge made a stupid decision," Helen said. "Rob wasn't entitled to half my future income. He wasn't entitled to anything of mine. He lived off me for years. He just had a better lawyer than I did and he won."

"And you ran away," Phil said. "Come back with me to St. Louis and fight the decision."

His voice was soft. Helen wanted to say yes, but then she saw the pale guy eating the salad was eavesdropping. His mouth was open and his fork hovered in the air. Great. What if he reported their conversation to the police? Helen glared at him, and he went back to shoveling in salad.

"Phil, I can't leave Mom alone in Florida," Helen said, lowering her voice. "She hasn't regained consciousness in the three months since our wedding. What if she does come to? I can't let her wake up alone in a nursing home. My sister, Kathy, and Tom can't afford to travel here again after our June wedding didn't come off. Mom's so-called husband, Larry, is too cheap to fly down and see his sick wife. I haven't been the best daughter, but I can't abandon Dolores."

"When are you going to see your mother next?" Phil asked. "Maybe the doctor can give you some clue to her condition. You're running out of time here, Helen, and if you wind up in jail, you can't help your mother at all."

"The store will be closed tomorrow," Helen said. "It's still a crime scene. I can go to the nursing home and talk to the doctor when he makes his morning rounds. The home didn't call you today, did it?"

"Not a peep from Dr. Justin Lucre," Phil said. "Is that really his name—Lucre, like money?"

"Yep. The nurses call him Dr. Filthy, but not to his face. They like him even less than I do. You don't find a lot of great healers working as nursing home doctors, but the nurses say he'll take good care of Mom until her insurance money runs out. I'm glad she bought a long-term policy for catastrophic illness."

"So is Larry, I bet," Phil said. "She won't be dipping into her savings."

"I think Larry married Mom for her money," Helen said. "She had worse luck with men than I did."

Phil raised an eyebrow, and Helen said, "Except you, of course.

ward after Rob. I know you're not interested in my
se I don't have any."

ss poured more decaf for Helen, then slapped down
ie salad eater. His cell phone rang. He answered it,
le.

our table neighbor got a sudden attack of good
said. "Speaking of neighbors, was Jordan home
?"

"Her boss at the restaurant called at four thirty
is. Jordan didn't answer her cell phone or show
lled Jordan's boyfriend. Her boss was mad. I
ired."

e's no shortage of breastaurants in Fort Lau-

nt?" Phil asked.

oked puzzled. "A place where pretty wait-
res, like Hooters. Beach Buns Bar & Grill
ove king lot, but promises 'a brew and a view.'
The Jordan in a bikini."

"She must save money on dry cleaning if that little bikini is all
she wears," Phil said.

"Jordan says the leg and bikini waxes cost a fortune," Helen
said. "Guys don't like hair with their beer, unless it's long and
firmly attached to a female scalp."

"I'd like to go to Beach Buns," he said. "I hear they have good
spicy wings."

"Margery had lunch there one afternoon. She said the customers were mostly married men old enough to be Jordan's father. She
never saw so many Tommy Bahama shirts. I think Tommy Bahama is the official shirtmaker for overweight adulterers."

"Nice slogan," Phil said.

"You can go to Beach Buns," Helen said. "I wouldn't care."

"Will you go with me?" he asked.

"Not unless they add cute waiters in Speedos."

"I'd feel silly staring at scantily dressed young women," he said.

"That's why I love you," Helen said.

Phil reached across the table and squeezed her hand.

"Excuse me," the waitress said. "Did you see the guy eating his salad here?"

"His cell phone rang right after you brought him the bill," Helen said. "He went outside."

The waitress looked out the window. "Damn. Nobody's there," she said. "He's gone and he didn't pay. I got stiffed by a new twist on an old scam—the disappearing cell phone caller. They used to say they were going to the restroom. He'll get away with it, too."

Helen flashed on Chrissy hanged in the dressing room, and hoped her killer didn't get away.

CHAPTER 6

Jordan was stretched out on a chaise by the pool at the Coronado Tropic Apartments, like a Victorian lady on a fainting couch. There was nothing Victorian about her figure-hugging dress. It was so tight, Helen thought it might be holding Jordan together. It had a slightly grubby look, like a used bandage.

Jordan had combed her long, dark hair and put on fresh makeup for her dainty crying scene after her ordeal with the Hendin Island police. She gently blotted her eyes with a tissue. Helen, relaxed and refreshed after dinner with Phil, watched the performance.

Jordan sniffled delicately while a well-built young man patted her arm with strong callused hands. Her live-in boyfriend, Mark, was handsome enough to be a male model. But the dark lines on his knuckles revealed his profession. Mark was a mechanic at Warren's Wrecks, and could never quite scrub the grease stains off his hands.

When Mark's comforting hands strayed too near her tight white dress, Jordan gently brushed them away.

Funny, Helen thought, Mark's paycheck was never too soiled for Jordan to spend.

Peggy, the Coronado's exotic red-haired tenant, was drinking white wine. Her Quaker parrot, Pete, perched on her shoulder like a green imp. Even his Quaker-gray feathered head couldn't make him look serious.

"The police asked me questions like I was a criminal." Jordan wept artistically.

"Awk!" Pete said. Peggy tried to soothe the bird by petting him, but he hopped restlessly from foot to foot.

Jordan ignored the interruption. "They kept me so long I missed going in to work. Now my boss is mad at me."

"You don't have to go back to Beach Buns if you don't want to, honey bear," Mark said.

Jordan quickly turned off her tears. "But I have to work," she said. "I don't want to live off you."

"I wouldn't care," Mark said.

The poor sap was besotted. Helen wanted to take him aside and explain that honey bear was prowling for a rich, upscale lover. But she knew her warning would be useless. How many people had tried to clue in Helen about Rob? She didn't listen. You only open your eyes when it's too late, she thought. I was Jordan's age when I fell for my rotten ex. She is awfully young. Maybe Jordan will wake up and appreciate the good man she already has.

Helen tried to catch Peggy's eye, but her friend was listening intently. Peggy had had her own problems with men. Her current man was a rare breed, a likable lawyer. She deserved him after too many heartbreakers.

Helen tuned out Jordan as her thoughts drifted back to her ex-husband. Rob was aptly named. The man had robbed her of her peace of mind. He'd stolen seventeen years of her life in St. Louis. He nearly got her money.

Helen had kept her eyes firmly closed to his faults. It was a shock when she came home early from work and found Rob with their next-door neighbor, Sandy. They were having sex on the back deck.

No, "having sex" sounded too polite, like having tea. Rob and Sandy were in a sweaty, rip-off-their-clothes rut when Helen walked in on them.

She was stunned. The pair were oblivious. They didn't notice that Helen had picked up a crowbar. Finally, Sandy looked over and screamed. Rob, pale and naked as a new seedling, abandoned his lover for the protection of his SUV. Helen had started swinging and reduced the SUV to rubble. Then she filed for divorce.

She'd been surprised again when the judge had awarded Rob half her income. She'd expected to lose the house, but never thought the court would give fifty percent of her future salary to her scum-sucking spouse. For the last seven years of their marriage, Rob had lived off Helen while pretending to look for work. She tried to get her lawyer to fight back, but he sat there like a cardboard cutout.

Helen swore in court that Rob would never see a dime of her future income. Then she'd tossed her wedding ring into the Mississippi River, ditched her six-figure corporate job and driven off in frantic zigzags across the United States. She wound up in South Florida at the Coronado, where she had a new name and a new life, and worked for cash under the table.

The Coronado was an Art Moderne apartment building with sweeping white curves, rattling air-conditioner units and turquoise trim. Helen loved the old building and its raffish inhabitants.

Rob, desperate for his share of Helen's money, eventually tracked her to Fort Lauderdale. He wasn't too proud to demand his share of the pittance Helen made at her dead-end jobs.

It was her landlady, Margery, who tried to save Helen. She introduced Rob to a fabulously rich older woman, Marcella, known as the Black Widow. The pair sailed away together on her yacht. Margery figured Rob would join the Black Widow's long string of late husbands. But Rob's amazing luck worked again. The Black Widow didn't want another messy murder investigation. She set him free with a million dollars and his promise to disappear.

Helen hadn't seen her ex in almost a year. Phil said the Black Widow had only pretended to pension off Rob. She'd really added one more "accidental" death to her tally of former spouses. Helen disagreed. She believed Rob had the survival instincts of a cockroach. She knew he'd crawl back to ruin her new life.

Helen had spent her time in that special purgatory South Florida had for single women, dating drunks, druggies and deadbeats. Then she met her prince, Phil. Helen was finally ready for a happy ending. She and Phil planned a small, perfect wedding at the Coronado in June. They were nearly pronounced man and wife when Helen's mother had appeared like an Old Testament prophet and stopped the ceremony.

As Dolores called down God's wrath and the weight of the law on her daughter, the frail woman had a heart attack. Helen's attempted wedding was canceled in a welter of accusations and unsolved legal issues.

The ambulance roared off to the emergency room with Dolores. Helen was left with her ruined reception—and Phil. He swore he loved her and promised to go to St. Louis and help Helen fight her unfair divorce. So far, her mother's illness had prevented that trip.

Jordan's soft, insistent saga sliced through Helen's unhappy memories. Helen was forced into the present and Jordan's melodramatic tale of her day. "The police wouldn't even let me take the pink dress." Jordan produced two perfect tears. "I offered to pay for it. But they said it was evidence."

"You do realize a woman died," Helen said.

Margery, lounging nearby, heard the righteous edge in Helen's voice. She suddenly stood up and asked, "Who'd like a homemade brownie? I can nuke some."

"Me!" Phil said.

"Me," Peggy said.

"Me, too," Mark said. "I love your brownies."

"Not me," Jordan said, as if Margery had offered her cat food on a cracker. "They're fattening."

"Some risks are worth it," Helen said. "I'll take one."

"Good," Margery said. "Five brownies, coming up. Helen, you can help me."

"I'll help, too," Phil said.

"What can I do?" Peggy asked.

"You can help eat them," Margery said. "Stay right where you are."

Helen followed her landlady as she marched briskly across the short, tough grass to her apartment. Margery might be seventy-six, but Helen saw her as ageless rather than old. Three thousand years ago, Margery would have been sucking in the fumes escaping the rocks at Delphi and making pronouncements. Now she inhaled cigarettes and sucked down screwdrivers by a Florida pool. She was a modern wise woman in purple clamdiggers and orange gladiator sandals.

Margery knew Helen was stirring up trouble. She shut the old-fashioned jalousie door to her kitchen hard enough that the glass slats rattled. Then she turned on Helen. "What is the matter with you, going after that innocent girl?"

"Innocent, my aunt Fanny," Helen said. "If you want to feel sorry for anyone, save your sympathy for Mark. Poor little Jordan's playing that man for a sucker. She came into Snapdragon's today and announced she wanted to buy a dress so she could date a rich man. Mark isn't good enough for her. He does something useful."

Margery opened the freezer, slid five cold brownies onto a plate and popped them in the microwave. "If being useful is so important, get out the plates, napkins and forks," she said.

The microwave beeped. Margery continued her lecture in a softer tone. "Mark's love life is none of your business. You have enough problems without borrowing his. Mark won't wake up until it's too late. He's in love with Jordan."

"He's a fool," Helen said.

"So were you, as I recall. If someone had told you the truth about Rob seventeen years ago, would you have listened?"

"No." Helen hung her head.

"Mark has to make his own mistakes," Margery said. "You can't save someone who doesn't want to be rescued. Mark will fall out of love someday soon, and I hope it's not a hard landing."

"Why are you defending Jordan?" Helen asked.

"I'm not defending her," Margery said. "But she's harmless. And young. There's still hope for her. She may grow up. If not, the only person she'll hurt is Mark—and maybe herself if she drops that man for a better catch.

"The person I'm worried about is you. This is my property. I won't have you sniping at my tenants around my pool. I like peace in my own backyard. If I may say so, you are not yourself these days. You're going to lose Phil and your friends if you don't pull yourself together."

"I'm sorry," Helen said.

Margery put the warm brownies on a plate. "I've made excuses for you, but I'm running out of patience."

"I apologize," Helen said.

"Good," Margery said. "I don't want to see this Helen around here again. Now, help me carry out these brownies." Margery had the brownie plate in her hand when her kitchen phone rang. She put it down and picked up the phone.

"You!" she said into the phone. "I thought you were gone." Her face was taut with anger. She listened for a moment, then said, "You want to speak to Helen? I'll see if she's here. Just a minute."

Margery pressed the MUTE button.

"Sorry you got that call," Helen said. "I bought a cell phone after Rob tracked me here so you wouldn't have to take my calls. I figured there was no point in hiding anymore."

"Maybe not from Rob, but what will you do when that Hendin Island detective finds out you're running from the court?" Margery asked.

Helen didn't want this discussion. "I can't leave my mother now. I gave all my friends my new cell number."

"This is no friend," Margery said. "Brace yourself. It's Rob."

"He's back?" Helen said.

"I'm afraid so. Do you want me to stay here with you?"

"No, thanks," Helen said. "He's as hard to get rid of as athlete's foot. Go take the brownies out. I'll take his call."

CHAPTER 7

"Hi, sunshine." Rob's voice was slick with contempt. "I'm sorry about your wedding."

Stay cool, Helen told herself. Don't lose your temper. He's not worth it. She remembered a sign a secretary used to keep over her desk: ONLY YOU CAN LET SOMEONE RUIN YOUR DAY.

She was not going to let Rob ruin hers.

"What do you want?" Helen's voice was freezing rain on a winter day.

Remember the last time you fought with him, she told herself. You nearly were arrested for murder.

Helen pictured Rob the way she'd seen him that night at the Superior Club. It was midnight, and a thunderstorm was rolling in. Flashes of lightning lit the sky. Helen had worked twelve hours straight, wearing the ugly polyester uniform reserved for servants. Sweaty, tired and rumpled, Helen was forty-one and looked it.

Rob had seemed sleek and smug. He'd looked tanned and lean, thanks to Marcella's personal chef and fitness trainer. Even his bald spot was gone now that he could afford Rogaine. His skin glowed from frequent facials. Naturally, he was wearing a Tommy Bahama shirt. It was almost a uniform for players: Team Swine, the big-league cheaters.

Rob had taunted her that night and she'd punched him in the mouth, an indulgence for which she'd paid dearly. Now her hand itched to hit him again, though he wasn't in slugging distance. She took her red-hot temper and sealed it into an ice cave.

"Hey, you don't have to be that way." Rob's words seemed to slither out of the receiver. Her ear felt soiled listening to him. "I was trying to be polite. I heard your wedding didn't come off and I'm sorry. That's all. I also wanted to know how your mother was. She's in a nursing home in Florida, right? That's too bad. Dolores always liked me. I can't help that."

Helen's hot temper shivered and stirred, but the ice cave held.

"Who told you about my mother and my wedding?" Helen asked. "You haven't talked to my friends."

She had surrounded herself with people she trusted. Margery wouldn't have said anything. Neither would Phil. Helen's sister, Kathy, couldn't abide Rob. Marcella, the Black Widow, didn't know what Helen was doing these days and didn't care.

"Your mother's second husband told me," Rob said. "I'm the son that old Lawn Boy Larry never had. I stopped by his place and we shared a couple of brews. Larry gave me the news about your mother. He's worried about her."

"So worried he never bothered to see her in the nursing home," Helen said.

Oops. She could feel the ice cave cracking. A burning red ten-tacle tried to break out. She stamped on the ugly thing and sent it scuttling back into the cave.

She took deep breaths in Margery's cozy, brownie-scented

kitchen. The polished copper kettle, the microwave, the bowl of fruit on the kitchen table, were all signs of ordinary life.

"Well, Larry is not young anymore," Rob said in that lazy drawl. "Your mother is sick in Fort Lauderdale. Eight hundred miles is a long, hot trip for an old geezer. Larry isn't well enough to take the bus. Look what it did to your mother."

"It's no hotter in Florida than it is in St. Louis," Helen said. "And he can buy a plane ticket."

"The farthest Larry goes these days is to the supermarket and church," Rob said. "It wouldn't hurt you to be nice to him, Helen. He'll get your mom's money when she passes on. Though I hope she won't die," he added quickly. "You know Dolores made out her will in his favor."

"That's all Larry cares about," Helen said. "Mom and I both married men who were only interested in our money." Oops. Her hot temper was flaring up, trying to bust out of the ice cave.

"That's harsh," Rob said. "It was your idea to divorce me. Otherwise, we'd still be happily married."

"You'd be happy," Helen said. "I was happy, too, as long as I stayed stupid." She could hear the ice cave cracking. Helen fought to seal it, but the heat was too much.

"Your mom was a lonely widow when she married Lawn Boy Larry," Rob said, his voice still silky cool. "She needed a companion. The new marriage didn't work. When Dolores asked Larry to move back into his own home, he did. Larry is a gentleman. He still makes himself useful. He cuts your mother's lawn, cleans the gutters, paints the fence, rakes leaves, little chores like that."

"So he can sell her house as soon as she dies," Helen said, with more heat than she intended. Her temper was sizzling. She tried to shut it away, but it was getting too hot to handle.

"You can't judge Larry for that," Rob said. "He's almost eighty.

Dolores has been in a coma for what—three months now? Larry told me she was his wife in name only for most of their marriage. Larry and Dolores weren't exactly red-hot lovers. Your mom only did it once with him. That was enough for her. Think it was that little flat cap he always wears when he cuts the grass? Could be quite a turn-on for an older woman. When she got him into bed without that cap, well, all his charm vanished."

Ping! That was it. Helen could hear roaring in her ears.

"Are you here in Florida?" Helen asked, her voice lethally quiet.

"Why? Do you miss me?" Rob said.

"Hell, no. If you're staying at a nearby hotel, I want to come over and rip your face off. If you ever talk about my mother's sex life again, I'll kill you."

She'd lost it. She was flaming mad, all caution forgotten.

"You're feisty," Rob said. "I've always liked that about you. Here's some advice: Do be careful. Talking about killing me could be construed as a threat if anything should happen. As to your question, I'm a free man, Helen. There's no reason to tell you where I am.

"You've got to admire Larry, though. He made sure he consummated his marriage to your mother. Dolores wouldn't dare ask for an annulment after they did the deed. A lesser woman would have lied. But Dolores was legally married to Larry and she doesn't believe in divorce. She disapproved when you divorced her favorite son-in-law. She wasn't happy with Larry, but she's no hypocrite.

"Larry made sure he and his new bride were well and truly hitched. Must have been worth the effort. Nice piece of property he'll get when your mom passes."

"Shut up," Helen said. Her voice sizzled and died in the powerful heat of her rage. She tried to remember if Rob had been this obnoxious when they were married, but she couldn't think.

"You won't get her house, but at least you didn't inherit Dolores's dislike of sex," Rob said. "You used to go at it hammer and tongs."

Helen couldn't say anything. A sheet of red flame shut out her vision. She didn't know who she loathed more—her ex-husband or herself for marrying Rob.

"Shut up and tell me what you want, or I'll slam down the phone," she said.

"There's a serious failure in your logic," Rob said. "How can I tell you what I want if I shut up?"

"I'm counting to ten," Helen said. "Then I'll hang up if you don't start talking. One . . ."

"Don't do that," Rob said, his voice slippery with satisfaction. "What's his name—the guy who wants my used goods?"

"Phil," Helen said. "My fiancé is Phil."

"Right. He will be very unhappy when the law hauls you away."

"Get to the point," Helen said.

"I want my money," Rob said. His voice was flat and hungry. "The divorce judge awarded me half your income. You've disobeyed him. It's hard to keep track of what you've actually made since our divorce, Helen, since you were paid with cash under the table. There's one exception: your job at the country club. Based on your Superior Club salary, you earned eleven dollars an hour."

"That's the most I ever made," Helen said.

"So you say," Rob said. "But you can't prove it. You don't have any other payroll records."

"I only made about six hundred dollars every two weeks at the Superior Club. And that was after taxes."

"We've been divorced a little over two years," Rob said. "By my calculations, you made thirty-one thousand, two hundred dollars. You owe me fifteen thousand, six hundred dollars. But I'm in a generous mood. I'll only ask for an even fifteen thousand dollars to settle your past debt. And I won't tell the IRS about your employers."

"I didn't make enough money to pay taxes," Helen said.

"I understand, but the government gets crabby if they don't hear from a potential taxpayer," Rob said.

"What if my mother needs money?" Helen asked.

"She has a husband," Rob said. "Larry is legally responsible for her bills. He can pay them."

"That skinflint will ship her off to someplace cheap and horrible the moment she costs him money. Mom has a long-term-care policy."

"A prudent move," Rob said. "Dolores showed great forethought. No one wants to be kept alive beyond their time. Even if Larry puts her in a cheaper home, what difference will it make? She'll never know. I mean no disrespect, but your mother is broccoli in a hospital bed."

"You bastard!" Helen said.

"Let's leave my mother out of it," Rob said. "She's dead."

Now his voice was harder than granite. "These are the facts, Helen. I'm entitled to half of your earnings. It was a court ruling, and you've run from it for more than two years. The law will not look kindly on that.

"I'm sure your boyfriend will pay your old debt of fifteen thou. Once that is taken care of, you still owe me half your income, even if you remarry. It's time I collected my little court-ordered annuity. I'll expect that big check, then smaller ones each month."

"The Black Widow gave you a million dollars," Helen said. "What happened to that?"

"Lost it all. Bad investments," Rob said cheerfully. Helen could almost hear him shrug. "I'm cold, stone broke. Do you know what a Belvedere martini costs these days? I can't ask Marcella for more money. We had an agreement: a million bucks and she'd never hear from me again. And Marcella knows how to deal with people she doesn't like."

"I should have shot you when I found you with Sandy," Helen said. "I'd only have to serve eight years for murder."

"But you didn't," Rob said. "Like your mother, you're too moral."

"You son of a bitch," Helen said.

"There you go, picking on my mother again," Rob said. "Don't even think of threatening me, Helen. Remember when you hit me? The charges were dropped, but that assault is on your record. If anything happens to me, you'll be the first suspect."

"It was expunged!" Helen cried.

"Not from the police officer's memory," Rob said.

He stripped away the last shred of silk. "I want my money in thirty days, Helen Hawthorne," he said. "You owe me fifteen thousand dollars."

"Do you have an address in St. Louis?" she asked.

"Not sure where I'll be. But I'll let you know where to send it. I'll keep in touch. Remember, thirty days for the big payment, then the little ones once a month. Keep them coming. And don't be late."

Helen threw the cordless receiver across the room.

CHAPTER 8

"Want a cigarette?" wheezed the skinny white-haired man in the wheelchair.

Joe's big hands were dotted with yellow nicotine stains. Joe zipped around the Sunset Rest Retirement Home in his "Ferrari"—a red motorized wheelchair with black racing stripes and a miniature marine flag flying proudly. He wore a black baseball cap and held his cigarette at a jaunty angle.

"No, thanks, Joe," Helen said, and laughed. "I still don't smoke."

"Smart girl," Joe said. "You're young. You've got some good times left. Cigarettes can't hurt us old coots. They're one of the few pleasures we have left. Oh, I see you brought me flowers. You shouldn't have." He batted his eyelashes flirtatiously.

"They're for my mother," Helen said.

"Don't listen to this old fool," Rita interrupted. "How is your mother, dear?" Rita wore red lipstick and a matching bow probably filched from a flower arrangement. Rita's thin hair was the same color as her swirling cigarette smoke.

"That's what I'm hoping to find out this morning when I talk with her doctor," Helen said. "He ordered a CT scan. He'll tell me the results today. Thanks for asking."

Joe and Rita were two of the smokers who gathered in the palm-shaded Sunset Rest courtyard. They lit up at dawn and puffed happily until the doors were locked at night.

"Have fun with old Filthy," Joe said.

Rita elbowed him with a chubby arm. "Quiet," she said. "If Dr. Lucre takes a dislike to you, your bony ass will be out on the street."

"Such language from a lady," Joe mocked. Rita giggled.

"Filthy can't afford to throw me out," Joe said. "I have too much money. I'll leave here feetfirst."

Helen wished her mother had been well enough to enjoy her neighbors. Dolores, determined to stop Helen's wedding, had taken a long, hot bus ride from St. Louis to Fort Lauderdale. She achieved her goal, but at great cost. Helen's mother had a minor heart attack and hit her head on the Coronado's concrete sidewalk. At the hospital, when the doctors treated her heart, they also found a brain bleed from the fall.

A neurosurgeon operated to relieve the pressure. After a month, the doctors said they could do nothing more at the hospital and suggested a nursing home. Helen visited four recommended nursing homes. She'd walked out of the first two because they smelled like urine and stale soup. The third home had lines of older people tied into wheelchairs and parked in the aisles. Her mother wasn't going to a human warehouse.

Sunset Rest's lobby was painted a pretty pastel blue and had a tropical fish tank. The halls had photos of Florida beaches. Helen had eaten two meals in the dining room and thought the food was fairly good. She hoped her mother would get well enough to play bridge, go to the weekly music nights, then go home to her grandchildren.

It never happened. Helen's mother never woke up after her surgery. The neurosurgeon said the bleed had damaged her brain stem. Even after the pressure was relieved, he said it did not look hopeful that Dolores would recover.

Helen's sister, Kathy, and her brother-in-law, Tom, stayed another week after Helen's interrupted wedding, but both had to return to their jobs in St. Louis. Helen promised to look after Dolores and call if there was any news, good or bad.

The surgeon had explained, "Your mother is in a shadow world of partial consciousness. She may answer a few simple yes or no questions. She may sometimes open her eyes and look at you. She may be agitated if she's roused. But she probably won't come back." He assured the family Dolores was in no pain, but she had little hope of recovery.

Helen arranged for Catholic sisters to come by once a week and pray in her mother's room. A priest gave Dolores the sacrament of the sick (which her traditional mother would have called extreme unction). Helen asked parish priests in Florida and in St. Louis to say masses for her mother's recovery.

Arranging these small comforts for her religious mother had given Helen a sense of peace and some hope of reconciliation. Her late father had called Helen "my little firecracker" and enjoyed her spirit. Dolores saw her daughter as dangerously rebellious. Helen tried hard, but she could never please her mother. Taking care of her mother in her final illness was Helen's last chance to be the daughter Dolores wanted.

Helen visited her mother every two or three days in the nursing home. She would sit in the tall turquoise chair by her mother's bedside and talk as if Dolores could really listen. Helen had read somewhere that some patients in comas could hear what people around them were saying. Helen told Dolores only news that she would want to hear.

Dolores's nursing home roommate was Ruth, a seventy-five-year-old who'd had a stroke. She, too, was unconscious. Ruth's daughter, Muriel, looked like a hen with a perm. Muriel fussed around the room each visit, then turned up the television so loud it should have awakened the residents of the nearby Lauderdale cemetery.

"Mama loves her television," Muriel insisted as she ramped up the volume. Helen flinched at the blasting soap opera. Ruth didn't move. Neither did Dolores.

Helen turned off the set as soon as Muriel left. It stayed off until Muriel's next visit. Neither woman mentioned this silent battle over loud noise. Muriel must have visited her mother this morning. Helen could hear the TV blaring from the courtyard.

She stopped by the nurses' station and checked in with Maria, the brown-skinned Jamaican nurse. "How's Mom?"

"The same, Miss Hawthorne." Maria's island accent made Helen think of vacation beaches and rum drinks with paper umbrellas. "The doctor is making his rounds. Would you like to speak to him?"

"Yes, please," Helen said. "I'll wait for him."

"It shouldn't be long," Maria said. "Dr. Lucre is only three rooms away from your mother's. I'll tell him you are here."

Dolores had the bed with the view, though she'd never seen it. Her window overlooked the courtyard with the palm trees, pots of red impatiens and jolly smokers. The room's walls were painted pink, Dolores's favorite color. The corkboard on her side was covered with homemade cards from her grandchildren, Allison and Tommy Junior.

Helen clicked off the blaring television and studied her mother.

She could hardly find Dolores's frail body in the tangle of lines, tubes and plastic bags. Dolores's skin was yellow and her eyes were ringed with dark circles. Her chest barely moved under the hospital gown.

She had only a few feathery wisps of white hair. Dolores had worn a brown wig for nearly twenty years. Helen had had the wig washed and styled. It waited on a stand in the closet.

Dolores's hands were crossed on her chest, as if she were already dead.

"Hi, Mom," Helen said, and kissed her mother.

No movement.

Helen tossed out the dying flowers she'd brought last week, and filled the vase with fresh water and pink carnations. She sat down and took Dolores's small, bruised hand in hers, carefully avoiding the IV line.

"I hope you've had a good week, Mom. I've been working. I like my job. Kathy and Tom send their love. Your grandchildren miss you. Allison asks for Grandma all the time. Kathy is shopping for Tommy Junior's school supplies. I can't believe school will be starting soon."

Silence.

"We didn't always get along, Mom, but I love you and want you to get well."

Helen's mother didn't answer.

Dolores had loved Rob. She saw all of Helen's faults, and none of Rob's. Dolores had stayed in touch with her former son-in-law, giving Rob information he used against her own daughter.

Kathy had supported Helen's decision to divorce Rob. When Helen was on the run, her sister was the only person who knew how to reach her.

During her divorce, Helen endured her mother's harsh lectures.

When the judge decreed Helen would lose half her home and her future earnings, she fled St. Louis. She called her mother occasionally. When the lectures started, Helen would break off the calls, claiming she couldn't hear her mother through the cell phone static.

Dolores pursued her daughter with hateful letters. "You have broken your promise and you will die," she wrote. Her religious mania grew worse after her unhappy second marriage to Larry. Her parish priest rebuked her for lack of charity.

As Dolores deteriorated mentally, Tom and Kathy considered placing her in a home. Dolores sneaked away, took a bus to Fort Lauderdale and showed up at Helen's wedding at the Coronado. Her visit was an unwelcome surprise. Dolores told Helen—and the assembled guests—"I'd rather see you dead than burning in hell for divorcing your husband." Those were her last words to her daughter.

Helen used these one-sided conversations with Dolores to ease her pain. She repeated her mother's arguments, trying to escape the stinging criticism.

"I know you disapproved of my divorce, Mom," she said. "You told me a wife had a duty to stay with her husband, no matter how unfaithful he was. But I'm not strong like you. I couldn't stand living with a lie. I couldn't forgive Rob."

More silence. To Helen, it seemed accusing.

"You said it was my fault that Rob strayed, Mom, because I didn't stay home and keep house like a proper wife. But we both had to work. We couldn't afford to have me stay home."

Not if we wanted that cracker-box mansion your son-in-law loved so much, she thought. Helen bit back those bitter words.

"I wouldn't have been a good homemaker like you were, Mom. I was happier in an office."

She clamped down her lips so the next thoughts would not escape: You stayed home and Daddy cheated on you anyway, and the whole parish knew it. Especially after he had a heart attack in a no-tell motel during an illicit encounter with the head of the altar society.

"You forgave Dad many times for his failings," she said. "I hope you can forgive me. I'm sorry our last words together were—"

Helen was relieved to hear a man clearing his throat. She turned to see Dr. Justin Lucre in the doorway, holding a chart. He was a fit forty, graying at the temples. Helen thought he could be in one of those old commercials that said, "Nine out of ten doctors recommend . . ."

Dr. Lucre pulled out a stethoscope and began examining Dolores.

"How is Mom?" Helen asked. "What were the results of the CT scan?"

"Not good. Your mother's brain is bleeding again, Helen. You and your mother's husband decided that 'comfort care only' was the best course. The bleeding is growing. She may go quickly."

"Is she hurting?"

"She's not in pain," Dr. Lucre said. "She'll drift away. It's good that you visit her, though I doubt if she knows you're here."

"How much time does she have left?" Helen asked.

"It's difficult to predict. Maybe a day, maybe two or more."

"Is there any chance she'll come to?" Helen asked.

"I doubt it. Miracles have happened, but they're unlikely. That's why we call them miracles."

"Oh," Helen said. She thought she'd been prepared for this, but the news felt like a blow.

"You've gone out of your way to give her the best care," Dr. Lucre said. "You've been a good daughter."

"A good daughter," Helen echoed.

But the doctor's words were no comfort. She knew the truth.

CHAPTER 9

Helen drifted out of her mother's room like a sleepwalker. She wiped away a tear, then realized she had walked all the way through the Sunset Rest Home to the lobby.

An old man snored softly on a fat sofa, a newspaper on his lap. Only the tropical fish saw Helen crying, and they were used to water.

She picked up the dozing man's paper and hid her face until she quit weeping. Helen didn't like to cry, especially in public. She wouldn't take the bus home until the tear storm stopped. Bus riders had their own troubles.

Then she realized she didn't need the bus. She was engaged. Phil, her fiancé, had begged Helen to let him drive her to the nursing home. She was too used to handling everything on her own. Helen stopped sniffling, opened her cell and called Phil.

"I've been waiting to hear from you," he said. "How's your mom?"

"Not good," Helen said. "The doctor says she maybe has a few days left. She's not in any pain, but that's the only good news."

"I'm sorry she won't recover," Phil said. "Can I pick you up and take you to lunch?"

"I definitely need a ride. But I'm not hungry," Helen said.

"I'll be there in twenty minutes," Phil said.

While Helen waited, she called her sister, Kathy, in St. Louis and told her the news. Kathy was silent for a moment, then said, "This isn't a surprise. Why do I feel like I've been punched in the gut?"

"Me, too," Helen said. "And Mom and I didn't get along."

"I wish I could be there with you," Kathy said. "But Tom can't get more time off work and we can't afford more plane tickets."

"I'll send you the money," Helen said.

"You aren't rich, either."

"No, but Phil and I can come up with enough for two plane tickets."

"Helen, if Mom were conscious, I'd be there," Kathy said. "But she never woke up."

"No, she didn't. Sometimes Mom opens her eyes, but it's obvious nobody is home," Helen said. "The doctor said it would be a miracle if she regained consciousness. She won't be alone when she goes. I'll be with her. Stay home with your family."

"Tommy Junior will take his grandmother's death hard," Kathy said. "Mom loves our kids and enjoys doing grandma things with them—making cookies, taking them to the park, letting them sleep over at her house.

"The holidays were so much fun, until she married Lawn Boy Larry. That Grinch stole our Christmas. He didn't like the kids making noise. He didn't want a real tree because it would shed needles. Larry complained when Allison got cookie crumbs on the kitchen floor. He wouldn't let Tommy play with his soccer ball in Mom's backyard. Larry said my boy might break a window. He's a mean man. I miss Mom. I didn't always agree with her, but I miss her."

Kathy's voice wavered and turned watery. "I'm not going to cry."

"You should," Helen said. "She's your mother. She was a good grandmother and she gave your children wonderful memories."

"I just hope Tommy fits into his best shirt and pants for the funeral," Kathy said. "The boy is growing like a weed." She let out a startled gasp and said, "Oh, no. I just realized Larry has the legal right to make Mom's funeral arrangements."

"Didn't Mom leave instructions?"

"Sure," Kathy said. "She wants her funeral at the parish church and she wants to be buried in the cemetery plot next to our father. Mom's name and her birthday are already carved in their joint tombstone."

Helen shuddered. "That's creepy. You feel like you have to die to fill in the blanks."

"Larry will know where to find Mom's instructions," Kathy said. "They're in the envelope with her will. I'll have to suck it up and tell him she's dying. Larry doesn't like me. He is afraid Mom will change her mind and leave everything to our kids."

"Can't happen now," Helen said.

"Word of Mom's impending demise must be out on the local WIC," Kathy said.

"Wic?" Helen asked. "Do you mean Wicca, as in witches?"

"No, WIC is what I call the widows' information circuit, though there are a few witches in that group. The parade of home-made meals for Lawn Boy Larry has started already. Larry loves pot roast. I can't pass his house without seeing a widow with a foil-wrapped dish ringing his doorbell. Mom's funeral will be jammed, and not only with her friends. Every unmarried older woman in the parish will be in her best dress, trying to bag Larry. They'll proposition him over Mom's casket."

"Larry?" Helen asked. "Who would want him? The guy is bald and built like a broomstick."

"You've overlooked his assets," Kathy said. "Larry has all his own teeth, plays bridge, has a fat pension, and best of all, he can drive at night. He's the Daniel Craig of the senior set. I'd be surprised if Mrs. Raines didn't tackle him at the burial. She's the front-runner—excuse me, hobbler—for his hand in marriage. Her pot roast is said to be fork-tender."

"I'd better give Larry the news before his new flame flies to Florida and puts a pillow over our mother's face," Helen said.

Kathy started giggling, then said, "I shouldn't laugh."

"Why not? The thought of any woman pursuing Larry is hilarious. Instead of making pot roasts, they should wave their bank statements at him. I'll call Larry."

"You're a good sister," Kathy said.

Right, Helen thought as she hung up. Like I'm a good daughter.

Before she could dial Larry's number, her cell phone buzzed. It was Vera, Snapdragon's owner. "Helen, can you meet me for lunch today?"

"Uh, no," Helen said.

"Are you okay? You sound funny," Vera said.

"I'm at the nursing home. Mom is worse. She only has another day or so."

"I'm sorry, sweetie."

"I shouldn't be so upset," Helen said. "I've been expecting this."

"My mother died of cancer," Vera said. "No matter how well prepared you think you are, it's still a shock. Let's forget lunch."

"How about tomorrow?" Helen said. "I could meet you for breakfast."

"Sure," Vera said. "The shop will still be closed. Swarms of cops are crawling all over the place. How about nine o'clock? We could go to the Coral Rose Cafe in Hollywood. Best breakfast in Broward County. I'll pick you up at nine."

"See you then," Helen said, and shut off her phone as Phil's black Jeep pulled up under the Sunset Rest portico.

Helen felt like she was running toward life when she jumped into the Jeep. She admired her fiancé as his Jeep plunged into the stream of traffic. The wind ruffled his silver-white hair. The man was hot as Florida, but in a good way. Helen sighed with happiness. Phil was her reward after her wretched marriage to Rob.

"Margery has a cold glass of wine for you," Phil said. "There's a beer waiting for me."

"I can use it," Helen said. "I need to fortify myself before I call Larry, Mother's husband."

"Margery and I will be at your side." Phil reached over and squeezed her hand.

"Good. You can restrain me from reaching down the phone and tearing out his throat," Helen said.

At the Coronado, Helen was touched to find that Phil had fixed lunch for the three of them. The food was set out on Margery's kitchen table.

"I got you and Margery salads with grilled chicken and made an onion-and-rye sandwich for myself," Phil said. "There are cupcakes for dessert."

"What else is on your sandwich besides onion?" Margery asked.

"Irish butter," Phil said.

"You're eating a butter-and-onion sandwich?" Helen said.

"You're always telling me to eat healthy," Phil said. "This is a Bermuda onion. It has powerful antioxidants."

"It has something else powerful, too," Helen said, waving her hand. "At least it's not Limburger."

"I can't find that cheese down here." Phil looked innocent as a puppy.

"Good," Helen said.

"Listen, I don't want to ruin your appetite further," Margery said, "but you should start making arrangements to ship your mother's body home to St. Louis."

"She's not dead yet," Helen said.

"She will be soon, if the doctor's right. It's better to make those decisions now than trying to reach a funeral director at three in the morning. Trust me, that's when old people pass. You'll be too tired and upset to make rational decisions then."

"Do you know a good funeral director?" Helen asked.

"I do, and a couple of bad ones. I'll go with you, if you want."

"Thanks," Helen said. "But I can't deal with that today."

"How about tomorrow?" Margery asked. "We can leave about noon."

Fortified by two white wines, one salad and a cupcake, Helen was ready to call her stepfather. She could see Larry now, his bones covered with wrinkled skin like a baggy shirt, his hairless head hidden under a flat brown cap. Larry made polite noises of regret when she told him about Dolores. Helen thought she'd heard people sound more upset when their cat died.

"I'll make the arrangements to send Mother home," Helen said.

"Well, dear," Larry said, in a voice that rustled like old paper, "I was thinking of having Dolores cremated."

"Mother wants to be buried in St. Louis, Larry. She left her funeral instructions in the desk in her living room, along with her will."

"I know, dear, but it's so expensive to ship her body home. Cremation would be much better."

"You mean cheaper," Helen said, her voice getting higher.

"Well, yes, there are cost advantages. And we must be practical."

"You'll cremate my mother over my dead body." Or over Mom's, Helen thought. She took a deep breath. Margery hovered in the background, frowning at her. Phil rubbed her back to calm her. Helen knew if she fought with Lawn Boy Larry, she'd get nowhere.

She softened her voice and said, "Larry. Lawrence. Sir. You're right, of course. But Mother was old-school Catholic. She was taught that cremation was wrong. I understand the Church has changed its view and cremation is allowed as long as you believe in the resurrection of the body. But Mother has already bought a plot next to her first husband and had her name carved on the tombstone. It's paid for."

"But I have a coupon," Larry said. "My friend Bert lives in Pompano Beach, which I think is near you. He sent me a coupon for a low-cost cremation. It's good anywhere in Broward County, where you live. You can get Dolores cremated for only six hundred dollars. That includes the coffin."

Helen squeezed Phil's hand so hard it turned red, then said, "Larry, this is my mother's funeral, not a sale at Costco. She will not be thrown away like a full ashtray. She wants a funeral in her parish church with all of her friends there and she will have it."

"But Helen, dear, that's so wasteful. We can have a memorial service at church, and the ladies' sodality will serve tea and sandwiches. Those are free. I'd have to make a slight donation, of course, but . . ."

"I'm sure your donation will be skinnier than a heroin addict," Helen said. Margery frowned at her, and Helen tried to rein in her rage. "Larry, my mother has left you her money and her house. Surely there should be enough money for her wishes."

"Well, dear, housing prices aren't what they used to be—"

Helen interrupted the dithering and shrieked, "I'll pay the freakin' shipping costs myself."

"And where will you get the money, dear?"

"I'll sell my body on the street, Larry. I'll hold up a gas station. I'll get the money some way. And my sins will be on your soul!"

Margery clamped her hand over Helen's mouth. "Shut up and think before you say another word," she whispered in Helen's ear, then took her hand away.

"Larry," Helen said slowly. "I'm sorry. My mother's illness has upset me. I will pay for her funeral. It won't cost you a penny."

"Well, that's very generous, dear, but—"

"And if you don't say yes, my sister and I will start dialing all the women on the parish calling tree. We'll contact every widow and tell them how you are treating our mother. Those women will be shocked. The parade of pot roasts will stop. No more free food, Larry. You'll starve before you see another home-cooked meal. Do you understand?"

"Yes, Helen. Your mother said you could be forceful. Dolores can be buried in St. Louis. But I get to pick out the funeral home."

"Knock yourself out. Maybe you can make it a double ceremony."

Margery glared at Helen.

"I'm sorry," Larry said, "but I didn't get that last sentence. Something on the double?"

"I said thank you for a decision on the double," Helen said.

CHAPTER 10

The Coral Rose Cafe was small and simple: two rooms scented with coffee and warm sugar. It was very Hollywood. The other Hollywood, the casual beach town between Miami and Fort Lauderdale. Helen's breakfast with Vera was a break between death duties—her mother's lingering exit and Chrissy's violent end.

Helen's plan to order fresh fruit was derailed when she saw blueberry pancakes arrive at the next table. They were made with blueberries, not canned fruit. That counted as fresh fruit, didn't it?

"I have to order those," she said to Vera. "After all, how often do I get blueberry pancakes with real maple syrup?"

"As often as I snowmobile on Hollywood Beach," Vera said. "I'm going for the eggs Benedict with portobello mushrooms."

Vera told the waitress, "Please don't skimp on the hollandaise sauce. I'd like the fried potatoes and could you bring extra fruit bread?"

How could Vera look so trim and muscular when she ate like a linebacker? Helen wondered. The woman was a mystery. Helen still hadn't figured out how Vera managed frizz-free hair in the Florida humidity.

When the waitress left with their order, Vera said, "How are you? You look a little ragged."

"I am. The doctor says Mom doesn't have long." Helen felt the tears rush in and said, "Let's talk about something else."

"You were right," Vera said. "Chrissy didn't commit suicide. She was murdered. Detective McNally confirmed it. Chrissy was stunned with that Limoges pineapple, then hanged."

Helen winced.

"At least she was unconscious when she died," Vera said. "Poor little thing."

"Are the police still at the shop?" Helen asked.

"I run into one every time I turn around," she said. "Cops make me nervous. Detective McNally keeps asking questions like he thinks I killed Chrissy. I'm going to need a lawyer soon and there's no money coming in."

"Why would he suspect you? You wouldn't kill a good source," Helen asked. "Chrissy brought in prime merchandise."

"McNally said I was in the back of the store when Chrissy was killed," Vera said. "I was messing around with the silk scarves that morning. That's true, but so were Roger and Commissioner Stranahan."

"But Loretta left before Chrissy was killed, didn't she?" Helen said.

"I personally let her out the back door. I gave her an alibi and let the cops loose on me," Vera said.

"I know Danny the developer killed his wife," Helen said. "I wish we could prove it. You saw how he treated Chrissy. He yelled at her. He dragged her to the back like a caveman and bruised her arm. She was afraid of him."

"Chrissy was so afraid of him, she bruised my arm," Vera said. "She grabbed it and made me promise I wouldn't tell Danny about the money she made at my store. She even gave me the pony-hair purse as a bribe. I'm keeping it, too. I earned it. I showed my bruises to McNally, but the detective said I could have gotten them from anyone, even a boyfriend.

"Danny is as protected as the manatee. The police will be gone tomorrow, or so they say. I think they'll be harder to get rid of than roaches. At least I can open the store again at ten o'clock. I hope I'll have customers. Can you work tomorrow?"

"Unless Mom takes a sudden turn for the worse," Helen said.

"Are you sure you're ready to come to work?" Vera asked.

"Please," Helen said. "It will take my mind off things. I have to make my mother's funeral arrangements this afternoon."

Helen was grateful when plates of fragrant food arrived with a basket of warm breakfast bread and the conversation ended. She slathered on butter and poured half the Vermont syrup crop for 2009 on her cakes. The two women dined in blissful silence for a few minutes.

Then Helen asked, "I don't understand why Detective McNally is going after you. Isn't the husband the chief suspect when a wife dies?"

"I thought so, but the cops are all over me like fleas on a hound. Aw, crap. I've dripped hollandaise on my Lilly Pulitzer shirt." Vera dunked her napkin in her water glass and dabbed at the stain on the turquoise-and-white-striped shirt.

"New shirt?" Helen asked.

"New old shirt," Vera said. "Mrs. Vanderbilt brought it in. I think she wore it once."

"Why did you code name your Lilly Pulitzer source Mrs. Van-derbilt?" Helen asked. "She's a dreadful snob, right?"

"Right. She sees herself as the social arbiter of Hendin Island. She's pleased to be named after the creator of the Four Hundred. My Mrs. Vanderbilt has never seen any photos of the society leader. The real Mrs. V. was no size two."

"Your major jeans source is Sookie Stackhouse," Helen said, "but she doesn't look anything like Anna Paquin, the *True Blood* actress."

"My Sookie dates a real bloodsucker," Vera said. "My code names are little jokes, and the jokes are on my ladies. But they don't know it." Vera's smile was a hard bloodred slash.

"Why name them at all?" Helen asked.

"Helps me keep track of things." Vera took another sip of coffee. "In their world, it would be a disaster if anyone found out Mrs. Big Bucks was buying Mrs. Fat Cat's castoffs. Planets would collide and stars would fall from the sky. So I choose buyers from outside their orbits.

"My Glenn Close serves on a lot of boards and wears serious suits. Emily usually buys them. She's a drug rep who needs to dress well when she visits doctors' offices, but she can't afford designer suits. The rest of Glenn's suits are usually bought by Commissioner Stranahan and Tara, an up-and-coming young lawyer."

"What if your Glenn's husband had an affair with Tara?" Helen asked. "Wouldn't he notice she was wearing his wife's old suit?"

"That's the sad part," Vera said. "Once the honeymoon is over, the trophy wives are invisible to their husbands. Glenn's husband would rip that secondhand suit off Tara so fast, he'd never see it."

Helen forked in another mouthful of blueberry pancake. "What I don't get is why Chrissy had to sell her clothes at Snapdragon's in the first place. Her maneuvers cost Danny a fortune, just so she could have some spending money. Danny would have been better off giving her three grand rather than having her collect two hundred fifty after you sold a purse that he bought for three thousand dollars."

"It's not about money," Vera said. "It's about control. Some of these rich men give their wives allowances like little kids, but the women have no money of their own. The wives have unlimited shopping at places like the Galleria. They're on a tight leash. The clever ones figure out how to get off the leash. They buy expensive things, wait until the store's return policy expires, then sell the clothes to me on consignment. They only get a fraction of the money back, but it's *their* money, not their husband's. The husband keeps the illusion that he's in control. The leashed wives have their secret bank accounts or stashes for their cash. Maybe they use it to buy gold cigarette lighters for their boy toys, or drugs, or maybe they're saving it to pay a divorce lawyer. But they are desperate for money of their own."

"My grandmother did that," Helen said. "She wasn't rich, but she was a traditional wife. My grandfather wouldn't give her spending money. She was on a tight household budget, figured down to the last can of cleanser. She'd wait until Grandpa had a few beers and fell asleep. Then she'd tiptoe into their bedroom and take his pocket change. But that was almost a hundred years ago."

"In the world of the rich, marriage hasn't changed that much," Vera said. She mopped up the last of her hollandaise sauce with a triangle of English muffin.

"What about murder?" Helen asked.

"That's why Chrissy's murder is so complicated," Vera said. "All the suspects are either rich or politicians."

"Don't forget bargain-hunting Jordan," Helen said. "She was there, too, and alone in the back."

"She's poor but weird," Vera said.

"What about Roger?" Helen asked. "He's not rich."

"He's a hanger-on. Or maybe that's banger-on. He likes to bed his rich ladies. There are no normal suspects."

Helen was home before noon. She changed into a dark pantsuit and climbed into Margery's big white rectangular car. The cozy, sugar-scented Coral Rose Cafe vanished in a cloud of Margery's cigarette smoke as they drove to the Florida Family Funeral Home.

Even on the porch, the air smelled of hothouse flowers and felt heavier, as if accumulated sorrow weighed it down. A grandfather clock gave a single, solemn *bong!* as Helen and Margery entered the funeral home.

"Why do grandfather clocks sound so gloomy in funeral homes?" Helen asked.

"What do you expect?" Margery asked. "It's a place for grieving. Though some funerals I've been to needed a cuckoo clock—and a referee."

Helen barely recognized her landlady this afternoon. Margery wore a pale lavender shirtwaist. Matching pumps hid her orange pedicure. Her fingernail polish was a subdued pink. She'd left her wild outfits and gladiator sandals at the Coronado.

Margery had stubbed out her cigarette on the porch, but Helen thought smoke still trailed after her.

"Why are you staring at me?" Margery asked.

"You're dressed for a June Cleaver look-alike contest."

"I'm trying to look like a respectable citizen who can fork over enough dough for a funeral," Margery said. "You don't have any money."

"I have eight hundred dollars in cash," Helen said.

"Hah. This will cost five thousand minimum. Where will you get the other forty-two hundred?"

"Phil gave me the money."

"Good," Margery said. "That's what a fiancé is supposed to do."

"His gift comes with strings," Helen said. "He made me promise that when we fly to St. Louis for the funeral, we'll hire a good lawyer to fight my divorce. He wants all the paperwork in order so we can get married legally."

"Thank the Lord," Margery said. "And why are you whispering? We're not in church."

"It's all the stained glass and candles," Helen said.

A sober-suited receptionist appeared. "We have an appointment with Cassie, your preneed specialist," Margery told her.

The receptionist seated them in an office the size of an upright coffin, painted a lugubrious shade of pink. There was room for an undersized desk, two client chairs and a rack of pamphlets headlined *Plan for Dignity at the End of Life.*

Cassie squeezed in between the wall and the desk and sat down. The preneed specialist looked like an overgrown cheerleader: small, smiley and chirpy. She had a perky dark bob and a cat pin on her gray suit. A black cat.

Cassie arranged her smiling face into a professionally sad expression. "Now, how may we help you—Miss . . . ?"

"I'm Helen Hawthorne and this is my friend Margery Flax. We're here about my mother. She's in a nursing home in Fort Lauderdale. Her doctor says she hasn't much time left. Mother was down here on a trip and took ill suddenly. She wants to be buried in St. Louis, where she's lived all her life. I want to make the arrangements now, while I can think clearly."

"Wise," Cassie said. "We offer thoughtful care and affordable dignity. Let me explain the process.

"When the time comes, we would pick up your mother and bring her to our care. She will be washed, embalmed and dressed here. We will have her transported by plane to St. Louis. We will ask that you call the St. Louis funeral home to receive her at the airport. Picking her up and preparing her in our care is twenty-eight hundred ninety-five dollars."

Helen wondered why the home didn't round out the price to a flat twenty-nine hundred dollars.

"That price will include a one-hour viewing for the immediate family," Cassie said.

"I'm the only one here and I've seen her," Helen said. "I mean, alive."

"You don't have to have a private viewing if you don't wish one," Cassie said. "Our caskets start at eight hundred ninety-five dollars and go up."

Again that ninety-five dollars. Helen felt a wild urge to giggle.

"The actual cost of returning your mother home will depend upon the casket you choose," Cassie said. "You can make that choice today. When your mother is ready to leave, we will drive her to the airport."

Cassie made it sound like a taxi service. Maybe they had a special airport shuttle for the dead, Helen thought, using black vans.

"Will she fly on a cargo plane?" Helen asked.

"Your mother will fly commercial," Cassie said. "It's a well-kept secret, but most commercial flights have at least one casket on board, especially here in Florida, where so many of our citizens come from other states."

"Will the passengers see her getting on the plane?" Helen asked. She had a vision of her mother's casket waiting on the tarmac, piled high with rolling suitcases, baby strollers and golf bags.

"No," Cassie said. "The casket will be placed in an air tray, which has a wood cover."

"So the airline won't roll the casket out with the luggage?" Helen asked.

Margery looked at her strangely.

Cassie said smoothly, "Nothing like that. The air tray, which is required by the airlines, is one hundred twenty-five dollars. No one on the flight will know there's a casket on board. We will make sure that your mother travels with dignity. The airfare will be about five hundred dollars."

"How soon after she . . . uh . . . passes," Helen began. Suddenly, "dies" seemed too difficult to say. ". . . can Mom go home?"

"She could go home within the week after the certificate is signed by the doctor. There probably won't be an autopsy, since your mother is under a doctor's care. Any death certificates needed are ten dollars each. Would you like to see our caskets now? We offer dignity no matter what your budget."

"Let's go," Helen said. The room was claustrophobic. Helen hoped if she moved around, she would lose the urge to giggle.

The showroom reminded Helen of a used-car lot, with polished caskets lined up in rows. She settled on a midpriced wooden casket with a mahogany finish and silver handles.

"The lining has pink overtones to flatter the complexion. This is a very warm look," Cassie said.

"Right," Helen said. "We wouldn't want Mother to look cold."

Margery glared her into silence.

"Will you be purchasing a slumber robe?" Cassie asked.

"A what?" Helen said.

"She means a shroud," Margery said. "They look like nightgowns to me."

"They're very well made and dignified," Cassie said.

"I think Mother would be more comfortable in her own clothes," Helen said. "I can ask my sister to FedEx our mother's favorite dress."

"Very good. Do you have a recent picture of your mother? That will help us prepare her hair and makeup so she looks as natural as possible."

"My sister can send that, too," Helen said. "Mother has her own wig, and that's been washed and styled."

"Good," Cassie said. "Then her hair will look just the way she always wears it."

They were crammed back in the sorrowful pink room. Cassie reached into the undersized desk and pulled out a pile of papers and a black pen.

"If your mother passes in the night after our business hours," she said, "it would help if you signed the paperwork now so that you could contact us and we could take her into our care. The total, including preparations, casket, airfare and air tray, comes to four thousand, nine hundred seventy dollars. Would you like to order any death certificates in advance?

"You will need one death certificate for every life insurance policy," Cassie said, "if your mother has them, as well as pension plans, any property in her name, the IRS, all her credit cards, checking and savings accounts, CDs, stocks and bonds. Some banks require an original certificate for every account."

Helen was adding up the money Larry would need for the death certificates to claim her mother's small estate. She'd make sure Larry would buy every certificate he needed. Each ten-dollar charge would hurt that skinflint as if it were stripped from his hide.

"I'll take three death certificates," Helen said. "Might as well make the price an even five thousand. I'll write you a check."

"Very good," Cassie said. "And could I interest you in our preneed payment plan? For just ten dollars a week—"

Helen interrupted. "Cassie, right now, I can barely afford to live, much less die."

CHAPTER 11

The line straggled halfway down the block from Snapdragon's, and it was only nine in the morning. Two television vans were parked out front. Helen nipped around the back and knocked on the store's door. Vera peeked out and unlocked it.

"Quick!" Vera grabbed Helen by the wrist and hauled her into the back room. In the dim light, Helen could see Vera was not her usual stylish self. Her silky straight hair was badly frizzed. She had an ugly zit on her chin, and lint on her black clamdiggers.

"You look a little harried," Helen said. "That forest green microfiber dustcloth clashes with your lime top."

"Only old ladies like matchy-matchy," Vera said. "Have you seen that crowd outside?"

"Tons of people. That's good, right?" Helen said.

"Bad," Vera said. "For two reasons: A zillion reporters want interviews and I don't need that kind of publicity. And those aren't customers. They're tourists. They're wearing more polyester than a seventies disco dancer. Half that crowd is carrying foam boxes from the Flo with dripping leftovers. Lookie loos will leave greasy fingerprints on my stock. They won't buy anything. I need money. I have to make the rent and pay Roger."

"Roger?" Helen asked.

"You met Roger the day Chrissy died," Vera said. "The guy in the back room. The one you thought I was dating."

"Oh, right. The muscleman with the tan," Helen said. "I remember now."

"Any woman with a pulse would remember him. Now that Chrissy's gone, he's my best designer source. Last month he brought in three instant sellers: a little white size-two Moschino with the tags still on it, the beaded Versace evening gown and the 7 For All Mankind jeans. They practically flew off the racks. Then he brought me True Religion jeans and T-shirts."

"Where's he get those clothes? Does he work in retail?" Helen asked.

"He parks cars at Cheri, the posh salon down the street. Roger makes minimum wage and tips. He probably charms the clothes off the women at the salon.

"Roger says he has a gift for picking bargains at garage sales in rich neighborhoods. I believe him. With those blue eyes, I'd believe anything he says. I have to come up with three hundred dollars to pay him for last month's sales, and he'll be in for his money this afternoon."

"Do you think he shoplifts clothes?" Helen asked.

"Honey, I can't afford thoughts like that," Vera said. "Besides, some people tell the truth. I had an older man bring in a fabulous size-two Escada suit with a belt, scarf and shoes. All the pieces had the tags on them. The man said his wife wouldn't be wearing them. He had on saggy jeans and a stained T-shirt. The dude looked like a bum.

"I thought, right, and figured he's stolen them. Later, I learned his wife was a businesswoman who'd died of a stroke right before an important trip to New York. He was telling the truth."

"While we're on the subject of dead wives," Helen said, "what do we do about the dressing room where Chrissy was killed? Is it closed off?"

"Can't afford to close it," Vera said. "We only have two. I've fixed it up."

The back dressing room smelled of patchouli. A framed pastel print of a seashell hid the spot where Chrissy had been hanged. The floor had a pale blue rug. The chair was replaced by a white wicker stool. The new additions were all Snapdragon's stock.

"Did you repaint the room?" Helen asked. "The walls are extra white."

"Wasn't time to repaint," Vera said. "I hired Marquita and Evie to clean. Those two women have been working since six this morning. They washed down the walls and have been dusting like crazy. There was so much fingerprint powder, it looked like a black snowstorm."

"I like the seashell print there," Helen said.

"The cops cut the hook right out of the wall," Vera said. "The print covers the hole. I bought another dress hook and put it up on the opposite wall. Chrissy's blood dripped onto the tile grout. Marquita and Evie couldn't scrub it out, so I added the rug. The black fingerprint powder made the chair grungy. It's in the back until I can repaint it."

"The room looks fresh," Helen said.

"I'll probably have to redecorate the other room, too," Vera said. She sounded gloomy.

"What can I do?" Helen asked.

"Straighten and size the women's shirts while I put more summer shoes on display."

Helen worked at buttoning shirts and returning the sizes to the right racks. She shook her head when she found a sharp hanger thrust through a sheer top, tearing the delicate fabric.

"More loss," Vera said sadly. "I'll ask our alterations woman if she can mend it."

At nine fifty-five, Vera paid the two Latina cleaners and let them out the back door. At ten oh one, people impatiently rattled the front door. "I'd better let them in before they break the glass," Vera said. "Battle stations. I'll handle the reporters."

A human waterfall poured through the pink door.

"May I help you?" Helen asked a woman with orange hair. Not red. Orange. She could have been a Sunkist spokeswoman.

"Just looking," Ms. Orange said.

So was the woman behind her in a peach pantsuit. And the two women in strawberry tops. The shop looked like a fruit stand.

If Helen had a dollar for every time she heard "just looking," Vera could have paid the rent and Roger.

The ghouls were worse than the lookie loos.

"Is this the dressing room where that lady . . . you know . . . died?" a breathy blonde asked. Her skin was so pale Helen was sure she bunked in a coffin. Her bloody lipstick was unsettling. She licked her lips. Helen thought Vampira was excited by this distant brush with death.

"Which scarf was she hanged with?" Vampira slid her hands along the silk scarves. Her nails were red, too.

"It's not here," Helen said. "The police took it."

"Oh." Vampira left.

Vera had cleverly positioned herself outside to talk to the reporters. She faced the street so the television viewers would see a family restaurant in the background. "It's a terrible loss," Helen could hear Vera say, "but the police will catch him. He wouldn't dare come back here."

By noon, Helen had had four women who wanted to see the "death dressing room." Two more wanted to buy the "death scarf." When the latest ghoul left at twelve thirty, Helen ran up front to Vera. "How are sales?"

"Nothing," Vera said. "Nada. Zero. I told you all we'd have were lookie loos."

"Would you mind if I lied to sell something?"

"Honey, you can strip naked and dance in the window if it will help make a sale. Just split your tips with me. We need the money."

"I'll need to cut off the scarf tags," Helen said.

"Take the scissors and cut me a deal," Vera said. "I need to make five hundred dollars minimum. Save the tags so I can keep track of the stock."

Helen bird-dogged two more lookie loos before an older woman with a Bride of Dracula hairdo materialized. Her hair was dyed black with a dramatic white stripe and poufed like Elvis's pompadour. Her long white cotton dress was a shroud.

Dracula's Bride picked out a black Ferragamo scarf with dead-white flowers. "Is this the scarf she was hanged with?" Her voice fluttered like moth wings.

Helen's skin crawled. She looked around, then whispered, "Don't tell anyone, but that's the death scarf. The police returned it this morning."

"Was it cleaned?" Dracula's Bride spoke in a cobwebbed whisper.

"No," Helen said. "Not since Chrissy's death."

"How much?" Dracula's Bride asked.

"We can't sell it," Helen said.

"I'll pay anything." Her eyes gleamed like a cat's in heat.

"Not for sale," Helen said.

"Please." A cold, bony hand clutched Helen's arm.

"Well, if you promise not to tell anyone . . ."

"Yes? Yes?" Dracula's Bride asked.

"It's five hundred dollars. Nonreturnable. But only if the shop owner says yes. I'll ask Vera for you. Wait here."

Helen hurried up front. "I've sold her this for five hundred bucks," she whispered. "Act reluctant to sell it."

"You're kidding," Vera whispered.

"Start acting," Helen said, "if you want your money."

"No!" Vera said loudly. "I can't let that scarf go! It's too precious."

"Please," Helen said, equally loud. "She'll take care of it. She'll respect it."

"Five twenty-five!" cried the Bride of Dracula from the back of the store.

She streaked up front and burst into a scary smile when Vera said, "Sold. But only if you keep your promise not to tell anyone its origin."

"Can I tell my boyfriend?" Dracula's Bride said. "I'll swear him to secrecy. But Brad will find it . . . exciting."

"What if he blabs?" Vera asked.

"He never tells anyone what we do," the Bride said. "I'll sign a paper if you want. And I'll make it five hundred fifty." She stroked the scarf, then quickly counted out the cash. Helen was wrapping the scarf while Vera made an award-winning show of reluctance. "All right, if he can keep his mouth shut," she said.

"Oh, he'll be quiet," Dracula's Bride said. "He likes to—"

"Here's your purchase," Helen interrupted. She shoved the pink Snapdragon's bag at the Bride and pushed her toward the door.

After she left, Vera said, "You wuss. I wanted to know what her boyfriend liked to do."

"If I found out, it could ruin my love life," Helen said. "I might have to take the veil or live in a lighthouse or something. And was his name Brad, or Vlad, as in Vlad the Impaler?"

"I don't care if he's Stone Cold Steve Austin," Vera said. "You got me five hundred fifty dollars for a thirty-dollar scarf. Now I can pay Roger."

After the sale to the Bride of Dracula, the lookie loos seemed easier to tolerate. Two teenage girls spent half an hour trying on rings and giggling while Helen stood guard. Rings were one of the store's most shoplifted items. The brown-haired girl bought her birthstone—an amethyst—for the second sale of the day.

Helen wrapped up the ring. She was ready with a "May I help you?" when the door opened. The words died on her lips. This was a tough customer and an unwelcome one—Detective Richard McNally.

"Is Ms. Salinda here?" he asked.

Vera came out of her office carrying six shirts to be tagged. She hung them on the dry-cleaning hook at the counter.

"You want to talk to me?" There was a touch of defiance in Vera's voice. Helen tried to slip away, but Detective McNally said, "Don't go far, Ms Hawthorne. We may have a question for you, too.

"We want to know where you get your clothes, Vera," he said.

"This shirt is from a Palm Beach woman," she said, indicating her lime top. "I got some things from Chrissy, as I told you before. A Hendin Island woman is another good source."

"So your sources are all women?" he asked.

"Desperate housewives. Well-dressed women who need cash," Vera said.

With that, Roger walked in. He looked like he'd stepped off a Malibu beach. He was carrying a soda can and three evening dresses, carefully wrapped in clear plastic. Even ten feet away, Helen could see expensive beading and sequins on the long dresses.

Roger's blue eyes widened when he saw the detective, and he started to back out.

"May we help you, sir?" McNally said, blocking his exit. "Or maybe I should say 'ma'am.' Vera told me she only buys clothes from women."

"Uh, no. Yes. I brought these in for dry cleaning." Roger was stuttering.

"They look a little small for you, Roger," McNally said.

"I'm running an errand for a lady at the salon. I said I'd drop off her dry cleaning."

"She keeps her dry cleaning in plastic?" McNally asked.

"The beads and sequins fall off if you aren't careful," Roger said.

"Funny how clothes get dirty on hangers in the stores," McNally said. "I see tags on these."

"I—she—uh, the lady likes them cleaned before she wears them. You never know who tries them on in a store. They might have bugs or something."

"Right," McNally said. "Neiman Marcus is infested with bedbugs. But one escaped and is standing in front of me."

"Uh, can I leave my dry cleaning and go?" Roger asked.

"For now," McNally said. There was a trace of a smile. A smirk, actually.

"I'd like them back Tuesday," Roger said, hardly pausing between words. He set down his soda can, then dropped the dresses on the counter as if they were on fire. He was out the door.

"Well, he seemed desperate all right," McNally said. "But I don't think Roger is a housewife."

As if on cue, a size zero appeared lugging a green shopping bag brimming with clothes. She was blond as a Christmas angel. Vera seemed to regard her as a heavenly savior.

"Kelly," she said, "what a pleasant surprise." Helen had never heard Vera give such an effusive welcome.

"I'm cleaning out my closet," Kelly said, "and I wanted to bring you some summer clothes while you can still sell them. I have Versace, D&G, Gucci and—oopsie, this Vera Wang still has the tag on it. Please don't tell my husband. Jason would have a fit if he knew I never wore it. These are shopping errors. My head cleared when I got home, so I didn't wear them in public. I don't know why I ever bought that hot pink Ed Hardy shirt. There are too many imitators. My maid bought one almost like it at Target. I was mortified. And these white clamdiggers make my ass look wider than Roseanne Barr's."

She looked up and saw Detective McNally. "Excuse my language." She attempted a blush.

"I'm sure he's not offended," Vera said. "Let's talk price quickly and I'll send you on your way."

Vera made an offer that Helen thought was overgenerous. She suspected it was out of gratitude for Kelly's timely arrival. The woman didn't argue. Kelly signed the agreement and flew out of the store.

"Well, I hope that answered your questions about my sources, Detective," Vera said. "Now, may I ask you one? Why hasn't Danny been arrested for Chrissy's murder? I thought the husband was always a prime suspect. Or do you give developers a pass?"

Helen could hear the anger in McNally's voice. "He would be, Vera, except for one complication. He was in a meeting for the

Orchid House development fifteen blocks away at the time of his wife's death. Danny has thirty witnesses."

"And how did you know the time of death?"

"His wife told us," Detective McNally said. "The victim's watch stopped when she was attacked. It fell to the floor and broke. Oh, one more thing. Ms. Hawthorne, your fingerprints were on that watch. And on the murder weapon."

CHAPTER 12

A shattering silence followed Detective McNally's statement. The street sounds outside Snapdragon's Second Thoughts disappeared. A flock of chattering tourists passing the shop seemed to make no sound.

Helen's shocked brain scrambled to hold on to Detective McNally's words: *Your fingerprints. On that watch. And the murder weapon.*

Finally, Helen managed to ask two questions that made sense: "Why would my fingerprints be on a scarf? Can you get fingerprints off a scarf?"

"Your fingerprints weren't on the scarf, Ms. Hawthorne," McNally said. "Mrs. Martlet was coldcocked by a white porcelain pineapple. We found her blood and hair on it and your fingerprints on the bottom of the ornament."

"I dusted it," Helen said. "I hated it, too. I never thought pineapples were ornamental, but rich people put them on everything. They like those stupid monkeys, too. They bring in monkey lamps, bookends and candlesticks to sell. Some of them are wearing turbans. The monkeys, not the rich people. I don't get it."

Detective McNally interrupted. "Now that we have your opinions on decorating," he said, "let's go back to your fingerprints."

Helen had bought enough time to gather her scattered thoughts. "My fingerprints should be on that pineapple," she said, and grew more confident. "They should be all over this shop. It's my job to dust the stock. You should be surprised if my fingerprints aren't on anything in this shop."

"Mrs. Martlet's watch wasn't part of the stock," McNally said.

"I thought the glass on Chrissy's watch face was broken," Helen said.

"We found your thumbprint on the metal back."

"Oh. Right. Chrissy dropped her watch. The clasp was broken. I picked it up, followed her to the dressing room and handed it to her."

"And you didn't tell me?" McNally asked.

"I forgot."

"How many times did you go over the events on the day of the murder?"

"Five," Helen said. "Or maybe six."

"And you forgot six times?"

"There was a lot happening," Helen said.

"What about you, Ms. Salinda? Did you see Ms. Hawthorne pick up the watch belonging to the victim?"

"Yes. But I forgot, too," Vera said.

"Perfect. Double amnesia. What about Ms. Drubb and Ms. Stranahan? Did they see anything?"

"Who's Ms. Drubb?" Vera asked.

"That's Jordan," Helen said. "I don't think those two women were nearby."

"Amazing," McNally said. "And convenient."

"Look, I'm sorry I forgot," Helen said. "I only talked to Chrissy the day she died, but she seemed like a nice lady. She dropped her watch. I took it back to her while she was accusing her husband of cheating on her. She said he'd been staring at another woman's chest the night before.

"Commissioner Stranahan showed up back there after I returned the watch, and there was another fight. Chrissy told Danny she knew about the three thousand new jobs his project would bring into the city and also the house of the seven toilets. That made him mad, but I don't know why."

"We checked that, too," Detective McNally said. "Danny Martlet owns a house in the Idlewyld neighborhood. It has four bathrooms and two in the pool house. That's six total. I'd call it a mansion, but what do I know? Place looks like a Greek temple."

"Are you sure Danny isn't guilty?" Vera asked. "He was really mean to his wife."

"He may be mean, but he's not guilty," McNally said.

"But they fought in front of us," Vera said.

"Lady, if every squabble resulted in murder, we wouldn't have a married couple left in Florida. Let me repeat. We have no evidence that Danny killed his wife."

"Did you decide that because he's rich?" Vera burst out. "Are powerful people exempt from police scrutiny? Is that why you aren't bugging Commissioner Stranahan? Are you here because it's easier to harass us? This murder is ruining my business."

Helen winced. She didn't like McNally, but she didn't think he was a crook. Vera was foolhardy to antagonize him.

McNally spoke through gritted teeth. "I'd be the first to run in Danny Martlet if he was guilty. The same goes for Ms. Stranahan. I want this case closed even more than you do. I want these politicians off my back. Half of them are screaming that we're going to ruin the deal of the century and destroy Florida's future if we don't stop investigating Danny Martlet. The other half swear Ms. Stranahan couldn't kill an ant at a picnic. You know what? If either one were guilty, they'd be sitting in jail now so I could get the second-guessers to shut up.

"But until I find the killer," McNally said, "and enough evidence to convict that person—and I do need evidence, Ms. Salinda—I plan to be a pain in the ass to all parties involved, no matter how much money they have, or don't have. Sorry that poor woman's death inconvenienced you. Good day, ladies. I'll be back. And that's a promise."

He slammed the door on the way out and the bells jingled. It was not a merry sound.

"Guess you think I was stupid to say something," Vera said.

"You were brave," Helen said. "But maybe a little impulsive."

"I couldn't stand it," Vera said. "He was so snide and sarcastic. And he scared Roger after he brought me these beautiful dresses." She hung the gowns in the dry-cleaning section.

"Are they dry cleaning?" Helen asked.

"Hell, no. They're going out on the racks as soon as I can tag them."

"Do you think Detective McNally knows Roger?" Helen asked.

"Yes," Vera said. "He called Roger by his name. And Roger looked scared when he saw the detective. McNally must know Roger from somewhere. You know what else is weird? Roger's soda can is missing. He dropped it on the counter with the dresses and I didn't throw it away. I think McNally took it."

"It could be a possible source of DNA," Helen said. "McNally wouldn't need a warrant for Roger's fingerprints if he took a discarded soda can."

Vera groaned. "We have to solve this murder, Helen, before I lose my store. I need help."

"Let's go through who was here that morning," Helen said. "Maybe we can remember something useful. I was too scared talking to the police. No wonder I forgot to tell them about the watch."

"From the top," Vera said. "Chrissy arrived right after the shop opened with the pony-hair purse. You came and got me. I was talking to Roger. Chrissy looked frightened when her husband drove up. They got into a fight about money at the front counter. Then Loretta arrived. I told Danny and Chrissy to take their fight elsewhere, and Danny dragged his wife to the back. Chrissy lost her watch on the way."

"I followed them back to the dressing room to return the watch," Helen said. "Chrissy accused Danny of looking at another woman. Did Chrissy sign a prenup with Danny?"

"Yes," Vera said. "She told me she'd only get a measly two hundred thousand if she divorced him. She acted like she'd be living on welfare. I wish I could have her poverty."

"Then Danny wouldn't lose any money if he divorced Chrissy," Helen said.

"He'd lose a little," Vera said, "but he'd lose a lot less if she were murdered. Go back to remembering."

"Loretta the commissioner walked into the middle of Danny and Chrissy's fight," Helen said, "and started trading barbs. Chrissy did not like Loretta. She thought Loretta was after her husband. Chrissy said she knew about the three thousand new jobs with Danny's project and the house of the seven toilets."

"The police said Danny didn't own a house like that," Vera said.

"Maybe the cops overlooked it," Helen said. "Phil is good at property searches. I can ask him to check the records."

"Good," Vera said. "Back to what happened. You stepped into the three-way fight between Danny, Chrissy and Loretta. I tried to get everyone to cool off. I gave Danny the Bruno Magli shoes, showed Chrissy a summer dress and took Loretta to the back to look at new arrivals."

"Danny threw down the shoes," Helen said, "and had a tantrum like a two-year-old. He walked out. Do you think Danny is having an affair with Commissioner Stranahan?"

Vera laughed. "She'd make a lousy corporate wife. She'd have to give up her power to marry him. Poor Chrissy never understood that some women don't need men to have money."

"How much does Danny need Commissioner Stranahan's vote for his project?" Helen asked.

"He doesn't," Vera said. "He has a majority of the county commission already. Loretta has publicly denounced his hotel project. She's fought him every step of the way. That's why I tried to keep those two apart in here."

"Then why did Chrissy say Danny was on the phone with the commissioner a hundred times a day?" Helen said. "Wouldn't he avoid Loretta?"

"He's trying to negotiate with the commission," Vera said. "He's revamped the project designs twice, because Loretta said the luxury hotel looked like a shoe box. Six neighborhood associations agreed with her and that made Loretta a hero. She got the voters what they wanted. Next Loretta and Danny fought about the hotel complex adding more traffic to an already clogged road. Danny caved in and said it would be routed through the hotel garage. Loretta won that fight, too.

"Sometime while he was changing the designs, Danny made the hotel project five stories above the legal height limit. Now he wants a height variance, which is really a change in the zoning laws. He says it's the only way he can make a profit after all the compromise changes he's had to make.

"Loretta's career took off when she started dogging Danny. If she's smart, she'll keep fighting him until the next election."

Dead end, Helen thought. She stared at the battery-operated toy chicken on the counter that ran around in circles. She had a lot in common with the tourist toy.

"What about your neighbor Jordan," Vera asked, "the one in the dress so tight it could have been a tourniquet?"

"She acted like she knew Danny and came on to him really friendly," Helen said. "He cut her dead. When he left, Jordan called him a prick. Maybe Danny didn't know her. Maybe he didn't want Chrissy to meet the woman he's been seeing behind her back."

"Is Jordan Danny's backstreet girl?" Vera asked.

"If she is, she's a fool," Helen said. "She's using her current boyfriend, Mark, to pay for dresses to snag herself a new man. Jordan is expecting this new guy to pop the question."

"That's lousy," Vera said.

"Danny and Jordan deserve each other if they're planning to marry," Helen said. "Jordan is using Mark's money to buy clothes to lure a rich man. She's a cold-blooded little thing. Margery says it's none of my business, but I think Jordan is ambitious and greedy enough to kill Danny's wife."

"Well, well," Vera said. "I think we found our murder suspect. Jordan killed Chrissy. It would be a lot easier for Danny to marry Jordan if he was a widower."

CHAPTER 13

The limo pulled up in front of the Riverside Hotel on Las Olas, long as a funeral procession and just as black. Even the windows were dark.

That's odd, Helen thought. Why was the limo parked on busy Las Olas Boulevard, blocking traffic? Usually drivers went to the hotel entrance on a quieter side street. Helen had had a day of odd occurrences at Snapdragon's. Now she encountered a mystery limo on her walk home from work. She stopped abruptly for a better look, and the man behind her nearly dumped his drink down her back.

"Watch it, bitch," he said as he passed her on the sidewalk. Mr. Rude stank of beer, and more brew sloshed out of his plastic cup as he staggered down the street. His temper was as ugly as his neon green Hawaiian shirt. Mr. Rude had to be a tourist, Helen decided, or color-blind. Even Floridians wouldn't wear a shirt that ugly.

Helen saw a lithe young woman in a skimpy black dress slither out of the hotel, followed by men's stares. Her long brown hair shimmered in the evening sun. Her nose was slightly too long, but she was definitely sexy. It was Jordan, dressed for an evening on the town.

The limo seemed to swallow her whole. The last thing Helen saw was Jordan's black ankle-strap heels disappearing into the interior. Talk about killer heels. Did Jordan walk the six blocks from the Coronado to the hotel wearing them? Those shoes had to be four inches high, not counting the platforms. A woman could jump off them and commit suicide.

Helen couldn't see who else was in the limo. She wondered if it was the "special man" Jordan wanted to snag with her "slightly slutty" dress. Was Jordan having a fling with Danny the developer? Vera said the man had at least one sweetie on the side. Was Jordan his current playmate? She certainly wasn't dressed for a quiet dinner with a new widower. Danny seemed cold and cruel, but was he bold enough to take his new cookie clubbing in South Beach so soon after his wife's death?

Helen had to know. Maybe Jordan and Danny had conspired to kill Chrissy. It would make sense: Danny had the perfect alibi and Jordan had the best motive.

Helen found an old grocery receipt in her purse and wrote down the license number. Phil could find out the limo's owner. Helen needed to confirm it was Danny's limo before she told Detective McNally.

The limo slid smoothly into the stream of traffic. The long walk home on the broiling sidewalk had left Helen tired and bedraggled. A block from the Coronado Tropic Apartments, she sat down on a bus bench, smoothed her hair, added fresh lipstick and put on a smile. She didn't want Phil to see her so bedraggled.

Helen felt cooler just looking at the Coronado. The pink glow of the setting sun turned the old building the color of peach ice cream. The Coronado crowd saluted the sunset whenever possible.

Tonight, four residents were sitting by the pool—Phil, Peggy, Margery and Mark, the mechanic who lived with Jordan in 2C. Five, if you counted Peggy's Quaker parrot, Pete, a bright green bird with sober gray feathers on his head.

Mark and Margery were stretched out on chaise lounges. Helen was relieved to see her landlady in her customary purple caftan. The timid pink polish Margery wore to the funeral home was replaced with screaming tangerine. Her brass earrings were the size of temple gongs. She was once more wreathed in Marlboro smoke. Her drink looked a little pale. That screwdriver probably had more booze than orange juice, at least the way Margery made it. Helen's landlady was back to her colorful self.

Mark was leading-man handsome. Put him in a tux and a limo and he would turn heads with his dark good looks. Too bad he was wearing khakis with a name tag on the pocket. Mark was never quite able to remove the oil and grease from his fingers. The mechanic was too good for Jordan, but unless his work-stained hands were clutching stacks of Benjamins, she'd have no interest in Mark.

He raised his beer in greeting to Helen.

Peggy hoisted her wineglass. "Hey," she said. "Join us." Pete sullenly crunched a green bean.

The umbrella table was spread with potato salad, ripple chips, sliced tomatoes, onions and French bread. Phil was barbecuing chicken. Helen watched her man take a sip of Heineken, pour some on the chicken from the green bottle, then pour more into the cook. She waded through the beer-scented smoke and kissed him.

"That chicken smells luscious," she said. "How many six-packs before dinner is ready?"

"As soon as the chicken and I finish this beer, dinner is done," Phil said.

"What can I do?"

"Help us eat it," Phil said. "Change into something cool. And take this to my pal Thumbs." He handed her a paper plate with a grilled chicken neck.

"Thumbs will love that, but he'll smear chicken grease all over my floor," Helen said.

"Let the cat have some fun," Phil said. "I'll clean up if he makes a mess."

"The floor needs to be mopped anyway," Helen said.

Thumbs, her six-toed cat, greeted her at the door with a loud purr and a friendly forehead bump to her leg. Helen scratched his thick gray and white fur and said, "You're only making up to me because it's dinnertime. Phil made you a treat."

Thumbs chomped the chicken neck while Helen filled his water bowl, poured him dry food, then changed into yellow shorts and a black top. She inspected herself in the mirror. Helen wasn't a hard body like Vera, but she didn't look bad for forty-one. In fact, she decided, I look darn good.

She poured herself a cold white wine, found a can of mixed nuts for an appetizer, then rejoined the party.

"Can Pete have a cashew?" Helen asked Peggy.

"Too fattening. He's still a half ounce overweight," Peggy said.

"I should be so lucky," Helen said.

"That's a lot for a bird who's supposed to weigh six ounces tops. Pete can get hypertension, just like people. He's limited to nutritious snacks."

"Let me remove temptation," Margery said, reaching for the can. "Peggy, how's your lawyer friend, Daniel?"

"He may be a keeper," Peggy said. "And it's about time."

Peggy's love life had been chaotic for almost as long as Helen had known her. Peggy had been jailed for murdering one lover. When her name was cleared, Peggy had a romance with a hunky cop from that case. But he cheated on her with a stripper. Then Peggy fell for another cheater. This one took her for twenty thousand dollars.

"For a while, I thought Pete was going to be the only man in my life," Peggy said. "I spent my nights teaching him to talk."

"Hello!" the little parrot said.

"Daniel is working late tonight on a contract," Peggy said.

"Jordan has a modeling job tonight," Mark said. He was touchingly proud. "She looked hot when she left here. She says she may have to stay out late while they take photos in South Beach."

That lying little witch, Helen thought. She hoped her feelings didn't show.

"How nice," she said out loud.

"Your sister sent you a FedEx package, Helen." Margery was mining the mixed nuts for cashews.

"I asked her to overnight a dress and a recent photo of Mother," Helen said.

"Any word on your mom?" Margery crunched another cashew.

"No change. I'm sure the next call I'll get from the nursing home will be bad news."

"Dinner is ready," Phil said. He carried the platter of grilled chicken to the table and the five crowded around.

Helen listened while Mark bragged about Jordan—her beauty, her ability to photograph well from almost any angle, her unusual green eyes. The poor clueless sap, Helen thought as he recited Jordan's charms throughout dinner.

"She doesn't even have to wear false eyelashes," Mark said. "I'm going to support her until she's a supermodel. Then she'll support me. I'm hoping to start my own repair shop. Phil, want me to take a look at your Jeep? It sounds like the timing is off."

"The Jeep has been dying at stop signs," Phil said. "I can pay you or give you a couple of six-packs."

"Beer is good," Mark said. "I like Heineken."

Peggy, Helen and Margery shooed Mark and Phil off to work on the Jeep while they cleared the table. "You get a pass because you cooked tonight, Phil," Helen said. "And Mark, you're fixing the Jeep."

When the two men were in the parking lot, Helen said, "Mark is a nice guy. He doesn't know that his girlfriend is riding in a limo with another man."

"You didn't see anyone in that limo, man or woman, Helen Hawthorne," Margery said. "Maybe Jordan was getting a ride to her job."

"The only one being taken for a ride is Mark," Helen said.

"Been there, done that." Peggy tossed the paper plates in the trash. "Now, this is how I like to do dishes."

When the table was cleared and the grill cleaned, Peggy said, "Okay, Pete, it's bedtime. Show everyone I didn't waste all those lonely nights."

"Night!" Pete said.

Margery and Helen applauded, while Pete rode Peggy's shoulder triumphantly to their apartment. Margery gave Helen the box from Kathy.

Phil appeared at the door to Margery's kitchen. "Want to come to my place for a nightcap, Helen?"

Inside Phil's apartment, Helen said, "The curse of 2C has struck again. Margery has rented that apartment to every kind of crook. Now Jordan is cheating on poor Mark."

"Are you sure?" Phil asked.

"Well, not exactly. But she's been talking about dating another man."

"At least cheating on her boyfriend isn't illegal," Phil said. "It may be an improvement over everyone else who's rented 2C. Jordan is only scamming Mark instead of innocent citizens."

"She's a snob, like lots of pretty fashionistas," Helen said. "She won't get serious about a man who works with his hands."

"Jordan thinks it's a fair trade," Phil said. "Mark gets high-priced arm candy and she gets pretty clothes. 'Forever' is not a word in Jordan's vocabulary. But it works both ways. Soon some man will dump her because she's no longer young and pretty."

Helen found his words cold comfort.

"Would you like a back rub?" Phil asked. "It will get the knots out."

The back rub turned into a long session of love. Later, Helen said, "I feel guilty enjoying myself while my mother is dying."

"And denying yourself would help her how?" Phil asked. "You've done everything possible for your mother."

Helen drifted off to sleep in his arms until a buzzing sound woke her. She sat up, slapped Phil's alarm clock to shut it off, then realized the sound was her cell phone buzzing.

"Miss Hawthorne, this is Priscilla, the night nurse," said a voice with a gentle Southern accent. "I'm sorry, but your mother has taken a turn for the worse. Dr. Lucre doesn't think she'll last till morning."

"I'll be right there," Helen said.

Phil sat up in bed, looking adorably tousled. "What's going on? What time is it?"

"It's one oh three," Helen said. "The nursing home says Mom may not last until morning."

They threw on shoes, shirts and jeans. Helen picked up the dress box and they ran for the Jeep. The Coronado gleamed in the ghostly moonlight. The air was soft and flower-scented. A yellow light burned in apartment 2C. Helen wondered if Jordan was home yet or if Mark was alone there, drinking beer.

The Sunset Rest looked abandoned. The nursing home's lights were off except at the night entrance. Helen rang the buzzer. Priscilla's generous figure and short perm inspired confidence. The nurse led Helen and Phil through the dimly lit halls.

"We've moved your mother's roommate so you can have privacy," she said. "Dolores is fading, but she's peaceful."

Helen's mother looked like a small bundle of laundry in the white bed. "She's hardly there," Phil whispered.

Helen sat down, held her mother's nearly transparent hand and wished the IV could be removed. "Mom, I know you will go to a better world," Helen said to the still form. "You'll see Daddy again. Tommy Junior and Allison will miss you so much. They loved coming to your house."

Helen talked to her mother for what seemed like hours, while Phil alternately paced the room, then went down the hall for soda or coffee.

Suddenly, Dolores's breathing changed. It grew loud and rapid, then seemed to stop.

"Mom?" Helen asked. "Are you there?"

No answer, except another burst of loud, almost raspy breathing.

"I'll get the nurse," Phil said.

"What's wrong, honey?" Priscilla asked, running into the room.

"Her breathing is really loud and fast," Helen said. "Then it's almost not there. Then it starts up fast again."

"That's Cheyne-Stokes respiration," Priscilla said. "It happens near the end. They say it doesn't hurt the patient, but it sounds frightening."

At last Dolores's labored breathing stopped. "I believe she's passed," the nurse said. "I'm sorry." Priscilla left the room and closed the door.

Phil took Helen in his arms and she cried on his shoulder. "It's okay," he said, kissing away her tears.

"But we never made up," Helen said. "She died angry at me."

"If Dolores is in that heaven she believes in, she forgives you," Phil said. He gave her a cup of fresh coffee.

"Thanks." Helen wiped away her tears. She took a sip, then said, "What time is it?"

"Three fifteen," Phil said.

"Margery said Mother would die at three in the morning," Helen said.

It took nearly three hours for the grim formalities of death. Dr. Justin Lucre examined Dolores, declared her dead and signed the paperwork. Helen signed more papers and packed her mother's few belongings. She called Kathy for a tearful conversation. Her sister promised to call Larry in the morning and tell him he was a widower.

The funeral home took away Dolores's body, along with her wig, the photo and her dress.

It was six ten in the morning when Helen and Phil were ready to leave. The smokers were already puffing in the courtyard. Joe sat in his red motorized wheelchair with Rita at his side. She wore a perky pink bow today.

"What are you doing here so early?" Joe asked Helen.

Rita glared at him. "Have you smoked your brains out?" she demanded. "Why does any healthy young person come here in the middle of the night?"

"I'm an idiot," Joe said. "Your mother passed away, didn't she?"

Helen nodded. She was afraid she'd burst into tears if she said the words. Phil put his arm around her protectively.

"Give us a good-bye hug," Rita said. "We'll miss you. And you, too, big boy."

Finally, Phil and Helen climbed into the Jeep. "It's over," she said.

"Now you can take the day off," Phil said.

"I'm too keyed up to sleep," Helen said. "I'll get our plane tickets and hotel reservation online. The funeral home said Mom would be ready in about two days. I'll have breakfast with Peggy by the pool if she has time. Then I'll go into work at ten."

"I disapprove," Phil said. "You need rest."

"I need a distraction," Helen said. "I'll leave Snapdragon's early at two o'clock, come home and crash."

"We're home now," Phil said as the Coronado rose before them. "Please take a nap."

"You bitch!" a man shouted.

Phil slammed on the brakes at the edge of the Coronado parking lot. Jordan and Mark were screaming at each other in Phil's parking spot. Jordan was still wearing the same sexy outfit. She carried her high heels, but looked slightly shopworn. Her makeup was gone. Mark's handsome face was red and contorted with rage.

"I'm working my ass off while you're sneaking around with that big-time developer," Mark yelled.

"I told you. I was working," Jordan shrieked back.

"On your back," Mark said. "You've been sneaking out with Danny Martlet. Don't deny it. I found his phone number on your cell phone and called it. You slut! Danny's wife was murdered a couple of days ago. You didn't even wait until she was buried to hop in the sack with him."

"Danny auditioned me for his Orchid House campaign. But he wasn't at tonight's shoot."

"Really?" Mark said nastily. "I bet you saw plenty of him before tonight."

"No, I swear," Jordan said, then went on the attack. "You're drunk."

"So are you," he said, slurring his words.

"You stink like cheap beer," Jordan said. "I had French champagne."

Margery materialized in a purple robe. "Why are you two brawling on my property?" she demanded.

"He said—" Jordan began.

"That bitch—" Mark said.

"I've already heard it," Margery said. "The whole street heard you. Jordan, go to your room." Jordan went upstairs to 2C like a sulky child.

"And Mark, go to work."

"I can't," Mark said. "I've been up all night worrying about that slut. She isn't worth losing sleep over. I'm going to bed. Alone. She can sleep on the couch."

He stomped up the stairs after Jordan, and slammed the apartment door.

CHAPTER 14

By her fourth cup of coffee that morning, Helen was as wired as a stadium scoreboard.

She was too jittery to talk sensibly to Phil. He gave up and went inside while Helen drank more coffee outside by the pool. She nibbled on toast and waited impatiently for Peggy to appear. At seven thirty, her red-haired friend burst out of her apartment.

Normally pale and quiet, this morning Peggy seemed to crackle with energy. She moved so fast, Pete had trouble maintaining his perch on her shoulder. The parrot flapped his wings and let out a squawk of protest.

"Whoa, you're ready to fight the day," Helen said. "You must have had good news."

Peggy slid into a chair and opened a cup of blueberry yogurt. Pete settled down. "I won a thousand dollars in the Florida Lottery. It's my first win, ever."

"Congratulations," Helen said.

"Woo-hoo!" Pete said.

"Did he just say 'woo-hoo'?" Helen asked.

"Parrots learn to talk if you put a lot of emotion into your words. I'm glad that's what I screamed when I won yesterday."

"What kind of fun will you have with your money?" Helen asked.

"I'm using it to make more money," Peggy said. "I want to work at home and make five thousand dollars a month. That's twice what I make now. I bought my membership and supplies online. The first shipment will arrive this afternoon."

"I thought those work-at-home jobs were scams," Helen said.

"Most are lame pyramid schemes," Peggy said. "But not this one. It's called 'Make Work with Mike.' I start work when the first shipment of the product arrives after three o'clock today."

"What's the product?" Helen asked.

"Barbecue aprons. See?" Peggy showed Helen a photo of a smiling man at a smoking grill. His apron read, COME AND GET IT, CHOW HOUNDS! BILL'S BARBECUE. A barbecue fork and long-handled tongs were crossed under the letters.

"The aprons are made in China. I personalize them," Peggy said. "I add the name and the barbecue utensils. Or crossed beer bottles. Dog lovers can get the chow-hound breed of their choice, from Airedales to Yorkies. I add those, too."

"Why can't they do that in China?" Helen asked.

"Too far away," Peggy said. "Our buyers want a quick response. My membership is two hundred fifty dollars. I bought the industrial glue gun for another two fifty. I get the first shipment of aprons free. After that, I pay two hundred fifty per week for more aprons, but if I make my quota, I'll earn five thousand dollars a month."

Phil had been standing by the table holding a fresh cup of coffee. "How much do those aprons sell for in stores?" he asked.

"Not sure," Peggy said, "but they're in the finest specialty shops and cookery stores. Not Williams-Sonoma, but that same caliber."

"There has to be a hitch, Peggy," Phil said gently. "I've never come across a work-at-home scheme that wasn't a fake."

"Awk!" Pete said.

"No," Peggy said. "Not this one. I read the testimonials. Robert in Ottumwa, Iowa, made seven figures last year."

"Robert who?" Phil asked.

"Robert G.," Peggy said.

"Did you talk to this man?" Phil asked.

"Well, no. I tried to find him, but there are a lot of Roberts in Ottumwa."

"Exactly," Phil said.

"You don't have to be so negative," Peggy said. "This is my chance to escape a bad job."

"I thought you liked your job," Helen said, trying to find a safer topic.

"I do," Peggy said. "I mean, I did. But now my boss's wife wants a divorce. He spends all day on the phone with his lawyer. The staff is doing our work and his. And he's always in a rotten mood."

"Bad boy!" Pete said, shuffling along her shoulder.

"Pete and I could work at home together," Peggy said. "He'd never be lonely. And I wouldn't have to put up with my boss's moods."

"Peggy, I understand," Phil said. "But the Florida attorney general warns against these schemes."

"I didn't find Mike's company mentioned on the Web site," Peggy said.

"That's a start," Phil said. "Please promise me you won't quit your job until you've had a good money-making month." He knelt down beside Peggy and took her hand. Phil looked sincere, strong and, yes, humble. Helen's heart overflowed with love.

"When a man gets on his knees and begs me, I can't resist," Peggy said. She raised her right hand. "I solemnly swear I won't quit my job until I'm making at least three thousand a month working at home."

Pete flapped his wings.

"Now I'd better get to work," Peggy said. "Did I imagine it, or was someone fighting in the parking lot last night?"

"It was Mark and Jordan," Helen said, lowering her voice. "The fight was this morning around six. Jordan came home after being out all night. Mark was drunk—and furious. He accused her of seeing another man. Phil and I had just come back from the nursing home and we saw the fight. Margery intervened and sent them both to their room."

"Bad boy!" Pete said.

"Well, it's quiet up there now," Peggy said. "Let's hope they're asleep. I forgot to ask, Helen. How is your mother?"

"She died last night," Helen said, then tried to stave off the inevitable burst of sympathy. "Don't be sorry, please. Mom died peacefully. Phil and I were with her. We'll take her home, probably in two days. Really, it was the best way for a good woman to go."

"Then I'm glad it's over for you both," Peggy said. "I still have to go to work. And you, Pete, have to go back to your cage."

"Bye!" Pete said.

"He has an amazing vocabulary," Helen said.

"A testimony to my many lonely nights," Peggy said as she took her parrot back to her apartment.

When Helen heard Peggy's car start, she said, "You handled that well, Phil. Peggy's apron company sounds too good to be true. I wonder what the hitch is."

"She'll find out soon," Phil said. "How are the arrangements for the trip to St. Louis?"

"We're set for the day after tomorrow," Helen said.

"Then you have to keep your promise," Phil said. "We have to straighten out your legal problems, for better or worse."

"Are you going to get down on your knees?" Helen said.

"If you want," Phil said. "But they'll pop."

Helen took his hand. "I love you. I made a promise and I'll keep it. But I don't know where to start."

"With your divorce decree. What county were you married in?"

"St. Louis County," Helen said.

"It should be on record at the county courthouse," Phil said. "We'll start there. Then I'll research the judge and we'll look for a good lawyer."

"And we'll live happily—and legally—ever after," Helen said. "But in the meantime, I'd better get dressed for work and let Vera know when I leave for St. Louis. Will you check that limo license-tag number for me sometime today? If we can prove Jordan was out with Danny the developer, it would help solve Chrissy's murder."

She checked her watch. "It's time for me to go to work."

"And I have my assignments," Phil said. "Can I drive you to work?"

"Thanks. I need the walk," Helen said.

At Snapdragon's, Helen had her own second thoughts. Vera looked so bad, Helen wondered if the shop owner was sick. Instead of fit and thin, Vera looked washed-out and bony. Her arms were scrawny as Madonna's. Her red lipstick made her face seem sickly white. She was in a bad mood.

"I'm sorry about your mother," Vera said. "But if you go, you'll leave me here alone, pestered by the police and the lookie loos."

"I have no choice," Helen said. "I can work tomorrow, but then I have to leave. If you want to fire me, I wouldn't blame you."

"No, no. It's not your fault. I'll get by," Vera said. "My sister in Plantation is looking for work now that her kids are going back to school. She'll complain about the drive, but she'll help me out."

"Good," Helen said. "Thank you."

"But I want you back here as soon as possible," Vera said. "I hired you as a favor to Miguel Angel. I didn't expect to wind up needing you."

This odd mix of praise and blame was interrupted when a short, sturdy woman entered the shop. She looked like the perfect grandmother. Her blue pantsuit had a tabby cat on the front. She had fluffy white hair and a sweet smile. She opened a plastic grocery bag and brought out a purse wrapped in a white towel.

Perfect Grandma carefully peeled away the towel and said reverently, "This is a genuine Louis Vuitton."

Helen could tell it was a fake and a poor one at that. The classic brown monogram Vuitton bag had missing stitches on the leather handle tabs. The brass fittings were dull and the nylon zipper looked cheap.

"Was it a gift?" Vera asked.

"Oh, yes," Perfect Grandma said. "My dear son Edward and his wife brought it home from their Caribbean cruise. They bought me two designer handbags." Her face was pink with pride. "I wouldn't sell this one except that my Social Security doesn't stretch as far as it used to. And I have my Gucci." She patted another obvious imitation.

"The Louis Vuitton is a beautiful purse," Vera said. She held it up and pretended to admire it. "I wish I could buy it, but we're overstocked right now. But thank you for bringing it here."

"Maybe later," Perfect Grandma said, and swaddled the purse like a newborn.

When she left, Helen said, "You were sweet to her."

Vera blushed. "Hey, I know I can be a bitch sometimes, but I had a grandma, too. I hope nobody tells her the truth about sonny boy's gifts."

"Listen," Helen said. "Something happened last night that may solve Chrissy's murder and get the police off your back."

She told Vera about the limo and Jordan and Mark's fight. "What if Danny and Jordan murdered Chrissy?" Helen said. "They could be in it together. Danny had the perfect alibi. Jordan killed his wife for him—and herself. Her payoff will be marriage to Danny."

"Maybe," Vera said. "But I can't see Danny tying himself down with another wife. Why marry Jordan when he's already had her? A rich, powerful man can get all the sex he wants. Chrissy was useful. She ran their household well and that was no small feat. She served on the proper charity boards and the committees that advanced Danny's business. She was a genius at giving dinner parties. She could mend fences with some of the people Danny had angered. Jordan is too self-centered to be an asset to a difficult, ambitious man.

"If Jordan killed Chrissy, I think she acted alone," Vera said. "She wanted Danny single again. Personally, I don't care if the killer was Jordan or if both of them were involved, as long as it gets the police off my back. Now all we have to do is convince Detective McNally to look at them."

"We can call him," Helen said.

Vera found his business card, dialed a number, listened, then said, "It's Vera Salinda, Detective. Please call me."

"He's not there," Vera said to Helen. "I don't think I should say more in my message. He'll be back in here soon enough."

Helen sized stock and buttoned shirts until two o'clock. Then she said, "Vera, I've done as much as I can. I swear those shirts unbutton themselves at night."

"Go. I'll see you tomorrow," Vera said.

Helen ducked out the back door to avoid the ever-present television cameras, and wondered if she should remind Vera to lock it during the day. Chrissy's murder attracted some spooky shoppers. Walking into the heavy humid afternoon was like being smothered in wet wool. St. Louis wouldn't be any cooler, but Helen thought it would be a relief to get away for a few days, even if it was for her mother's funeral. This afternoon, she would catch up on her sleep. She'd work again tomorrow. Then she and Phil would leave the next day.

Her mother's funeral would mark the formal end to Helen's old unhappy life. Phil would help her start a new one here in Fort Lauderdale. By the time they returned home, Jordan would be arrested for Chrissy's murder. Helen and Phil could get married and their life would return to normal—or as normal as it would ever be.

She was nearly at the Coronado when a siren interrupted her thoughts. Then a second. And a third, all howling like a coyote pack. The speeding cars were heading toward her street. Helen ran through the heat to the Coronado. Nearly a dozen cars and emergency vehicles were parked haphazardly in front, like a child's abandoned toys. Phil stood at the edge of the parking lot, waving to the new arrivals.

"In here, Officers!" he said. "Right through the gate."

Helen ran up to him. "What's happened?" she asked.

"It's Jordan," Phil said. "She's dead."

CHAPTER 15

"Jordan can't be dead," Helen said. "I saw her this morning. She was fine."

"Margery found her in the pool," Phil said.

"She drowned? Jordan never goes swimming. She says the chlorine is bad for her hair."

"She wasn't swimming," Phil said. "She was bashed in the head with a beer bottle. A Heineken bottle."

"Oh," Helen said. She was too stunned to move.

Was it the heat or the horrible news? Helen had trouble following this conversation. She'd just seen Jordan a few hours ago—angry, arrogant and oddly beautiful. Now she was dead. Worse, murdered.

"Mark killed her," Helen said. "He killed her out of jealousy because she went out with Danny last night."

"Oh, it's worse than that," Phil said. "Much worse. You look kind of odd. Come over here in the shade and lean on Margery's car bumper. I can't take you inside to the patio. The police and techs are swarming over the Coronado like an overturned anthill."

Helen sat down on the bumper of Margery's big white Cadillac and felt a little better, but still dizzy. Mark had been drinking beer all night—beer that Phil gave him. Now Jordan was dead, murdered by a beer bottle. She could hear Phil talking, but he seemed a great distance away.

"I checked on that limo for you, like you asked," Phil said. "Jordan wasn't out with Danny—not last night. The limo was rented by a modeling agency. I tracked down the driver, Pat. I knew him from a drug case I did last year. His employer thought Pat was selling drugs and I proved him innocent, so he owes me.

"Pat said there were six people in the limo and Jordan was the last pickup. There were two other women models—a blonde and a redhead—along with a big-deal fashion photographer and his two assistants.

"Pat said the models posed for photos on South Beach until almost midnight. After that, the whole party hit the clubs, then went out for breakfast. He dropped Jordan at the Coronado about five fifty that morning. Pat said there was a lot of champagne, some drugs and no sex. He drives one of those block-long limos with a hot tub inside. He says he's seen some wild nights, but this wasn't one of them. Not by his standards."

"Jordan died for nothing," Helen said.

"Not quite. Mark was right that Jordan was having an affair with Danny," Phil said. "I also talked with a valet for a high-priced restaurant on Las Olas. His name is Taylor. You couldn't get out of the restaurant he works at for less than two hundred dollars, even if you ordered a hamburger. That would be made of organic beef and served with artichoke fries or mango salsa.

"Taylor said Jordan met Danny for dinner at least six times at the restaurant where he valets. After dinner, they'd drive off in Danny's black BMW. Danny drove his own car. He never rented a limo. Taylor didn't know where they went, but the valet thought Jordan was hot. He said Jordan stuck to Danny like Velcro. Her head would be bobbing up and down at steering-wheel level before the car pulled away from the curb."

"That's a little too much information," Helen said.

"Taylor seemed to regard Danny as his own personal soap opera," Phil said. "He waited eagerly for the next episode. Taylor says Danny called it off with Jordan about two weeks ago. Jordan tried to get into Danny's car as usual, but Danny said he wanted to go home.

"Jordan was 'acting clingy as usual,' Taylor said. She threw her purse at Danny. Other people were coming out of the restaurant. Jordan shrieked that Danny had promised to marry her and divorce his wife. They were gathering a crowd. Danny left Jordan right there on the sidewalk and roared off like demons were chasing him. The valet never saw Jordan with Danny again.

"According to Taylor, Jordan wasn't the first woman who tried to pressure Danny into marriage. Stupid move. He always ran away when women did that. Danny came back the next evening and gave Taylor a twenty to forget what he saw."

"But he told you anyway?" Helen asked.

"I gave him fifty to remember," Phil said, and winked.

"You were so clever finding Taylor," Helen said. "There are a lot of valets in Fort Lauderdale. How did you find him?"

"Some clever woman told me she'd heard Danny liked to meet his dates for dinner on Las Olas," Phil said. "I picked the over-priced restaurants and found Taylor after two tries."

"Poor Jordan," Helen said. "What a terrible waste of a pretty young woman."

"Jordan's murder is bad, but I'm also worried about Margery,"

Phil said. "Margery aged twenty years after she found Jordan's body. She looks like an old woman."

"She is seventy-six," Helen reminded him.

"I know, but Margery has never looked or acted her age," Phil said. "Even her wrinkles had style. Now she seems frail. She walks like she's old and creaky. Her colorful outfit just looks crazy. She's not making a whole lot of sense, either."

"I'd better go see her," Helen said, and started to stand up.

"You can't," Phil said. "She's with the police. They'll take her statement for hours. They should have isolated me, too, but the first responder was young and inexperienced. I offered to flag down the other emergency vehicles, and he let me go outside and help. I'll stick around for a statement, but that young cop will get his ass chewed when the detective in charge starts making sense of this scene."

"Tell me what's wrong with Margery," Helen said. "She's been like a mother to me since I got to Fort Lauderdale. Margery is prickly as a cactus, but she protects me in her own way. She always tells the truth, even if it hurts. I can't lose both mothers in one week."

Phil took a deep breath and said, "Margery blames herself for sending Jordan and Mark upstairs together. She says she should have taken Jordan to her home and protected her from her angry boyfriend. Margery feels like she sent Jordan to her death."

"I can see why she'd say that," Helen said.

"Here's what doesn't make sense," Phil said. "Margery claims Jordan was killed by a burglar. She says there have been break-ins in the neighborhood."

"Is that true?" Helen asked.

"There are always break-ins in this area," Phil said. "The burglary rates go up in hard times. But Jordan was beaten savagely. Her murder looks more like an enraged lover than a surprised burglar. Our landlady says Mark didn't murder Jordan because Margery found him passed out in bed. She wants me to investigate Jordan's death and save Mark. I'll go through the motions for her sake, but he's guilty as hell."

"What happened?" Helen asked. "Start from the beginning, so I can make sense of things. I'm hungry and groggy from lack of sleep."

"Margery took a nap after lunch," Phil said. "She woke up about one o'clock and went out to hose off the concrete sidewalks and pool deck like she does most afternoons. She saw dark drops on the sidewalk by the bougainvillea and thought coffee or paint had been spilled there. She looked closer and realized the drops were blood. She followed the trail of drops to the pool.

"Jordan was on the bottom of the pool. Margery called for me and we pulled her out. I tried CPR, but it was no use. One look at Jordan's crushed skull and I figured she was dead when she went into the water.

"After we got Jordan out of the pool, Margery called 911. While we waited for the paramedics to arrive, Margery and I followed the blood drops in the other direction. They led straight upstairs to 2C.

"Margery opened the apartment door—it wasn't locked—and found Mark passed out on the bed, surrounded by empty beer bottles. There was blood spatter all over the living room, bloody towels in the bathroom and diluted blood running down the sink. Even the soap was bloody. I thought it was obvious what happened: Mark killed Jordan while she was sleeping on the couch, dragged her outside when Margery and I were in our apartments and threw her body in the pool. After that, Mark tried to clean himself up, then drank himself into a stupor. Margery didn't agree.

"We couldn't wake him. Mark kept flopping back on the bed. His skin was clammy and his breathing was shallow. He'd drunk the two twelve-packs I gave him and a six of Coors. That's enough to give a man his size acute alcohol poisoning. The paramedics took Mark to the hospital and two police officers went with him."

"I don't understand. Why does Margery believe he's innocent?" Helen asked.

"Margery said Mark didn't know Jordan was dead because he was unconscious. The burglar came into their apartment, attacked Jordan, dragged her body to the pool and Mark slept through it."

"Then who tried to wash off her blood in their apartment sink?" Helen asked.

"Margery said it was the burglar. I'm sure the bloody fingerprints in that bathroom will show Mark was the killer. Margery insisted on calling a lawyer, Colby Cox, to be with Mark when he wakes up in the hospital."

"Was the murder weapon in 2C?" Helen asked.

"There were lots of beer bottles," Phil said, "but the cops found the murder weapon in the trash can near the pool. Mark had carried it outside, possibly to finish off Jordan, then dutifully followed Margery's rules about not leaving glass near the pool. It was dropped in the trash can. He didn't even try to hide it. The bottle is covered with blood and fingerprints and has some long hair on it. I'd bet you my next paycheck the fingerprints will turn out to be his."

A white Crown Victoria screeched up in front of the Coronado and stopped defiantly under a NO PARKING sign. Helen's heart sank when she saw the driver. Detective Richard McNally, tall, gray and somber, unfolded from the seat and walked up the drive.

"What a surprise," he said.

"I thought you were on the Hendin Island force," Helen said.

"I was called here because a person of interest in my investigation was murdered—Jordan Drubb," he said. "And what do I find? Another person of interest happens to be on the scene. The Queen of Coincidence, Helen Hawthorne."

"I told you Jordan lived here," Helen said.

"Yes, you did," Detective McNally said. "But you didn't say she'd die here, too."

CHAPTER 16

"You have True Religion!" The woman had the glowing eyes and long, pale face of a young novice nun.

"I do?" Helen said.

"Yes," she said. "You have the True Religion jeans with the horseshoe-flap pocket. The same ones Halle Berry wore. Except hers cost three hundred dollars and yours are only seventy and they're my size. I can't believe it."

"We have Gucci and Versace, too," Helen said.

"No, these are all I want," the novice said, and plunked them on the counter.

Helen's fingers moved slowly over the cash register keys as she rang up the jeans. She had the IQ of a squid this morning. She'd been questioned by the police and Detective McNally until six o'clock last night. McNally had even called Vera to ask what time Helen left work.

Then Helen spent three long hours with Margery. She was shocked by the change in her landlady. Margery had refused any food, even toast. She insisted on drinking a screwdriver. Then another. And another, until Helen refused to make more. She tried to give Margery straight orange juice, but her landlady wouldn't touch it. Margery chain-smoked cigarettes instead. Worse, she never cussed or chewed Helen out.

Margery had become an instant old woman, just as Phil said. She mumbled, lost her way in sentences, wept that Mark was innocent and that she had killed Jordan. No one believed that last part but Margery.

Helen was glad that Mark was under arrest. As far as she was concerned, he was guilty of two murders: He'd killed Jordan and he'd killed Margery. The landlady Helen loved was gone.

Margery either fell asleep or passed out about nine o'clock. Helen had removed the burning cigarette from her landlady's fingers, covered her with a blanket, carefully shut Margery's door and gone to her apartment.

There she fed her cat, Thumbs, and scrambled herself an egg for dinner. Just when Helen thought she could get some sleep, Peggy came over with her box of aprons. Helen told her the awful news while Peggy worked on her aprons. At least her friend had left Pete at home. A prowling Thumbs made the little parrot nervous.

Tired as she was, Helen found comfort in Peggy's company. Peggy insisted Margery was resilient and would soon be her old self. Helen wanted to believe her. It was midnight when Peggy finished the last apron. "I'm overnighting these tomorrow," she told Helen. "Then the money will roll in and I'll be free."

"I hope so," Helen said. She shut the door and finally fell asleep.

Morning came too soon. Now she was at Snapdragon's, walking in a fog, wishing she could go to sleep and selling to a woman ecstatic over a pair of jeans.

The True Religion buyer carried off her purchase as if she were bearing frankincense and myrrh. A pocket-sized brunette breezed up to the counter holding a pair of high heels with polka-dot bows.

"These are so cute," Ms. Pocket said. "How much? I don't see a price tag, but they were with the summer bargains."

Helen turned the shoes over, then said, "There is no price. Let me ask the boss."

Vera, on the phone in her back office, waved Helen away.

"She'll be here in a second," Helen said.

"Sorry," the miniature brunette said. "Gotta run. I see the parking patrol."

Helen had barely stashed the polka-dot shoes under the counter before a tall dishwater blonde announced she was looking for a summer dress. Helen didn't see many women her own height. It was refreshing to look another female in the eye.

Ms. Dishwater riffled through the racks, then picked the white gown Helen had worn for her aborted wedding. "This is lovely," she said. "It looks new."

"Only worn once," Helen said. The words were torn from her heart. She'd been so happy when she'd put on that dress. Then, with a few words from her mother, Helen's dreams were destroyed. She could no longer bear to look at the dress. Hiding it in her closet was a luxury she couldn't afford. Vera had given her a generous consignment deal and Helen put the wedding dress out for sale.

Ms. Dishwater came out of the dressing room in Helen's wedding gown and admired herself in the mirror. "I'll take it," she said.

"Excellent." Helen fixed a smile on her face, carried the dress up front and wrapped it. She felt like she'd sold a piece of her heart for fifty bucks.

A Latina with dark eyes and blond highlights said, "Excuse me. How much is that Blue Willow jar?"

She pointed to a handsome ginger jar on a shelf out of her reach. Helen stretched to read the tag. "One hundred dollars."

"That would be perfect for my neighbor," the Latina said.

"She collects Blue Willow china?" Helen asked.

"No, her husband could use it for his wife's ashes. She was shopping at Wal-Mart and she died."

The Blue Willow woman made it sound like shopping at Wal-mart led to her death. From the pricey designer logos on her clothes, the Blue Willow woman was safe. Helen wondered if the lively Latina planned to fill another vacancy in the widower's life. Too bad she left without buying anything.

"I see you sold your white dress," Vera said, checking the sales receipts.

Helen was glad Vera didn't call it "your wedding dress."

"I'll write you a check while I have the money," Vera said. "Thanks to your sales, we may make it through the month."

"I can use the check for my trip," Helen said. "Mom should be ready to leave this evening. I have to give a death certificate to Detective McNally. He told me I couldn't leave town, just like in the movies. He wanted the certificate for proof."

"That jackass," Vera said.

Helen shrugged. "At least I can go to her funeral."

"Jordan's murder has been a double loss for me," Vera said. "She was a good customer and a good suspect. I thought we'd have this murder wrapped up."

"No way McNally will consider Jordan the killer now," Helen said. "Danny broke up with Jordan two weeks ago. He dumped her after a loud argument with lots of witnesses. Even she must have understood he'd never make her Mrs. Martlet."

"Did your fiancé, Phil, find that out?" Vera asked.

"He did, but so did McNally," Helen said. "The detective told me last night when he interviewed me about her death. The police knew Jordan had had an affair with Danny and that it was over. They'd interviewed the restaurant staff about the couple's very public breakup. I hate to say it, but McNally is good."

"He may be good, but he's not fast enough," Vera said. "Some of my trophy wives are afraid to come here since Chrissy's murder. They won't even pick up their husbands' shirts. One sent her Latina maid. Mrs. Hamilton called me and said it was okay to let Graciela get the shirts, because she lived in Little Havana and was used to dangerous places."

"Incredible," Helen said.

"It's already cost me one canceled event," Vera said. "I was supposed to hold a fashion show for the Sexy Sixty Singles meeting. Now they've backed out. 'Other plans,' their event chair said. But I know it's the bad publicity."

"Would women age sixty and over buy your dresses?" Helen said. "You have lots of size twos."

"There are mature small-sized women," Vera said. "And any woman can carry a Dior purse, no matter what her dress size. We have first-rate shoes and accessories."

"I didn't mean to be weightist," Helen said "Or ageist."

"I could have made major money at that event," Vera said. "Those ladies love designer purses. The only good thing about Jordan's murder is I'm old news. The press has switched to staking out the Coronado instead of trying to interview me."

"I know," Helen said. "I had to slip out of my own apartment this morning like I owe a year's back rent."

"I'm still worried," Vera said. "Snapdragon's is a fragile business in a risky economy. How do we solve this murder and save my reputation—and your job?"

"Phil and I talked that over this morning," Helen said. "Chrissy told Danny she knew all about the house of the seven toilets. She said it like a threat. The police couldn't find any properties in Danny's name besides his home, but Phil is a whiz at ferreting out facts. He'll look at Danny's property records today."

"I thought he had his own job as a detective," Vera said.

"He just finished an assignment," Helen said. "Phil broke up a ring of thieves who were hiding stolen computers in the company's Dumpster. The computers were still in the boxes. One of their cohorts would come by with a pickup truck about midnight, remove the computers and sell them. Phil worked as a janitor for a month before he cracked that case. He got his pay from the agency as well as his wages as a janitor. Now he has a little free time. If anyone can find that mysterious house, Phil can."

Helen realized she sounded like a proud wife. Well, she was. Almost.

"How long will you be in St. Louis?" Vera asked.

"Four, maybe five days," Helen said. "I have some legal matters to straighten out. Then Phil and I can marry."

"Too bad you sold your wedding dress," Vera said.

"I wouldn't wear it again," Helen said. "Too many bad memories."

The jingle of bells signaled another customer. That ended their last chance to talk until closing time. At five fifty-five, Vera was straightening the front of the store when she saw the polka-dot heels Helen had left on a shelf under the counter.

"Why are these high heels here?" Vera asked.

"A customer asked about them. They don't have a tag. You were on the phone, remember? She had to leave."

"Oh, that one," Vera said. "These need a little work. I'll see if I can freshen them. Have a safe trip. Come back to work as soon as you can."

Helen barely felt the smothering heat on her walk home. Her mind was focused on the St. Louis trip, news of Phil's records search and a cold glass of wine. She saw the two television news vans when she was a block away from the Coronado, and took a shortcut through the alley. She picked her way gingerly through a maze of spiderwebs and broken lawn furniture into the yard.

The regulars were relaxing around the Coronado pool. Phil saluted her with a beer and a kiss.

"Good boy! Pete's a good boy!" the parrot said, eyeing Phil's spicy chips from his perch on Peggy's shoulder.

"Pete's a fat boy," Peggy said. "You're still on a diet. You have to eat like a bird. Have another asparagus spear."

Helen felt sick when she saw Margery. At least, she thought that worn, wrinkled woman was her landlady. All the bold colors were gone. Margery wore beige pants, a plain white shirt and no nail polish. Her gray hair was dull as unpolished silver. The only sign of the old Margery was the low-hanging cloud of cigarette smoke.

"Sit down and have a drink," Margery said, patting the box of wine. Her voice lacked its usual authority. She sounded like—Helen hated to even think it—a sweet old woman.

"The funeral home left a message for you," Margery said. "Your mother is ready to go home tomorrow. You can pick up the death certificates anytime. The home asked again, are you sure you don't want a private viewing before your mother goes home?"

"No," Helen said. "I don't want to see her body. Is that awful?"

"Not really," Margery said. "You've already said your good-byes. Better to keep her alive in your memory."

What if your last memory of your mother was the worst? Helen wondered. It would never be erased. She couldn't ask this meek, frail Margery.

"You'll be at the wake in St. Louis, won't you?" Margery said. "You'll see her then. This is a good funeral home here. They'll do good work on your mother. You need your rest tonight. When do you leave for St. Louis?"

"Tomorrow morning," Helen said. "Will you watch the cat while we're gone?"

"Of course," Margery said. Helen wished her landlady had made her usual snarky remarks about disliking cats.

"I can look in on Thumbs, too," Peggy said.

"Bad boy!" Pete said, and moved restlessly on her shoulder. The mention of a cat frightened him.

"I have news," Peggy said. "I sent my first shipment of aprons off this morning and ordered a hundred more. I'm on my way to making five thousand dollars a month."

"Shouldn't you see how they like the first shipment?" Phil asked.

"I'm just gluing things on the aprons," Peggy said. "What can go wrong?"

In Helen's experience, that question always led to trouble, but she wasn't going to burst her friend's bubble.

Phil kept pressing. "When do you find out if your work is accepted?" he asked.

"They'll send me an e-mail tomorrow morning," Peggy said. "Why are you being so suspicious? I'll keep my job until I make three thousand dollars a month with this new project."

Helen heard the exasperation in her friend's voice and quickly switched the subject. "How did your property search go today, Phil?"

"Not so good," Phil said. "The only house I can find is the one Danny lives in. I've checked his name, Chrissy's name and his corporation's name."

"Well, that's it," Helen said.

"Not quite," he said. "When we get back, I'll check Dade and Palm Beach counties. That's a bigger job. I'll need more time."

Everyone ignored the subject of Jordan and Mark, though their names seemed to be flashing overhead in neon. After an awkward silence, Helen said, "Think I'll go pack."

"How can I help?" Phil asked.

"Would you pick up Mom's death certificates and drop one off at the Hendin Island police station?"

"No problem," Phil said, kissing her. "Go get some sleep."

"Don't forget to lock your door," Margery said. "There's been a series of burglaries in this neighborhood."

Helen studied her landlady's dull clothes and wan face. For the first time, she felt real fear. Margery—feisty, funny Margery—might be gone forever.

CHAPTER 17

"I can't believe St. Louis has a Hustler store," Helen said.

Helen and Phil had picked up a rental car at the airport. Helen left the rental lot and was driving past the Hustler Hollywood store. The huge neon-lit shop stood out among the square utilitarian buildings like, well, a hustler in church.

"What's wrong with it? It's by the airport," Phil said. "I don't see any kids around here. Besides, we have one in Fort Lauderdale."

"That's different," Helen said. "Lauderdale is a tourist town. St. Louis is a family city."

"How do you think people get children?" Phil asked. "Is St. Louis a sinless city?"

"Heck, no. Dad was the neighborhood skirt chaser," Helen said. "No one but Mom was surprised when he was caught in the sack with another woman. But that was straightforward Midwestern sin, not cheap, flashy Hustler sin. I can't see a St. Louis soccer mom sneaking into Hustler to buy a *Slutty Senoritas* video or a crotchless tanga."

"No one will see her there except other sinners, who also have to be discreet," Phil said. "And you seem to know a lot about cheap, flashy sin."

"Peggy told me," Helen said, hoping she didn't blush. "She went with Daniel, her lawyer boyfriend, to the Hustler Hollywood on Federal Highway. Just to look at things."

"Uh-huh." Phil grinned at her. "We're on Natural Bridge Road. Where is the natural bridge?"

"Legend says there used to be one nearly two hundred years ago, but it's long gone," Helen said. "The only bridges around seem to be overpasses. Natural Bridge Road has some cool vintage architecture, though, like the Goody Goody Diner."

After several turns, Helen wound up on a major highway.

"Are you lost?" Phil asked.

"There's a lot of new highway construction," she said. "I think I can still find Kathy and Tom's house from here."

"Why not stop and ask directions?" Phil said.

"No, I'll find something I recognize soon," Helen said. She felt a little frantic driving in her former home, as if she was trying to find the city she used to know.

"I thought only guys refused to ask directions," Phil said.

"Wait! Here's Lindbergh Boulevard," Helen said, hailing it like an old friend at a party. "Now I can find Kathy's house."

"I don't mind driving around," Phil said. "This is a good-looking city. Are we going to see the arch?"

"That's downtown," Helen said. "We can make time to see it, if you want."

"I want to drop my bags at the hotel and get to work on your divorce research. That's our priority."

"Look at that," Helen said, more to herself than Phil. "Schneithorst's has morphed into three restaurants with a rooftop beer garden."

She turned to him and said, "Schneithorst's is an old German restaurant."

"I kind of guessed that," Phil said. "Can I get a beer there?"

"Sure. It's a watering hole for the old rich, and not just their money is old. Your silver-white hair would fit in nicely, but you're younger than most of that crowd."

"Jeez, you don't have to insult the place because I wanted a beer there," Phil said. He looked hurt.

"Sorry," Helen said. "I didn't mean to snap at you. Coming home stirs up old memories."

"It must be tough after more than two years," Phil said. "You didn't leave here with a happy good-bye party from your friends."

"I didn't have any friends," Helen said. "Just people I worked with. I ran away from St. Louis late at night, and didn't care where I went. I just wanted to get away. The only people I miss here are Kathy and Tom and their kids. Mom had sided with Rob during the divorce and that hurt. It's unsettling to be back home. I recognize some places, but others are gone or changed. The city looks like a new photo superimposed over an old one. It's confusing."

They drove in silence that was oddly comforting, until they passed a series of estates. "Look at that house," Phil said. "It has a stainless steel beer keg for a mailbox. I wouldn't mind getting my bills out of one of those. Do people that rich drink beer?"

"I think beer bought that mansion. If I remember right, it was owned—maybe it still is—by someone in the Busch family. The beer-baron Busches, not the politicians."

"I'm not used to a place where everything is old," Phil said. "South Florida was built yesterday."

"And will be torn down tomorrow," Helen said.

"Sad but true," Phil said. "Refresh me on our plans for today."

"After we drop our suitcases at the hotel, I'll drive us to Tom and

Kathy's house. I'll stay there and help Kathy with the final arrangements for Mom. The wake is tomorrow at noon and the funeral is the next day. This afternoon, you'll take my car and drive to the St. Louis County Courthouse to start researching my divorce. You'll meet us back at Tom and Kathy's for a barbecue tonight."

"And I can have a beer," Phil said.

"I hear a theme," Helen said. "Beer garden, beer mailbox, beer and barbecue."

"This city was built on beer," Phil said. "It's the home of Anheuser-Busch."

"Which has been sold to a Belgian conglomerate," Helen said. "Now Tom Schlafly is the town's biggest beer baron. He owns the Schlafly brew pubs."

"We can go there, too," Phil said. "I should know St. Louis culture."

"Not today," Helen said. "Here's our hotel. And believe me, you won't admire its architecture."

They checked into their beige hotel and ten minutes later were driving toward Webster Groves, a St. Louis suburb built in the 1890s.

"Look at those old trees," Phil said.

"We have trees in Florida," Helen said.

"We have mostly boring palm trees. These are big, burly and twisted. They shade the whole street. The streets are cleaner here than in Florida. And quieter. Nobody honks or flips us off."

"Wait till we're on the highway at rush hour," Helen said. "It's only eleven in the morning."

"I like the flowers in these older yards. Florida plants are scary-looking."

"Excuse me? You find flowers scary?" Helen asked. "Did the flight attendant put something in your coffee?"

"No. It's true. Florida flowers are loud, rubbery things that look like they're going to either eat you or poison you. These are gentle, old-fashioned flowers: hollyhocks, black-eyed Susans, geraniums, and what's that one there that looks like a purple daisy?"

"Echinacea, I think. I'm trying to drive."

Helen was irritated by Phil's praise for her former home and wasn't sure why. "It's only eighty degrees today," she said. "Don't think this is a typical St. Louis summer. In an ordinary August, the temperature will hang around a hundred for days."

"Well, it's pleasant now," Phil said. "Maybe we could get married here."

"I'd rather not. My first wedding was in St. Louis," Helen said. "It was a disaster. This isn't my home anymore."

She parked their rental car in front of a two-story house with a wide white porch. Pink rambler roses cascaded over the picket fence.

"It looks like a Hallmark card," Phil said.

For the final sentimental touch, a sturdy blond boy came running out of the backyard, carrying his aluminum baseball bat and yelling, "Uncle Phil! Uncle Phil! Can we play baseball?"

"Later this evening, Tommy," Phil said. He hugged the boy, then his small blond sister, Allison, who trailed shyly behind her big brother. Phil waved to Kathy, who was standing in the front doorway, and drove off.

"Hi, Aunt Helen," four-year-old Allison said.

"Cool red-checked playsuit," Helen said. "Beyoncé has one like it."

"Who's she?" Allison asked.

"A famous singer. But you're cuter."

"Enough compliments," Kathy said. "I want to talk to your aunt Helen. Allison, go play in the backyard with Tommy."

Kathy had fixed a salad for lunch and the sisters settled in for a chat. Kathy was two years younger, four inches shorter and thirty pounds heavier than Helen. Kathy's plump figure radiated contentment. Helen had a nervous racehorse energy. Today, Helen thought her younger sister looked tired.

"Has it been difficult making the plans for Mom's funeral here?" Helen asked.

"The real strain has been fighting with Larry," Kathy said. "I want to kill him and make it a double funeral. Tommy's taking his grandma's death badly. He's got a chip on his shoulder the size of a school bus. Oh, hell. He's tormenting his sister again."

Helen could hear the children arguing under the kitchen window.

"Gamma is too in heaven with Jesus," Allison shouted, her voice shrill.

"Grandma is dead. They're going to put her in a box in the ground," Tommy said.

Allison burst into tears. "She's not in a box. She'll catch cold. She's in heaven with Jesus." Helen heard small feet stomping up the porch stairs.

Kathy sighed, rose wearily to open the kitchen door and gathered Allison into her arms. "Grandma is with Jesus, honey," she said, kissing away her daughter's tears. "She's been sick for a long time, but now she won't hurt anymore. Jesus took her home."

"He didn't have to take my grandma," Tommy shouted. "There are lots of other people. Why didn't he take Larry? Larry wouldn't even let us play in Grandma's yard. Nobody likes Larry, not even you, Mom."

"Tommy, we've talked about this," Kathy said. "Grandma is in heaven now, but time is different there. You'll live to be an old, old man, but it will only seem like a blink of an eye to Grandma before she sees you again. We don't know God's plan. He may have something else in store for Larry."

"Something bad?" Tommy asked hopefully. "Something badder than what happened to Grandma?"

"It's possible," Kathy said.

"I hope God runs him over with a dump truck," Tommy said. "Or puts him in a concrete mixer. There's a bunch of construction at church, and there are giant trucks all over. If one of them ran him down and squashed him, would that be part of God's plan?"

"It could be, but we can't expect miracles," Kathy said. Helen worked hard to suppress a smile.

"Now apologize to your sister for making her cry," Kathy said.

"It's not my fault she's a baby," Tommy said.

"She's younger than you. Say you're sorry."

"I'm not sorry. She should grow up."

"Then if you won't apologize, go sit in your room. And leave your bat by the porch."

"Oh, Mom," Tommy said. He dropped the aluminum bat with a thunk and stomped upstairs.

Later, Helen wished he'd dropped the bat in the Mississippi, where she'd dumped her wedding ring. She wished she'd never seen that bat.

Before the night was over, it would kill someone. Whether that was God's plan or the devil's meddling, Helen would never know.

CHAPTER 18

"**K**ill the fatted calf!" Phil shouted into the phone.

"Kill the what? Where are you?" Helen asked. "How did you get Kathy's number?"

"I'm a highly skilled detective," he said. "Also, it was in the phone book. I'm at the St. Louis County Courthouse with a copy of your divorce decree." Phil was talking so fast, Helen had trouble following him.

"Wait till you hear my news, Miss Helen Janet Geimer."

"That's my name," Helen said. "I haven't heard it in so long, I almost forgot. Quit dragging this out, Phil. Tell me."

"I have information about your divorce judge, Xavier Smathers," Phil said. "Do you know he was arrested for bribery eighteen months ago?"

Helen could see the man who had turned her old world upside down: His well-fed face was a waxy, heart-attack red. His wispy white hair barely covered his square skull. She remembered his smug words as he gave away her hard-earned money to the worthless Rob.

"Judge Smathers took bribes?" Helen said. She sat down hard on her sister's kitchen chair and stared at the rooster clock on the wall. It was twelve forty-five.

Kathy hovered over Helen. "What's wrong?" she asked.

Helen covered the phone and said, "It's okay. It's good news."

"Then why are you white as a sheet?" Kathy asked.

"Sh. Pick up the extension and listen in," Helen said.

"Are you there?" Phil asked.

"Yes, yes," Helen said. "Now tell me." She heard Kathy's footsteps on the stairs to her bedroom, then a small click as her sister lifted the extension.

"Judge Xavier Smathers was convicted of bribery in July of this year," Phil said. "The story was in the *St. Louis City Gazette*. How did Kathy miss it?"

"Oh, I don't know," Helen said. "Maybe she was preoccupied with a dying mother, a greedy stepfather, a part-time job, two kids and a husband."

Helen thought she heard a gentle snort from Kathy.

"You sound sarcastic," Phil said.

"I was just giving you a few reasons," Helen said. "Besides, most people don't read newspapers anymore." The last of her patience vanished and she raised her voice. "Now tell me the rest before I die of old age."

"You don't have to be angry," Phil said. "This is good news. Judge Xavier Smathers's bribery trial focused on one person, a real estate broker who wanted sole custody of his son. The broker paid the judge two hundred thousand dollars in cash. He got custody of his six-year-old boy despite two experts who testified that the broker's wife would be a better caretaker parent. The judge also overlooked the husband's cocaine addiction and anger-management issues.

"The prosecution's investigators found nearly two million dollars in cash in shoe boxes in the judge's weekend home near Lake St. Louis, so they're pretty sure he made more crooked deals. Your ex-husband's name wasn't mentioned during the trial, but I think Rob bribed the judge."

"How? Rob didn't have any money," Helen said. "He still doesn't. He spends everything he gets his hands on."

"He got half the proceeds of your St. Louis house sale, didn't he?" Phil asked. "That's what it said in the decree."

"Yes," Helen said. "We'd sold the West County house just before the divorce for six hundred thousand dollars. The money went into our joint account. I'd expected to split the sale proceeds with him as part of the divorce. I put my share in a money market account for Helen Hawthorne, the name I use now. I didn't have time to reinvest any of it."

"You used a fake name back then?" Phil said.

"Just that once. I liked it and used it when I left town," Helen said. "Rob didn't know about my new name. Another name would make me harder to find."

"And the money is still there in the account?" Phil asked. "Why didn't you spend it when you were on the run?"

"I couldn't do anything that would help the court or Rob find me," Helen said. "I'd expected a fair divorce."

"Really?" Phil asked. "That's why you hid your money under a fake name?"

"I didn't hide it," Helen said. "The money was legally mine. But maybe some part of me expected the worst. When the judge gave Rob half of my future earnings, I was so furious, I took whatever cash I had on hand, then maxed out the advances on my credit cards and the cash limit at the ATM. I left St. Louis late at night with about ten thousand dollars. I never used my old accounts or credit cards once I left my hometown.

"I didn't go near that money market account, afraid it might lead Rob to me. Even after he tracked me down to Fort Lauderdale as Helen Hawthorne, he could have taken some of that three hundred thousand dollars, claiming it was owed to him as part of my earnings while I was on the run."

"Then you have money!" Phil said. "You must have at least three hundred thousand dollars in your account. Maybe more, if it paid interest for nearly three years."

"Only if Rob didn't know about my personal account at National Bank and Trust on New Ballas Road," Helen said.

"Your bank accounts are listed in the decree," Phil said. "There's a joint account for you and Rob at Commerce Bank. It also looks like Rob had his own account at Heartland Bank. Is there really a Heartland Bank?"

"That bank name couldn't sound more trustworthy if it tried," Helen said. "I'm sure that's why Rob used it. He's probably closed his account there by now. I don't know if he had others."

"No sign of any account at National Bank," Phil said.

"Oh," Helen said. "Maybe I forgot to list it for the decree."

"Good thing you were forgetful," Phil said. Helen could tell he wasn't buying her excuse. "Rob would have remembered that money. I'll need his Social Security number to check all his accounts."

"Is his Social on the divorce decree?" Helen asked.

"Not sure," Phil said. "It's thirty-one pages long. I'm still going through it."

"I can give you Rob's number," Helen said.

"You remember your ex-husband's Social Security number?"

"I'm an ex–number cruncher," Helen said. "I was better dealing with numbers than with men like Rob." She rattled off a nine-digit number.

"You're amazing," Phil said.

"Yes," Helen said. "Now go back to work."

"Only if you promise to check on the balance of your private account," Phil said.

"Easy. I can do it online at Kathy's house," Helen said.

Kathy ran downstairs, her face glowing with excitement. "I heard the news! The computer is in Tom's basement office. Follow me and watch where you step."

Helen sidled past Allison's folding baby crib, boxes of winter clothes and a broken chair, to a small office with fresh white walls. As Kathy bent to turn on the computer, Helen noticed the gray in her little sister's dark hair.

"You're ready to go," Kathy said. "Do you still remember your online password?"

"It's 'Cool Valley,' the town where Grandma was born," Helen said. "I figured Rob wouldn't know that." She typed it in, then shrieked, "Yes, it's there! I have $306,021.17."

"Then you're rich again," Kathy said.

"Nope. That money goes to pay Mom's Florida funeral expenses, the lawyers who might be able to get me out of this mess, and any back taxes and penalties I'll owe the IRS."

"Why would you owe the IRS?" Kathy asked.

"I haven't filed income taxes in more than two years," Helen said. "The feds don't like that, but with the right lawyer and the right attitude, they might show mercy."

"Let's work on dinner while we wait for Phil's next call," Kathy said. "We still have a bottle of white wine to finish."

Helen tore romaine and chopped onions, tomatoes and cucumbers for a salad. Kathy made potato salad. They finished most of the white wine while they prepared for the barbecue.

After an hour, Tommy Junior crept downstairs. "Mom, can I go play outside if I tell Allison I'm sorry?"

"There, that's my little man," Kathy said, and hugged him.

The two children played peacefully in the backyard. Tommy hit baseballs with his aluminum bat and said in his pretend sports-announcer voice, "It's Cardinal star Albert Pujols up at bat and he's having another great day, folks."

Tommy swung the bat, connected with the ball and shouted, "Pujols hits the ball out of the park. THERE HE GOES! ANOTHER HOME RUN!"

"The kid has quite a swing," Helen said. "Does he break any windows with that baseball?"

"It's a spongy thing. He can't use a real baseball in the yard," Kathy said.

Little Allison fetched the ball and presented it to the star. "She's nice to help him," Helen said.

"Don't worry," Kathy said. "She does more than wait on her brother. Tommy plays goalie and fetches the ball for his sister when Allison plays soccer."

"Is Allison good at soccer?"

"Better than her mother. She's young yet, but we hope she'll continue. There are good college soccer scholarships for girls."

Phil called Helen back at three thirty-two, talking faster than a tobacco auctioneer. "Rob had three accounts in his name that I can find. It took Rob three months to take out one hundred thousand dollars in cash in ways that looked sneaky but wouldn't have fooled an experienced investigator."

"Like yourself?" Helen asked.

"Maybe not as good as me, but they would have caught it, too," Phil said. "I gave the account numbers to the prosecutor's office. The accounts Rob routed them to are connected to the crooked judge. The prosecutor's assistant said if ex-judge Smathers admits he took bribe money from Rob, you're home free."

"Why would Smathers do that?" Helen asked.

"Smathers made a deal with the prosecutors that he would tell all to get better treatment. That means he'll get a name change, a transfer to a penitentiary in another state, and he won't be locked up with the hard cases. You don't want to know what they do to former judges."

"But Smathers wasn't a criminal judge," Helen said. "He never sentenced anyone."

"Think all those cons got along well with their wives?" Phil said. "They get divorced, too."

"When is Smathers supposed to spill the beans to the prosecutor's office?" Helen said.

"He's doing it now," Phil said. "He's been warned that if he's caught in a single lie, the deal is off. Because you were the victim of a bent justice system, the prosecutors will mention Rob's name and see what the judge says."

"And if Smathers doesn't admit Rob bribed him?"

"No chance," Phil said. "Smathers knows a lie is his death sentence. They'll ask His Dishonor tomorrow."

"That's the day of Mom's wake. The funeral is the next morning."

"Then I suggest we see a lawyer late that same afternoon," Phil said. "I did some asking around and found us two good ones. We can have an appointment at three p.m. with Tarragon Tyler. She's a family-law specialist."

"Her name is Tarragon?" Helen asked.

"Hippie parents," Phil said. "She rebelled against Mom and Dad by putting on a pin-striped suit and going to law school, but she has her parents' same distrust of the system. Her nickname is 'Terror' Tyler. After that, we can see a lawyer who handles IRS problems, Drake Upton."

"What's she famous for?"

"Drake is a he," Phil said. "Drake is good at getting the IRS off people's backs. Which you'll need if you're going to be a solid citizen again. Then we can go before a different judge to redetermine if you owe Rob money."

"Me!" Helen said.

"I wouldn't worry too much about that," Phil said. "Rob will be facing charges of judicial bribery. He might owe you his half of the house sale."

"No chance I'll see it," Helen said. "That money will be long gone."

"And so will Rob when he has to face the music," Phil said. "You'll never hear from him again. He'll be out of your life forever. How's that for a wedding present? Chill the beer and throw the steaks on the grill. We'll celebrate your freedom tonight. You don't have to run anymore. Ever."

Helen felt a great weight fall from her as she hung up the phone. She'd always known that her divorce decision was unjust. But she'd never thought it was crooked.

"Why are you crying?" her sister asked.

"Because I'm so happy," Helen wailed. "I'm free. Almost free. Rob will be out of my life forever."

CHAPTER 19

"Throw the ball again, Uncle Phil," Tommy Junior said. The future Albert Pujols held his bat ready for the next pitch.

"Okay," Phil said.

"No," Tom Senior said. "That's enough baseball for tonight, sport. Join your sister inside. Go watch TV, play Nintendo DS or something. The grown-ups need to talk."

"Oh, Dad," Tommy complained, but he propped his beloved bat against the back porch and went inside.

The adults waited until the light came on in Tommy's bedroom. Then Phil whispered, "I didn't mind tossing a few balls for the kid."

"He's taking advantage of your good nature," Tom said. "Besides, we're out of beer."

"Why didn't you say so?" Phil said. "This is an emergency. We'd better get more. We can take our car."

"Why don't you walk, guys?" Kathy said. "You've put away nearly a case. The bar is only a block away."

"But if we walk, we might be forced to have a drink or two at Carney's Bar," Tom said.

"Just don't let anyone step on your hand when you crawl home," Kathy said. She kissed her husband. "If you need a ride, call us."

Helen started stacking the dinner dishes on the picnic table. "Leave those alone," Kathy said. "Sit down and talk to me."

Helen settled into a lawn chair with an iced tea. "The barbecued pork steaks were terrific," she said. "I haven't had them since I left St. Louis. South Florida hasn't discovered pork steaks."

"They don't know what they're missing," Kathy said. "Pork steaks taste like ribs but have more meat. You can slather them in barbecue sauce. They're less messy to eat and quicker to barbecue. You can grill them in one six-pack."

"Pork steaks are the seedless grapes of barbecue," Helen said, and giggled.

Kathy heard someone stumbling up the sidewalk to her back gate and asked, "Are the boys back so soon?"

The man standing at the gate wasn't Tom or Phil. He was shorter and heavier. He was—oh, no, Helen thought. It couldn't be.

"Hello, girls." The man made a mock courtly bow and nearly fell over.

"Hell and damnation," Helen said. "It's Rob. And he's drunk."

Rob pushed open the gate and said, "A picket fence with pink roses. How sweet."

Kathy stood up, as if to defend her home.

"Get out of here," Helen said. "You're trespassing."

Rob used to have a certain teddy bear cuteness. Now he'd gone from boyish to old. Helen thought he looked hard up for money. His expensive Tommy Bahama shirt was two seasons old, a sartorial sin in his former circles. A beach bum would turn up his nose at Rob's boat shoes. Helen's ex had a potbelly. His twenty-thousand-dollar wristwatch had been replaced by one costing maybe three grand. Helen wondered if Rob had pawned the more expensive watch.

There was one more clue to his financial ruin: Rob was balding again. He could no longer afford Rogaine treatments.

"I'm sure my sister-in-law is happy to see me," Rob said. "You're looking good, kiddo. You've put on a few pounds, but I like a woman with curves."

He patted Kathy's bottom. She grabbed his hand, picked up a steak knife and said, "Try that again, and I'll slice it off. If you're lucky, it will only be your hand I remove. You've put on a few pounds yourself, Rob, unless I'm looking at a rare case of male pregnancy. And your head seems to be growing through your hair."

"Ooh, it hurts when you say it," Rob mocked.

Kathy dropped the knife on the picnic table, as if it had suddenly become hot.

"I came to offer my condolences, Kathy," Rob said. "I saw your mother's obituary in the *Webster-Kirkwood Times*. I stopped by earlier to see her husband, Larry, and we had a few beers. Larry's not happy that your sister hijacked Dolores's funeral, but at least Helen is paying for it."

"My mother wanted to be buried in St. Louis," Helen said through gritted teeth.

"I know. She told me," Rob said. "We always got along well, Dolores and me. She liked me better than her own daughter. Not that I blame Dolores. Helen is definitely short on charm."

"Leave, slime wad," Helen said. She thought she heard a small sound in the house and hoped Tommy wasn't listening.

"See what I mean?" Rob asked. "No charm." He slurred his words slightly and swayed. "Helen, is what's his name here?"

"Who?" Helen said.

"You sound like an owl, sweet cheeks. You know who. The guy who's getting my secondhand goods."

Helen stepped forward to punch his face, but she wasn't fast enough. Rob clamped his hand on her arm. She kicked him in the crotch, but he still held on, bending her arm back and forcing Helen to her knees.

"Ah, just the way I like my women," Rob said. "At my feet." He was surprisingly strong for a paunchy drunk. "You're so predictable, Helen. Remember the last time you tried to punch me? You got in a lot of trouble. You were in jail for a while, as I recall, until our friend Marcella sent a lawyer to rescue you. We have to talk. That's the other reason I'm here."

Rob dragged Helen over by a lawn chair and flopped into it, forcing Helen to kneel next to him. The pain in her arm was excruciating. Helen saw the long barbecue fork on the picnic table and thought she could stab him in the chest.

"Now, that's better," Rob said. "Let's talk."

"About what?" Helen said. Was that a creak behind her? Were Phil and Tom coming back?

"Why, the money you still owe me," Rob said. "I hope you didn't spend it all shipping your mother home. You know I can still put you in jail. And—"

He never finished the sentence. A blur came from beside his head. Tommy Junior swung his aluminum bat with all his might, hitting Rob's skull so hard the pop resounded through the yard. The swing would have done Albert Pujols proud.

Rob fell forward without a word.

Tommy stared at his unconscious uncle, then said in a small voice, "I'm sorry."

"Tommy!" his mother cried.

"Uncle Rob was hurting Aunt Helen," Tommy said. "He was hurting you, too."

"Go to your room and stay there," Kathy said. "Now."

Rob was still out cold. Kathy slapped his face with a little too much enthusiasm. Helen found a pitcher of ice water from dinner and poured it on his head.

Rob opened one eye and said, "What the fuck?"

"Please," Helen said. "There are children in the house."

He rubbed his head and said, "I know you didn't hit me. It must have been Kathy."

Helen burst out laughing. "You were knocked silly by my ten-year-old nephew. Tommy hit you with a kid's bat."

"Boy's got a powerful swing," Rob said, rubbing his temple.

"You should go to the emergency room," Kathy said.

"So I can tell them I was hit by a kid? No, thanks."

"Head injuries should be taken seriously," Kathy said. "Look what happened to that poor actress Natasha Richardson. She fell on a ski slope, said she was fine, and then she was dead from bleeding in the brain."

"We're not on a ski slope," Rob said. He picked up Tommy's bat. "This is a lightweight bat. I'm touched by your concern, but I'm fine."

"Besides," Helen said, "you need a brain to have brain damage."

"Rob, please go to the ER. We'll pay for it," Kathy said. "I'm worried."

"Christ on a crutch! I refuse all treatment," Rob said. "I'll put it in writing if you want. Now, for the last time, quit yammering about the ER. Go away. I want to talk to Helen."

"I need to talk to my son," Kathy said. "Will you be okay, Helen, if I leave you two alone?"

"Hand me the bat," Helen said, dragging a lawn chair near Rob. "I'll whack him in the head again if he starts trouble."

"Here's your cell phone, too," Kathy said, putting it carefully on Helen's chair arm. "Call 911 if he touches you."

Rob waited until Kathy had closed the kitchen door, then said, "Where's my money, Helen? And don't get cute. You know the judge awarded me half your income. You haven't paid me a penny yet. I need fifteen thousand dollars and I need it fast."

"Wrong," Helen said. "I don't owe you a dime, Rob. In fact, you owe me a fortune."

"Hah! Are you on drugs? Wanna see a copy of our divorce decree?" Rob asked. "That could refresh your memory. Or I could show it to the police."

"The police will be looking for you, probably by tomorrow. You're going to be arrested," Helen said. "I'll even tell you why. Consider it my last favor for old times' sake."

Rob's smug smile disappeared as she explained that Phil had found evidence of bribery and that ex-judge Smathers was expected to rat out Rob.

"So you will probably owe me ALL the money from the sale of our house," Helen said, "plus whatever was in our joint account when we divorced. And you're facing charges of bribery."

She looked directly at Rob. The smug grin was gone. He seemed asleep.

"Rob? Did you hear me?" Helen asked.

No answer.

Helen was furious. "Are you drunk?" she said. "Did you pass out? Answer me."

Rob didn't respond. His eyes were at half-mast and his jaw was slack. Helen started shaking him, then slapped him. "Wake up!" she shrieked. "Wake up!"

"Helen!" Kathy was on the back porch. "Quiet! I could hear you upstairs. What are you doing?"

"Rob won't answer," Helen said. "I'm sick of his games. He's pretending not to hear me."

Kathy came closer and examined Rob. She pinched the back of his hand. Rob didn't react.

"No response to pain," she said.

Kathy put a hand on his chest, then put her ear over his shirt pocket. "No heartbeat."

Kathy put her ear over his mouth. "No air movement," she said. "He's not breathing."

She lifted one eyelid. "His pupils are fixed," she said. "That's not good."

Kathy felt for a pulse, first in Rob's wrist, then at his neck. "He's dead. Definitely dead. Oh, my God. Oh, my God. My son is a killer," she said, over and over.

"It was an accident," Helen said. "We'll call 911 and explain that to the police."

Kathy grabbed Helen's arm, her eyes frantic. "We can't!" she said. "Tommy will be ruined."

"But he's not guilty," Helen said.

"Listen to me," Kathy said. "Remember Kevin, the kid at school who dropped his baby brother and killed him?"

"You mean—" The words died on Helen's lips.

"Yes. Killer Kevin. That's what everyone called him, didn't they? Kevin was a bright, sweet boy until his little brother died," Kathy said. "That was an accident, too, but Kevin never shook the nicknames. He's been Killer Kevin, or Klumsy Killer Kevin, or KKK, ever since.

"Kevin should have gone to college. But he never finished high school. He couldn't hold a job. Two years ago, he was arrested for armed robbery at a convenience store. Now he's in jail. I don't want my son's life destroyed. Tommy shouldn't suffer for that worthless Rob."

"Tommy was trying to defend me," Helen said. "I'll say I did it. It was an accident. Call the police."

"The police will never believe you," Kathy said. "They'll find out the court is looking for you after your divorce. They'll check in Florida and find the assault charges from the time you hit Rob."

"Those charges were dropped," Helen said.

"Someone will talk," Kathy said. "You'll be arrested. Then my son will tell the truth to save his aunt Helen and his life will be ruined. I won't allow it." She slammed her hand on the picnic table. Easygoing Kathy had turned into a lioness defending her cub.

"What are we going to do?" Helen asked.

"Get rid of Rob's body," Kathy said. "I have to save my son."

"I'll help," Helen said. "But this is so unfair."

"Why?" Kathy asked.

"I prayed for Rob to die for years," Helen said. "But nothing would kill him—not even when he moved in with a multiple murderess.

"Now when I need him alive, he up and dies."

CHAPTER 20

"What do we do with Rob?" Kathy asked. "We have to get him out of here fast."

Rob's body was slouched in the lawn chair like an overgrown doll. Helen wanted to pick up the baseball bat and keep pounding his body, but that wouldn't help Kathy—or Tommy.

"We could dress him up as a scarecrow and put him on the front lawn for Halloween," Helen said. A slightly hysterical laugh escaped her.

Kathy turned on her. "This is no time for you to get giddy. Your nephew's future is at stake. Tom and Phil could return any moment. They are such straight arrows, they'll call the cops."

Helen was instantly serious. "Can the neighbors see Rob in the backyard here?" she asked. "He may look drunk from a distance, but if we start packing him in a steamer trunk or something, the neighbors will call the cops. What if someone saw Tommy slug him with the bat?"

"I doubt it," Kathy said. "Old Mrs. Kiley next door is probably asleep. She goes to bed right after dinner. The house behind us belongs to the Kerchers, and they're on vacation. That leaves the Cooks on the west side, and their view of our yard is blocked by our house. We're safe so far. But we'd better move Rob soon. Let me pour you an iced tea and we'll decide what to do."

"Iced tea, my eye," Helen said. "I want a big glass of wine."

Kathy came out with another chilled bottle and poured generous glasses. The sisters sat at the picnic table. In the gathering dusk, Rob seemed to be watching them through slitted eyes.

"It will be dark in less than thirty minutes," Kathy said. "We need that."

"We could drag him around the corner to the bar's parking lot," Helen said. "Then he'd look like he was mugged."

"People don't get mugged in this neighborhood," Kathy said. "There would be a major investigation. The autopsy would show he'd been hit with a blunt instrument. We'd have cops everywhere."

"We could drop him in the river," Helen said.

"Bodies float back up," Kathy said. "The rivers are lower in August. You know Rob would be trouble. He was all his life."

"Then we'll have to bury him," Helen said. She surveyed Kathy's smooth green lawn and well-tended flower beds. "But we can't dig up your yard. I don't think we can put him in Mom's grave."

"The grave is already open," Kathy said. "But we'd have to dig down at least three feet in hard clay."

"That would take all night," Helen said, "and Phil and Tom would wonder where we were."

"Wait, I've got it! We'll bury him in the church's new hall," Kathy said. "It's an open construction site. They've torn down the old building. The new hall is being built on the same site. The concrete sides for the new basement have been poured. The drains and pipes are already in, and the basement floor is covered with crushed stone. They're pouring the concrete tomorrow. I had to tell the funeral director so he could direct the mourners' cars to the west lot, away from the construction. We could put Rob under the crushed stone. We won't have to do much digging."

"How do we get him there?" Helen asked.

"Tom has plenty of plastic drop cloths in our garage," Kathy said. "We'll wrap Rob's body in some, tie him to a dolly and wheel him to the hall basement. We can use my minivan."

Kathy slipped on her gardening gloves and handed Helen a pair of work gloves from Tom's workbench. "Put them on," she said. "Plastic takes fingerprints."

Kathy opened four drop cloths on the garage floor. Then she draped more plastic drop cloths on the van's front seats and put newspapers from the recycling bin in the foot wells. "To collect hair and fibers," she said.

The two women lifted Rob out of the lawn chair and draped his arms over their shoulders, carrying him as if he were dead drunk, instead of dead.

"Good thing I'm used to hauling Allison," Kathy said. "He's heavy."

"He stinks, too. And he's a deadweight," Helen said, and started giggling.

"Stop it!" Kathy said. "Concentrate."

With a grunt, they dumped the body on the drop cloths. "Let's go through his pockets and remove his identification," Helen said. "In case he's found, it will make Rob harder to trace."

Rob's wallet had a Florida driver's license, thirty-one dollars and two credit cards. His pocket held the keys to a rental car.

"You take the money," Helen said. She shoved the credit cards in her jeans. "I'll cut up the cards and drop them down a sewer by our hotel. We'll have to get rid of his rental. We can leave it at the gates of the car agency tonight and they'll think he left in a hurry. It's a shame to leave that expensive watch on his wrist, but it could be traced back to him if we take it."

Helen spotted a roll of duct tape on a shelf by Tom's workbench and reached for it.

"We'll have to throw out the whole roll," Kathy said. "Forensics experts can match up duct tape. I saw that on TV."

"You really do watch those *CSI*-type shows," Helen said.

"I also read murder mysteries," Kathy said. "I thought they were entertainment. Turns out they were educational."

They folded the drop cloths around Rob and crisscrossed them with duct tape, then strapped the plastic-wrapped body to the handcart with bungee cords. Kathy threw two shovels and a rake in the van. Helen stuck the nearly empty tape roll in her purse.

It was dark by the time they had Rob ready for his last ride. Kathy backed up her minivan and parked it sideways in front of the garage door. She and Helen rolled the body aboard.

"Let me check on the kids," Kathy said.

She came back and said, "I left a note for the guys that we'd run out of wine and will be back soon. Allison was already asleep. Tommy was engrossed in his Nintendo DS. He has my cell number if there's a problem. What kind of mother checks on her children before she goes off to bury their uncle?"

"A good mother," Helen said. "Anyway, Rob is an ex-uncle, and he wasn't much of one, dead or alive. Let's get out of here."

Kathy drove carefully through Webster Groves to the church. "I wonder what the neighbors would think if they knew what I had stashed in my minivan," Kathy said.

"Good thing women in minivans are invisible," Helen said. "I can't believe Rob died on me. I thought I was finally free. Now I have to worry about his body."

"You will be free soon," Kathy said. "We're at the church."

"Wait!" Helen said. "There's an SUV in the lot. On the other side of the church."

"Oh, that belongs to Horndog Hal," Kathy said. "He's having an affair with Mrs. Snyder. He tells his trusting wife he's at choir practice. She never checks on him. What Hal is practicing may have Mrs. S. hitting the high notes, but not in the church choir. Hal won't notice anything until his lady love staggers off to her Toyota, which she parks around the corner. I swear she'll be bow-legged before this affair is over."

"Kathy!" Helen said.

The lights were off inside the church building, the grade school and the rectory. The site of the new church hall was a deep hole surrounded by a chain-link fence. "There's no guard on duty," Kathy said. "The construction gate is padlocked, but I think we can squeeze through that gap in the fence. Just wish I hadn't had that extra helping of potato salad."

The open basement was covered with white crushed rock. Poured concrete lined the sides.

Kathy expertly maneuvered the minivan in front of the gap in the fence, then opened the van's side doors. She and Helen dragged the handcart with the wrapped Rob to the fence opening. Helen crawled through and emerged with a scratch on her right arm. She and Kathy pushed and pulled Rob until he fell over the edge into the huge hole, landing on the crushed rock with a loud crunch.

"Rob has hit rock bottom," Helen said.

"Shut up!" her sister said.

Kathy tossed the two shovels and the rake on the rock. She squeezed through the fence opening, muttering words she'd never say in front of her children. A ladder led down to the hall floor. Helen climbed down it and Kathy followed her. They dragged Rob's body to the closest corner. The handcart was hard to move in the rock. It tipped sideways when they hit a drain.

"Here," Kathy said. She was panting. "Let's put him here. There are no pipes or drains nearby."

Helen and Kathy shoveled and raked the rock out of the way until they had a shallow hole about six feet long. They took off the bungee cords, rolled Rob into the hole and covered him with the rock. Kathy raked the crushed stone several times until it was smooth. The two women walked over the site a few times so it would have footprints like the rest of the rock.

"Can you see the grave now?" she asked.

Helen climbed the ladder and surveyed their work. She saw no sign that Rob's body was under there. "I can't see any difference."

Helen helped Kathy carry the handcart and shovels up the ladder and push them through the fence hole. She climbed out, then lay down on her stomach in the mud and helped pull her sister out.

"I look like I've been mud wrestling," Helen said, back in the van. "Good thing you put plastic on these seats."

"Don't forget the rock dust," Kathy said. Her face was smeared with mud and white streaks. "We're covered in white dust from our shoes to our hair. If the guys aren't home, we can shower in the basement bathroom and wash these clothes. You can wear my clothes until yours are clean. The pants might be a little baggy."

Kathy drove back to her house with scrupulous care. "The lights are off in the living room," she said. "I don't think Phil and Tom are home yet. Let's sneak around the side and into the basement."

Helen and Kathy threw their clothes and tennis shoes in the

washing machine. They were dressed in twenty minutes. Their hair was clean and combed, but wet. Kathy's jeans were too big for Helen and her shoes were too small, but she could wear them.

Kathy checked on the children again. Both were asleep. She dug wool gloves and a hooded sweatshirt out of a closet. She stuffed the van's protective newspapers and drop cloths into a plastic trash bag, then cleaned off the shovels, rake and handcart with a garden hose. Finally, Kathy rolled the handcart through a flower bed to cover the rock-dusted tires with mud from her yard.

Helen found Rob's anonymous silver rental car easily, thanks to the license tag number on the plastic key ring. It was parked at the curb.

"Here," Kathy said, "put on this hoodie to hide your face, and wear these wool gloves. Your fingerprints can't be in Rob's rental car. And wipe those keys down so you don't leave your prints."

"You think of everything," Helen said.

"I hope so," Kathy said. "We have to save my son."

Helen started Rob's car and turned on the air-conditioning. She was sweltering in the heavy winter clothes. Helen drove to the nearest car-rental office, two blocks away, while Kathy followed in the van. The office had closed at six p.m. Helen parked the car at the edge of the lot, grateful her hoodie hid her face from the security cameras.

Helen climbed into her sister's minivan and they drove behind a failing strip mall.

"See any security cameras back here?" Kathy asked.

They drove through again carefully, but couldn't spot any. Helen tipped the plastic trash bag filled with newspaper and the drop cloths into the Dumpster.

"What time is it?" she asked.

"Ten o'clock," Kathy said.

"Is that all? I thought it would be at least five in the morning," Helen said. "We'd better stop at the mini-mart for some white wine. That's why we told the boys we were going out."

"And some Ben & Jerry's," Kathy said. "I'm hungry."

"What flavor?" Helen asked.

"Chubby Hubby, of course," Kathy said.

Soon they were at Kathy's with wine and ice cream. Kathy parked in her drive and said, "The living room lights are on. The guys are home. I'll go throw our clothes in the dryer. We can drink wine until they're ready."

"We have one big advantage," Helen said. "No one will be surprised if Rob never shows up again. No one will file a missing-person report. Nobody cares enough to search for him. And that church basement will be there for a long time."

"Swear to me that you will never mention what we did tonight to anyone," Kathy said. "Not even Phil."

"On one condition," Helen said. "If Rob's body is discovered, you will tell the police that Rob woke up after Tommy bopped him, and I hit him in the head again."

"But that's not what happened," Kathy said. "The police will think you killed Rob."

"So will Tommy," Helen said. "He won't sacrifice himself to save Aunt Helen. Swear to me. Do it now." Her voice was hard.

"I swear," Kathy said.

"Good," Helen said. "My nephew will not suffer for my mistake."

"But you didn't kill Rob," Kathy said. "He refused treatment for his head injury."

"And I refused to open my eyes while I was married to that man," Helen said. "That's the mistake I have to live with."

CHAPTER 21

Helen gathered the courage to look into her mother's coffin. Dolores was a withered wax doll, boxed for showing on pillowy satin. Her face was overwhelmed by the towering dark wig. Dolores had worn that style for years. Her friends wouldn't recognize her without it.

Funeral directors in two states had tried to erase the effects of Dolores's last illness, and failed. Only her hands looked good. Now the cruel IV bruises were gone. Dolores's favorite white rosary was twined around her hands, as Catholic tradition dictated. She would meet her maker in the pale pink dress from her second wedding. The collar looked too big for her wasted frame. Dolores wore the pearls her beloved first husband had given her on their wedding day.

Dolores would go to her grave with reminders of the three major influences of her life: her two husbands and her God.

The lower half of the casket was covered with a blanket of pink carnations from Helen and Kathy. Portraits of Dolores as a radiant bride, a smiling young mother and a proud grandmother were displayed near the casket. Pictures of Lawn Boy Larry were noticeably absent. Helen suspected that was Kathy's doing.

Helen felt a pang when she studied the photo of Dolores, Kathy and herself in sundresses from a long-ago summer. It was hard to believe the frail woman in the coffin had produced two robust daughters.

Helen bowed her head before the casket. Oh, Mom, she thought. You tried. I tried. We couldn't make it work. I am so sorry. Consider your St. Louis funeral my last gift and final apology. I hope you are happy now and reunited with Daddy.

A rainstorm of tears poured down her face. Phil materialized at her side and stood beside her, head bowed and hands folded, then led her to a chair in the second row. Helen wept on his shoulder. Phil handed her his white pocket handkerchief.

"I love men who carry handkerchiefs," Helen sniffled. "I don't know why I'm crying."

"I do," Phil said. "You only have one mother."

"But we didn't get along," Helen said.

"Then you have to cry twice," he said. "For the mother you had and for the mother you needed."

"Did I tell you I love you?" Helen said. "You look handsome in your navy suit."

She blotted her eyes and surveyed the St. Louis funeral home. Her mother would appreciate its old-fashioned style. The walls were a gloomy face-powder pink. The flowers were comforting, dated arrangements of gladioli and fat mums. Helen read the flower cards. Larry's dismal display was wilted. Helen wondered if the tightwad had fished it out of the funeral home Dumpster. She hid it behind a burly basket of yellow mums from Dolores's bridge club.

Lawn Boy Larry held court near the casket, surrounded by

well-dressed widows hunting for another husband. They hung on his words and fluttered their mascaraed eyelashes at him. Helen could smell their perfume two rows back.

A tall woman with quarter-sized rouge spots was glued to Larry's side. Helen wondered if she was Mrs. Raines, maker of fork-tender pot roasts. Could you be a shameless hussy at age seventy? Helen hoped Mrs. Raines won the hand—and stomach—of Larry.

"Oh, Helen, dear," Larry said. Her stepfather shambled over in a suit two sizes too big. "I wanted to talk to you about those pearls Dolores is wearing. I'll instruct the undertaker to remove them when the casket is closed."

"No, you won't," Helen said. "Mother wanted to be buried with her wedding pearls."

"But they're valuable, dear."

Helen looked Larry right in his rheumy eyes. "Take those pearls off my mother, Larry, and I'll make sure you get billed for shipping Dolores to St. Louis. You're legally responsible for her debts."

"But Helen, dear," he began.

"I'm not your 'dear' and you'll owe that Florida funeral home five thousand dollars, you cheapskate."

"Really, Helen," Larry said.

Phil had gone for coffee in the family room and hurried back to Helen. "Is there a problem?"

"Not anymore," Helen said. Her glare should have reduced Larry to a pile of ash.

Kathy had arrived with Tommy Junior in his best clothes: clean khaki pants and a white shirt. Both still fit, but they'd be too small after one more growth spurt. Tommy was trying hard not to cry, but his lower lip trembled. He straightened his back and marched toward the casket like a young soldier. Helen's heart ached for him.

His mother followed. Kathy looked seedy and pale in her black dress. She walked carefully, as if the carpet were land-mined. Kathy avoided looking directly at her sister. Helen guessed the law-abiding Kathy felt the same heavy burden of guilt.

Last night, Helen had been tempted to tell Phil about Rob, but he fell asleep too soon. After a sleepless night, Helen decided confiding in Phil would be an indulgence. She couldn't sacrifice Tommy's future for her comfort. She hoped this secret wouldn't hurt her impending marriage.

Helen took her place next to Kathy in the receiving line. The sisters greeted a parade of older women, many pointedly avoiding Larry. The women politely announced their connection to Dolores: "I was in your mother's prayer group." "We belonged to the Altar Society."

A woman about seventy in a neat gray dress with black buttons down the front held both sisters' hands and said, "I'm Mrs. Hurbert. I was your mother's bridesmaid when she married your father. Not," she sniffed, "when she made THAT mistake." Mrs. H. glared at Larry, but he was too busy being fawned over by the widows to notice.

"I wanted you girls to know that shriveled old coot is advertising an estate sale at Dolores's house," Mrs. Hurbert said. "The day after the funeral."

"What?" Kathy said.

"I couldn't believe it myself. But I saw the ad in the local paper."

Mrs. Hurbert gave their hands an affectionate squeeze. "I'm glad you brought your mother home. He'd be too cheap to do that."

At a lull in the receiving line, Phil said, "It's two thirty. When do you want to leave?"

"Now if we're going to make the lawyer's appointment," Helen said. "We can come back for the rosary service tonight."

"Good luck with the lawyer," Kathy said. "I have to check on

Allison. She's staying with Mrs. Kiley next door." Kathy dropped her voice to a whisper and added, "I have the key to Mom's house. I'm also going for a sneak preview of Larry's sale."

The bright afternoon sun stabbed Helen's eyes, but she was relieved to breathe air free from the stink of hothouse flowers.

Tarragon "the Terror" Tyler, her lawyer, had an office in an anonymous glass tower near the county courthouse. Tarragon didn't look like a terror, but Phil had assured Helen she was a tough negotiator on behalf of her clients.

The hippies' daughter wore a gray pin-striped suit, short brown hair and horn-rimmed glasses. There was a soft, pretty woman under that severe getup. Helen kept expecting Tarragon to whip off her glasses and turn suddenly glamorous, like in the old movies.

Helen presented her divorce decree to Tarragon, then stumbled through her complicated story of how she ran from her sorry past.

Tarragon listened without interruption, then skimmed the decree, while Helen and Phil sat in uneasy silence. Finally, she spoke. "If the judge who signed off on the decree took a bribe from your ex," she said, "that would be grounds to set aside this decree and go through the process again."

"But I'm still divorced, right?" Helen said.

"Definitely," Tarragon said. "I'm talking about the disposition of your joint property. That's what would be set aside."

"Rob's bribery wasn't mentioned at the judge's trial," Helen said, "but as I understand it, the prosecutors will expect Smathers to admit to accepting a bribe from my ex-husband today."

"If that's the case," Tarragon said, "the court will have no sympathy for your ex-husband."

"Good," Helen said.

"However," Tarragon said, "the court will still be pretty unhappy with you for ignoring its orders for more than two years."

"Oh," Helen said.

"But I can file a petition to set aside this decree." The lawyer patted the pile of papers.

"Then it's over," Helen said.

"Not quite," Tarragon said. "You've thumbed your nose at the court and skipped out on paying. They may not look kindly on you trying to come back and ask for a break."

"But the judge—ex-judge—is working on a deal now to get better treatment," Phil said. "Smathers is required to name everyone who bribed him. He's already been disbarred."

"I know," the lawyer said.

"I gave the prosecutors the bank accounts Helen's ex used and the dates he withdrew the cash," Phil said.

"If there is concrete evidence of the bribery," Tarragon said, "then the court will most likely set aside the divorce decree. Do you know where your ex-husband is now?"

Buried, I hope, Helen thought. "Rob has a habit of disappearing," she said, truthfully. "With the law after him, he may vanish for good." Also true.

"Well, if the ex doesn't turn up," Tarragon said, "there is no one to go to the court to ask for a new decree. You'll be off the hook for paying him a share of your earnings. But the court will still be pissed at you. It will also be embarrassed by the whole situation, so no one will be inclined to do anything about it. Do you know where Rob is living now?"

"He was living on a yacht with a woman named Marcella," Helen said. "She sails to South Florida occasionally. Rob told me she paid him a million dollars to go away, and he did. I don't think Marcella will know where he is now, but her lawyer might."

Tarragon's eyes lit up. "We may be able to recover some of that million on your behalf."

"He's spent it," Helen said. "I mean, he's probably spent it. That man runs through money the way you use legal pads. Anyway, he came into Marcella's money after our divorce."

"Oh," Tarragon said. "We might still be able to recover your share of the house-sale funds. Can you think of another way to contact him?"

"He stayed in touch with my mother," Helen said. "But Mom just died. Her funeral is tomorrow."

"I'm sorry," Tarragon said. "Will Rob be at the funeral?"

"Definitely not," Helen said.

She was picking her way carefully through the nuggets of truth, as if crossing a stream by leaping from one slippery rock to another.

"We can publish legal notices here in St. Louis and in Fort Lauderdale," Tarragon said. "Rob will have sixty days to respond. I just hope your ex won't show up."

"I can almost guarantee that," Helen said. "Based on his past behavior," she added quickly. Her heart was beating and she hoped no one could read her guilty thoughts.

"Then I'm free?" Helen asked her lawyer.

"You're free now," Tarragon said. "But if your ex-husband doesn't respond to our petition, your legal problem with the court will go away."

"That's wonderful news," Phil said, and hugged Helen. Helen tried to feel relieved, but she felt numb. Her rescue had come too late.

"Anything else?" Tarragon said.

"Yes, I want my name legally changed to Helen Hawthorne. It's the name I've been using for more than two years."

"Easy. I can do that online," the lawyer said. "Or you can."

"I'd rather you did it," Helen said.

Helen answered the questions on the form. No, she was not changing her name for fraudulent reasons, to avoid a civil judgment, or debts. Not anymore, she thought.

She felt slightly queasy about answering, "Have you ever committed a felony?" Well, she hadn't actually killed Rob. It was an accident.

"Next we'll file a demand letter with the small-claims court in Broward County, where you live now," the lawyer said. "Here's your case number. Call this phone number to find out when the change is completed. It should be less than thirty days."

"I'll need a legal driver's license, too," Helen said.

"You can get that in Florida," the lawyer said. "Did you file taxes while you were on the run, Ms. Hawthorne?"

"No," Helen said. "That's another thing I need to get straightened out."

"You were a CPA, correct?" Tarragon asked.

Helen nodded.

"Then you're going to need a good lawyer. The IRS has some amnesty programs. You may qualify for one. Do you need the name of a tax lawyer?"

"I've made an appointment with Drake Upton," Phil said.

"He's the best," Tarragon said. "You'll be in good hands. Good luck." She shook hands with Helen and Phil.

While they waited for the elevator, Helen asked, "When is the appointment with Drake?"

"Tomorrow afternoon, after your mother's funeral," Phil said. "The only other appointment was in two weeks. Is that okay with you?"

"Death and taxes," Helen said. "We can't avoid either."

CHAPTER 22

Candle wax, lemon polish and incense. The comforting scents of Helen's old church greeted her at the wide wooden door. Stained-glass windows cast colorful shadows on the soberly dressed congregation.

Red votive candles burned before the statue of the Virgin Mary. This Virgin was a joyous young mother, cradling her fat baby son. Helen had left a bouquet at Mary's feet when she'd married Rob. That day, she'd felt as happy as the innocent Mother of God looked.

Now Helen was returning after nearly twenty years, burdened with sorrow and a secret too deadly to tell Father Rafferty. The priest had grayed considerably since Helen was a bride. Helen was glad she'd fought to bring her mother's body home for this final ceremony. Dolores would be proud of her grandson. Tommy wore a blue shirt and a clip-on tie. His shirttail had escaped his khaki pants.

Tommy read a passage from the Old Testament in a singsong voice: "But the souls of the just are in the hands of God and no torment shall touch them." He'd chosen the passage himself from the approved list of readings. Helen heard it as an apology to Allison, who was too young to attend her grandmother's funeral.

"They seemed, in the view of the foolish, to be dead, and their passing away was thought an"—Tommy struggled with the next word—"affli-affilic-affliction!" he finished triumphantly. "And their going forth from us, utter destruction. But they are in peace."

I hope so, Mom, Helen thought.

Dolores's casket had been covered with a pall and blessed by Father Rafferty. Inside, Dolores was wearing her pearls. Helen had checked before it was closed. She didn't trust Larry.

Helen recognized many of her mother's friends—and a few of Larry's admirers—in the "memorial choir," the kind name for the church's second-string singers. Their voices wobbled in and out of key, but no pros sang with such sincerity. These women served their church faithfully.

Over the quavery choir, Helen heard the chunk and growl of the cement mixer as the floor was poured in the new church hall. Another burial was going on.

"Hurry up, dammit!" a man's voice yelled outside.

A fitting send-off for Rob, Helen thought, then felt guilty for her meanness. Rob would soon rest under rock and concrete.

Give him eternal rest, Lord, Helen prayed. Permanent rest, so Rob doesn't surface until that last trumpet, when Tommy and I are long forgotten.

Tommy had no clue he'd killed his uncle Rob. Helen hoped the boy never found out. At least Rob is buried in the church, she thought. A mad giggle rose in her throat. Helen strangled the sound and tried to turn it into a sob. Phil patted her hand in sympathy.

Helen and Phil, Kathy, Tom Senior and Tommy took the left

front pew. Larry, the new widower, sat on the right. Mrs. Raines, front-runner for the next Lawn Boy Larry consort, positioned herself close to keep her eye on her prize. The other widows clustered behind her, eyeing Larry like hungry lionesses at a watering hole.

At the Offertory, Tom Senior and Kathy brought up the wafers and wine. Tommy carried a basket of items that had been important to Dolores. Helen glimpsed family photos, a much-thumbed *Betty Crocker Cookbook* with a red-checked cover and a red racing car. Helen knew the story behind that toy. Two-year-old Tommy had insisted it be part of the manger scene under the Christmas tree because "Baby Jesus will like it." His grandma adored this historical inaccuracy. The red car, parked next to the Wise Men, became a family holiday tradition.

At last, the service ended. The memorial choir sang "May the angels lead you into paradise" and the pallbearers, priest and servers escorted Dolores's body down the aisle. The family followed behind the casket.

The undertaker's black limo doors opened, and Helen, Phil, Kathy, Tom and Tommy Junior slid inside. Lawn Boy Larry followed in his own car, accompanied by Mrs. Raines.

"Cool limo," Tommy said, obviously enjoying his first ride in the massive vehicle.

"You did a good job with the reading for your grandmother," Helen said.

"Proud of you, son," Tom said, and patted his boy's shoulder.

"After the burial, Larry is having a funeral lunch in the church basement," Kathy said. "I wanted the lunch at my house, but he said this would be better."

"Which means cheaper," Helen said.

"Probably," Kathy said. "But I'd fought with him so much, I let him have this victory. Mom knew all the church ladies, and I think she would have wanted it. He said he'd make a small donation to the sodality. Knowing Larry, it will be small. We'll have dinner at our house tonight, if your plans permit."

"We see the tax lawyer at two," Helen said. "We have to return our rental car and catch the first flight to Fort Lauderdale by eight tonight. But we have time for an early dinner with you."

Phil nodded agreement.

"It will be quick," Kathy said. "I can't figure out why sitting around a funeral home makes me feel like I've been digging ditches." Kathy blushed when she realized she had indeed been digging a ditch—to bury Rob.

Only Helen noticed Kathy's heightened color. Tom Senior sat there like a sweet, baggy-faced basset, patting his wife's hand.

"I want you both with us when we open the special gifts Grandma left the family," Kathy said.

The funeral procession entered the ornate wrought-iron gates of Calvary Cemetery. The limo drove past weeping stone angels, gray granite crosses and grand mausoleums with stained-glass windows their occupants never saw. The trees were a cool canopy over lush green grass.

"As cemeteries go, this one is a beauty," Phil said.

"Tennessee Williams is buried here," Tom said. "And Civil War general William Tecumseh Sherman and other famous people." Like many St. Louisans, Tom was proud of his city's history.

"We took a field trip to Calvary for school," Tommy said.

"To see the graves of the famous people?" Helen asked.

"No, cooler than that," Tommy Junior said. "Calvary Cemetery has some of the last prairie in the whole USA. It's being preserved and everything."

"Weird but true," Tom Senior said. "North America used to have a million square miles of prairie. One of the last known chunks survived in the city of St. Louis in the cemetery. The Catholic archdiocese has agreed to keep it intact for at least a hundred years."

"Grandma's in a famous place," Tommy said. "Where the buffalo roamed and the cowboys rode."

The black hearse stopped before a white tent sheltering rows of folding chairs. The burial ceremony was mercifully short. Kathy had brought a bouquet of pink carnations, their mother's favorite flower. She handed carnations to her family. They gently dropped flowers and symbolic clods of dirt onto the coffin. Helen hated the soft sound the clay soil made on the lid.

Larry tossed in a single limp rose.

Dolores shared a gray granite headstone with her first husband. Her death date would be engraved on it soon. Helen paused for a moment at the grave of her father, left a spray of red roses, then walked back toward the limo with Phil through the forest of granite headstones.

Larry, Mrs. Raines at his side, greeted the mourners at the funeral luncheon in the church basement. Kathy and Tom got a frosty smile. Larry managed a stingy nod for Phil and ignored Helen.

They ate slightly stale ham sandwiches, boiled coffee and sheet cake lovingly served by Dolores's friends. These women worked hard, but had no authority, one reason Helen had parted from the Church.

"Are we going to the reading of the will?" Helen asked Kathy.

"No. I don't want my son to know his grandmother cut him out for that jackass," Kathy whispered. "We'll open the things I swiped from Mom's house and tell the kids they were gifts from Grandma. I took things Larry will never miss. None of them had price tags yet."

"Will Tommy mention the gifts to Lawn Boy?" Helen said.

"Tommy never talks to that man unless he has to," Kathy said. "There's no reason now."

Helen and Phil thanked the church ladies, and Phil slipped Mrs. Hurbert, head church lady and archenemy of Lawn Boy Larry, a fifty-dollar donation. They left the church basement covered in lipstick kisses and flowery perfume.

On the way to their car, Helen checked out the new church-hall foundation. The basement floor was smooth and wet. No corpse stuck out of the concrete.

"We need to hurry to make the appointment with the tax law-yer," Phil said. Helen drove them to another glass office tower.

Drake Upton had a long aristocratic face, a lantern jaw and iron gray hair. His advice was short and no-nonsense.

"As a CPA, Miss Hawthorne, you will be held to a higher stan-dard, so it will be difficult for you to avoid penalties," he said. "Since you apparently made less than twenty thousand dollars an-nually during the years you were . . . gone . . . you may not have had to file taxes. That does not excuse what you did. You know better."

"I did and I'm sorry," Helen said. "I don't have much paper-work from that time. I do have the forms from when I worked at the Superior Club. I made eleven dollars an hour, the most money I earned during that time."

"But you can't prove that," Drake said.

"No. I took cash under the table for those other jobs," Helen said. "At least three of the seven companies are gone, and the rest are small businesses. I'm willing to pay the price, but I don't want the business owners to suffer because they did me a favor. I do have some money—three hundred thousand dollars left over from the sale of the house."

"The house was sold before your divorce, correct?"

Helen nodded.

"Did your ex-husband pay capital gains on that sale?"

"I can almost guarantee he didn't," Helen said.

"Then you are responsible for that, too. Here's what I recommend: Let's file returns for the real amounts of income. We will not over- or underestimate what you made. That would make it look worse. Then we'll wait for the audit notice that will most surely arrive. When that happens, you will go to the IRS with an attorney. It can be me, if you want to come back to St. Louis, or I can recommend a colleague in Fort Lauderdale. You and your attorney will tell the IRS about your emotional state, your small income, show proof of where the three hundred thousand dollars came from and give them information about your lifestyle, including all assets."

"I haven't any assets, except that three hundred thousand dollars," Helen said. "I rent a tiny apartment. I don't own a car."

"Good," the lawyer said. "That will help. Keep your life simple until this is settled. The IRS will calculate your penalties and interest. Interest cannot be waived, but the penalties can be if you can prove that you were unable to take care of your responsibilities during those years. Being on the run may be able to do that. It will help that your ex-husband bribed a judge to get a divorce decision.

"I'll check the years this took place and the filing requirements and see if there was an amnesty program then," Drake Upton said. "I'll also explain the sale of the house and the fact that your ex probably didn't file taxes for it. If you file taxes now, that will work in your favor.

"After I prepare your taxes, my office will send them to you. You can sign and mail them in with a check. Did you file state tax returns during the time you were gone?"

"No," Helen said.

"Then we'll have to file those, too. Give me a list of states where you worked. I'll research their laws and get back to you."

"There was just one, Florida," Helen said.

"That's good," Drake Upton said. "I believe Florida is one of the states that doesn't have personal income tax, but I'll check for you."

"Will the fines and penalties take the whole three hundred thousand?"

"I don't think so," Drake Upton said. "But taxes are a bit like opening a can of worms. One question leads to another and we have too many that need answering."

"How angry will the tax people be?" Helen asked.

"They're not the ogres most people think they are, Miss Hawthorne. They want citizens to pay taxes. That's what you're trying to do. With patience, time and money, we can get you out of this mess."

Helen and Phil walked to their rental car hand in hand.

"Our work here is done," Helen said.

"It's ironic, isn't it?" Phil said. "The last time you left St. Louis, you were on the run from the court. Rob was free and spending your money. Now Rob is running from the law, and you're free."

"Right," Helen said, "free."

Her heart twisted. Helen would never be free as long as Rob was buried in the church-hall foundation—and she'd go to jail if he was ever found.

She'd traded one trap for another.

CHAPTER 23

"Look at my new bat, Uncle Phil," Tommy said. "It's a wooden grown-up bat."

"Pujols better watch out," Phil said. "What happened to your old bat, slugger?" He ruffled the boy's straw-colored hair.

"Somebody stole it," Tommy said. "Mom bought me this one. She still won't let me use a real baseball in our yard, but I can hit one on a baseball diamond."

"Wanna show me what you can do with this new bat?" Phil asked.

"Yeah!" Tommy said. "You can pitch and Dad can play outfield."

"Daddy needs a beer," Tom said. "I'll get Uncle Phil one, too. Outfielder is thirsty work."

Helen followed her sister into the house to help with dinner. She waited until Tom left the kitchen with two cold beers, then said, "The aluminum bat disappeared, huh? There's been a crime wave in this neighborhood."

"I couldn't risk having it around," Kathy whispered. "DNA is dangerous. What if Rob's blood, hair or skin cells were lodged in the scratches on the bat? If—God forbid—they ever find his body, I don't want the autopsy to reveal he was bopped with a long, blunt bat-shaped object."

"Tommy still has no clue what happened to his uncle?" Helen asked.

"None," Kathy said. "He's used to Rob dropping in and then disappearing. If Rob never reappears, Tommy won't miss him."

"Nobody will," Helen said. " 'Nothing in his life became him like the leaving of it.' "

"*Macbeth*," Kathy said. "Classy epitaph for a worthless life. Nobody will cry for Rob."

"He triggered enough tears when he was alive," Helen said.

"Mom got a good send-off, didn't she?" Kathy asked. "It was a lovely funeral. All her friends were there. The church looked beautiful. And it was nice of Mrs. Hurbert to warn us about Larry's sneaky estate sale. I slipped out during the viewing and took some things from Mom's house before the sale."

"What if Larry discovers they're gone?" Helen asked.

"The only thing he might notice missing is the cookie jar, and it wasn't tagged. I know all Mom's hiding places, so I found her good stuff."

"Mom had hiding places?"

"She kept her good jewelry in a plastic bag in the flour bin."

"It was definitely safe from me there," Helen said.

"Larry, too," Kathy said. "He never lifted a finger to help or to cook. His loss. We'll check out our loot after dinner."

Dinner was quick and simple—spaghetti, salad and ice cream. After the dining room table was cleared, Kathy announced, "Grandma left special presents for everyone she loved. Let's look now."

Kathy opened a cardboard box. Helen swore she saw a light dusting of flour inside.

"Tom, these are Daddy's Cartier cuff links. They're for you."

"Classy," Tom said.

"Phil, this is my grandfather's diamond stickpin."

"Cool Art Deco design," Phil said. "Thank you."

"Helen, this is our grandmother's diamond brooch. You were her favorite."

"Gorgeous antique setting," Helen said.

"Tommy, this is your grandfather's pearl-handled pocketknife. I'm only giving it to you because you've been acting like a man. If I find you're misusing it, the pocketknife is gone."

Allison's chin was trembling, and Helen hoped Kathy had a present for her daughter. The little girl had been cranky and teary since her grandmother's death.

"Allison, this is the necklace your grandma wore when she was a little girl. It's a gold heart with a real seed pearl."

Allison's eyes lit up when she saw the delicate necklace. "Can I wear it now?"

"Tonight only," Kathy said. "Then you can wear it to church and for special occasions, like Megan's birthday party."

Kathy had also carried home a box of Christmas ornaments. "Mom knew how to celebrate Christmas," she said. "Some of these ornaments are nearly a hundred years old. Larry is too much of a Scrooge to know their real value."

Helen recognized the German glass ornaments from her childhood. "There's the fat Santa Claus," she said, "and the silver bells and the musical instruments, including violins and trumpets. We used to have a sleigh with reindeer, but I broke that."

"These antique glass-bead garlands were packed away in tissue paper," Kathy said. "Mom left us her manger scene, too." She opened a fragile white box with hand-painted figures.

"Here are the Christmas stockings Grandma made you kids

with your names on them. They used to hang on Grandma's mantelpiece, but now they'll go on ours."

"Grandma left us her Christmas," Tommy said.

"I also have Grandma's wedding album," Kathy said. "That's for Allison."

"With the Grandma Princess picture?" Allison asked.

"Yes, your grandmother did look like a princess in her white dress. I'll put it in your room, so you can see her all the time. Tommy, you can have Grandma's photo album of the two of you in Forest Park.

"And here's the best thing of all." Kathy held up a fat yellow china duck.

"Grandma's cookie jar," Tommy said. "Any cookies in it?"

"Not now, but I have her *Betty Crocker Cookbook*. I'll make cookies like she used to."

"Nobody can make cookies like Grandma," Tommy said. "Her cookies were the best. Even the water tasted better at Grandma's house."

He looked at his mother and said, "But yours will be good. You need practice to get better. Like me."

Helen saw her sister tear up and knew Kathy was tired after a long day. Tom must have recognized the same signals. "Bedtime, champ," he said. "Give your aunt Helen and uncle Phil a good-bye hug. They're leaving tonight."

"I don't want to go to bed," Tommy said, and stuck out his lip.

"You're an athlete. You're in training," his father said. "No whining."

Tommy hugged everyone and reluctantly retreated upstairs.

"Nice line about him being an athlete," Helen said.

"Hey, it works," Tom said. He carried a droopy-headed Allison upstairs to bed.

Kathy waited until both children were gone, then said, "Wait till you see what's in the cookie jar."

She lifted the duck's head. The jar was overflowing with currency. "It was Mom's stash," Kathy said. "I think there's about twenty thousand dollars in here."

"Sweet," Helen said. "Larry would have a fit if he knew that much cash escaped his clutches."

"Like I said, if Larry had spent any time with Mom, he would have known where she hid her money." She pulled out a fat wad with a rubber band around it. "Here's five thousand dollars to cover the Florida end of Mom's funeral."

"I don't want it," Helen said. "That was my gift to Mom. I have money now, remember? Put that cash in the kids' college fund, in case they don't get sports scholarships."

Phil checked his watch and said, "We have to return the rental car and fly home."

The St. Louis airport was easier to negotiate than the one in Fort Lauderdale. St. Louis didn't have mazes of parking garages attached to one another like tumorous growths, or masses of lost, confused, multilingual tourists. Helen and Phil went through security and were soon on the plane.

Helen felt her heart lift as the plane left the runway, as if she could really leave Rob's death behind. She liked flying at night, when the city lights looked like diamonds on black velvet.

When their plane was comfortably in the clouds, the flight attendant announced that the passengers could turn on their electronic devices. Phil stretched his long legs and let his seat settle back into a more comfortable position. The seat next to him was empty. The drone of the engines covered their murmured conversation.

"I hope Margery has recovered from Jordan's death and is her old self again," Helen said. "Peggy thinks she'll get better."

"I want Peggy to be right," Phil said. "But Margery isn't young anymore. I'm worried, too. Margery wants me to investigate Jordan's murder and prove Mark's innocence. I promised her I'd investigate. But Margery is not going to like what I find. She's convinced Mark was framed by a mythical burglar. I'm sure Mark killed Jordan in a jealous rage and there was no burglar."

"Jordan was sneaking around on Mark with Danny," Helen said. "Maybe not that night, but she'd had several dates with Danny before the developer dumped her. Mark was definitely jealous. I'm not blaming the victim, but Jordan gave Mark an excuse to kill her. I just hope Margery will believe you."

"Do you still want her to marry us?" Phil asked.

"Of course," Helen said. "She's a minister. Ordained by mail, but she can legally marry us."

"What else do we have to do to make you legal?" Phil said.

"I have a copy of my divorce decree," Helen said. "Now I need to get my Florida driver's license. That's my priority tomorrow morning. Then we can apply for a marriage license."

"How did you get on the plane without a driver's license?" Phil asked.

"I have one," Helen said righteously. "It just isn't mine. I borrowed it from the lost-and-found box when I worked at the bookstore." She opened her wallet and showed him a license for Wanda Tiffany Parker.

Phil squinted at the license that had belonged to a freckle-faced redhead. "That doesn't look like you."

"Women change their hair color all the time," Helen said.

"And add freckles?" Phil raised one eyebrow. "How did you fool airport security with that thing?"

"I added some freckles with an eyebrow pencil," Helen said. "You didn't even notice them."

"Beautiful," Phil said. "You used someone else's license to board a plane. What if it was reported stolen? What if Wanda was wanted for a crime? How much trouble would you be in then?"

"But it wasn't," Helen said. "And Wanda doesn't live at that address anymore. The store tried to contact her when she lost her license more than two years ago. Besides, my ticket isn't in Wanda's name. I used your credit card when I bought our tickets."

Phil groaned.

Helen was glad she didn't tell Phil she'd buried Rob in the church basement if he went ballistic over a driver's license.

"Those days are over," Helen said. "How legal do we want to get? Do you want to wait to get married until the tax situation is straightened out?"

"That could take years," Phil said. "You've set the process in motion. Rob can't come after you demanding money, and the law can't arrest you. That's good enough for me."

"The lawyer suggested we keep our lifestyle simple for now, so we should probably continue to live at the Coronado after our wedding," Helen said.

"Should we keep both apartments, or only one?" Phil asked.

"Between us we have a total of four rooms, two kitchens and two bathrooms," Helen said. "That gives us maybe fifteen hundred square feet, total. We'll need the two bathrooms. Let's keep both apartments for now. We can move to a larger place when my tax problems are settled."

"Also fine," Phil said. "Where do you want to go on your honeymoon?"

"I liked that vacation we took in the Keys," Helen said. "I want to stay at a hotel in Key Largo with an ocean view and room service."

"You won't get any argument against that from me," Phil said.

"But we have to solve Chrissy's murder first," Helen said, "or

Detective McNally will be going with us on our honeymoon. I don't care what he said—Danny the developer killed his wife. I know it. I heard them arguing. Her death has something to do with what she called the house of the seven toilets."

"That's where I'll start my search tomorrow," Phil said. "I'm going to look up the property owned by everyone who was at Snapdragon's the morning of the murder, not just Danny Martlet. We'll find Chrissy's killer and then live happily ever after."

He kissed Helen as the seat belt sign came on in the cabin and the pilot announced there was heavy turbulence ahead.

CHAPTER 24

lunk. Thunk. Rattle.

Helen yanked on the old red Samsonite suitcase wedged between the wall and the water heater in her utility closet at the Coronado. The suitcase popped free with a resonant *clang!*

She set the hard-sided suitcase on her kitchen table and opened it. It was stuffed with shabby old-lady underwear she'd bought at a yard sale for twenty-five cents. Helen shifted the graying circle-stitched cotton bras and snagged support hose, then picked up a pair of flower-sprigged panties big as a parachute.

"Your trousseau?" Phil said.

Her fiancé leaned against the kitchen doorjamb, looking adorably rumpled in his blue terry bathrobe. He was joined by a grumpy Thumbs.

"Sorry. I didn't mean to wake you up," Helen said. "The keys to my new life are buried in this granny underwear."

Helen held up the prepaid disposable cell phone she'd used to call her sister while she was on the run. "Won't need that anymore. It's out of minutes anyway." She tossed the phone in the trash.

The crinkled cellophane she'd kept to quickly end conversations with her mother went in after it. Helen would pretend that static had broken up their awkward chats to avoid a fight. There was no chance she could ever change Dolores's mind.

Heavy orthopedic hose hid two cards. Helen held them up. "My Social Security card and my Missouri driver's license. These will ease my reentry into respectable society."

"Isn't that license expired by now?" Phil asked.

"Nope," Helen said. "Missouri licenses are good for six years. And look! A hundred dollars from my original stash of ten thousand. I thought that money was all gone. It was hidden in this." She held up an ugly orangey beige girdle.

"A good way to stretch your money," Phil said.

"I'm glad we didn't get married in June," Helen said.

"Why?" Phil said.

"Because our marriage wouldn't have been legal. I was missing too many documents. I'm going today to get my Florida driver's license. Now I have everything I need: my Social Security card, my Missouri driver's license and my Coronado lease for proof of residency. My name change has been approved already. I can download those documents and take them with me."

"Are you going to keep the suitcase?" Phil asked.

"I can use it for storage," Helen said. "And I want it for sentimental reasons. Mom gave it to me for my high school senior trip to Washington, D.C. It's about all I have left from my old life."

Phil looked puzzled. "Why did you think a bright red suitcase was a good hiding place? What if the police had a search warrant for your home?"

Helen held up the mass of shabby underwear and twisted panty hose. It seemed to writhe in her hands. "No man would touch these, even with gloves on."

"There are women in law enforcement," Phil said.

"I guess I can dump the ugly underwear, too," she said, and dropped it in the trash. "Fortunately, my theory was never tested."

Phil kissed her nose and then her lips. "Your hair smells nice. You're letting it grow longer. I like that."

"I like your hair long, too," she said.

"We should go back to bed," he whispered. "We got home after midnight."

"I'm not interested in sleeping," Helen said.

"Me, either," Phil said, and kissed her again.

Helen forgot her plans to legalize her life for more than an hour. They fell asleep again after making love and woke up when Thumbs walked on their heads, howling for breakfast.

Phil scrambled eggs while Helen fed the cat. Thumbs had given them the cat cold shoulder for about ten seconds after they returned home late yesterday. When they'd been properly chastised, they were permitted to scratch his ears. He was still peeved and demanding this morning.

Over breakfast, Helen handed Phil a list of names.

"Vera Salinda. Danny Martlet. Roger Cardola. Loretta Stranahan," he read. "Why are you giving me these?"

"You asked who was in Snapdragon's Second Thoughts when Chrissy was killed," Helen said. "You're researching the house of the seven toilets today, remember?"

"No way I could forget. Who is Roger Cardola?"

"The hunky surfer guy who valet parks at the hair salon," Helen said. "He is Vera's best surviving source for high-end designer duds. The police are sniffing around him."

"He's definitely worth checking into," Phil said, tucking the list into his zippered leather portfolio. He poured coffee for himself and Helen, then kissed her again.

"Shall we face the day?" he asked.

They carried their coffee mugs outside by the pool. Purple bougainvillea blossoms floated on the water, and palm fronds whispered overhead. The humid Florida breeze felt like a caress on Helen's face. It had the slight salt tang of the sea. She breathed deeply and said, "It's so nice to be home. I love the humidity here."

"St. Louis has humidity, too," Phil said.

"But it's not bracing," Helen said. "Midwestern humidity is sticky. It drags you down."

"Bracing humidity," Phil said. "We must remember to tell the Fort Lauderdale Convention and Visitors Bureau. They can use that phrase in their ads."

Peggy had turned the poolside umbrella table into an outdoor assembly station. COME AND GET IT, CHOW HOUNDS! barbecue aprons covered the surface. Her red head was bent over her work. She was muttering to herself as she picked at the crossed beer bottles on an apron.

Pete the parrot peered from her shoulder like a small green supervisor.

"Good morning, lovebirds, and welcome back," Peggy said. "We missed you."

She moved a stack of aprons onto a chair and said, "Sorry. My work has spread like kudzu. Sit down. How was St. Louis?"

"Good," Helen said. "Or as good as a funeral trip can be. Mom had the ceremony she wanted with all her friends. I'm on the way to being legal at last. I'll apply for my Florida driver's license today, then go to work. Phil is going to research Chrissy's murder. Once we find Chrissy's killer, we're free to marry."

"Oh, is that all?" Peggy asked, and grinned. "The police haven't made any progress, but I suppose Super Phil can outdo two police forces."

"It's my job to do the impossible." Phil winked and sat beside her. "How's the apron business?"

"Not good," Peggy said. "Mike rejected my first shipment." She showed an apron to Helen and Phil. "See? He says this one is not up to his quality standards."

"What's wrong with it?" Phil asked.

"Mike said the crossed barbecue forks should be one-eighth of an inch lower," Peggy said.

"They look fine to me," Helen said.

"I prefer the crossed beer bottles, but the forks look okay," Phil said.

"My crossed beer bottles were crooked—according to Mike," Peggy said. "All twenty-five of them. I'd used a ruler, too. Every single apron had something wrong with it. I was so sure my work was good that I'd already ordered another shipment, completed the aprons and sent those back, too. I got another e-mail from Mike this morning. The second shipment has been rejected. I'm trying to see if I can dissolve the glue and reapply the barbecue forks, but they tear."

"Not worth your time," Phil said. "You'll never please Mike, or whatever his name is. That's part of the scam."

Helen waited for Peggy to say the aprons weren't a scam, but she seemed too discouraged to fight back. "How do you know it's a scam?" she asked in a small voice.

"How much was that glue gun?" Phil asked.

"Two hundred fifty dollars," Peggy said.

"I can buy it online for one hundred thirty dollars, including shipping," he said.

"But this is a cordless self-igniting hot-melt glue gun," Peggy said.

"That's right," Phil said. Somehow, he managed not to sound smug. Helen loved him for that. "Same specs, but a much lower price online. Work-at-home scammers make their money selling you overpriced 'professional' equipment and supplies."

"What do I do now?" Peggy asked. "I've lost a thousand dollars from the lottery on this scheme."

"You have some nice aprons," Phil said. "You could sell them somewhere else."

"Snapdragon's might take them on consignment," Helen said. "I could ask."

"Would you?" Peggy looked relieved. "At least I'll get some money back. Wouldn't you know it? The only time I've ever won anything in the lottery and I lost it anyway."

"Bye!" Pete said. He groomed a green wing feather with his beak.

"Right," Peggy said. "Good-bye to my money. The natural order at the Coronado has been upset. All the scammers used to live in apartment 2C. Now I'm the idiot who fell for a scam and we have a murderer in 2C."

"Who has a murderer?"

Helen heard the reedy voice and stared at the small, bent woman. "Good morning, uh—Margery," Helen said. She almost didn't recognize her landlady. Margery wore dull beige flats and a flapping flowered housecoat. It wasn't even purple.

"I said, who has a murderer living here?" Margery said. It wasn't a demand. It was a polite request.

"You do," Helen said. "Mark in 2C was arrested for Jordan's murder."

"That doesn't mean he did it," Margery said mildly. "You've

been arrested, too, and so has Peggy. Don't go calling someone a murderer unless you know what you're talking about. Where are my cigarettes?"

"In your hand," Peggy said.

"Awk!" Pete said.

"Right," Margery said. "I'd better have one to calm my nerves." Their landlady lit a Marlboro with trembling hands.

Helen wanted to weep for the ruin of the magnificent Margery. "Margery, you have no reason to blame yourself," she said. "You didn't kill Jordan. Mark did."

"I ordered her upstairs to her death," Margery said. "I should have kept Jordan in my apartment and she'd still be alive."

"You don't know that," Helen said.

"I acted like a fatheaded old fool, ordering people around without thinking about the consequences. Now that poor girl is dead. Where's Phil?" Margery asked in a querulous voice. "He's supposed to do some work for me."

"Right here," Phil said, raising his coffee cup. "What can I do?"

"Prove Mark didn't kill Jordan," Margery said.

"I don't know if I can prove that," Phil said. "But I will look into his background for you. I'll need Mark's last name, Social Security number, date of birth and previous address."

"I have that on his lease application. Here." She pulled the papers out of her housecoat pocket.

Phil read it. His eyes widened in disbelief. "His name is Mark Smith?"

"There's the copy I made of his driver's license," Margery said. "That's his picture on it. He used to live in Chicago. I checked. There is a Mark Smith in Chicago."

"There are probably five or ten of them there—and in every

other major city in the United States," Phil said. "Margery, I promised I'd investigate Mark, but I can almost guarantee you won't like what I find. I believe he killed Jordan. This 'Smith' driver's license only adds to my suspicions. I'll bet you it's a fake. You have a murderer living in 2C."

"Hah!" Margery said. "I know a murderer when I see one."

She glared at Helen until Helen wondered if her landlady knew about Rob's death. I didn't kill Rob, she thought. I just buried him.

"Margery," Phil said gently, "you know you've had some problems before with the renters who lived in 2C, and you never believed they were crooks. Some were ordinary thieves, others were scammers. One has infomercials on late-night television. Four are still in jail."

"So?" Margery said. "Florida is a rootless society."

"That makes it a perfect home for a murderer."

"Mark is not a killer," Margery screeched until her old voice cracked. "I want you to find who really killed Jordan. I ask you to do one little thing and you give me excuses."

Helen felt cold in the warm summery sunshine.

Where was her shrewd landlady? Would Margery ever return?

CHAPTER 25

"Well, well. You've decided to honor us with your presence today," Vera said. She wasn't dripping sarcasm. This was a flood.

"That's right," Helen said. "You knew I was in St. Louis for my mother's funeral. Is something wrong?"

Dumb question. One look at Vera, and Helen could see something was wrong. Vera's style had slipped from hobo-chic to plain hobo. Her eyeliner ran crookedly up one lid, as if her hand had shaken. Her pink cotton sweater needed washing. So did her hair.

"The cops arrested Roger, my best source." Vera spoke slowly, spitting out each word.

"The hunky valet who brought you the top designers?" Helen asked.

"That one." Vera ran her fingers through her unkempt hair. "Turns out he was stealing those terrific clothes."

Helen wasn't surprised, but she thought "I told you so" wasn't a good comment. She tried a neutral "How?" It failed to defuse the dangerous situation.

"Oh, Roger had quite a system," Vera said. More sarcasm. "When he parked women's cars at the hair salon, he'd go through their shopping bags in the backseats. He either knew where they lived or he'd get the address from the salon computer. Then he'd break into their homes, usually within a day or so after they were at the salon.

"That's how Roger got this season's styles so fast and sold them to me with the tags still on. If he saw anything else that looked new in his victims' closets, he took that, too. The greedy dumb ass did it once too often and got caught."

"And Roger said you were buying his stolen goods?" Helen asked.

"Didn't have to. The police already suspected him. Remember how weird Detective McNally acted when Roger dropped off those dresses?"

"Oh, yeah," Helen said. "Roger said he was bringing in a salon customer's dry cleaning, but even I thought he was lying. And you couldn't find the soda can Roger had left on the counter after McNally left here."

"Roger left his fingerprints behind at the last house he broke into," Vera said. "He was in a big hurry to get the clothes to me. That's why Detective McNally took that soda can. He had a hunch Roger was stealing clothes and selling them to me. McNally was right. He was in here crowing like a freaking rooster."

"So that's how the cops caught Roger?" Helen asked.

"No, it gets worse," Vera said. "Yesterday, one of his burglary victims was shopping here. Little size-two Mitzi, a bleached blonde who definitely needed that salon's services. Mitzi saw the dress she'd bought for her daughter's wedding on my 'new arrivals' rack. Roger had stolen it from her home two days before. Mitzi screamed so loud I thought she'd been murdered. Before I could calm her down, she called 911 and accused me of being Roger's partner in crime.

"Me!" The air seemed to glitter with Vera's electric anger. "That stupid bimbo. Thanks to Mitzi, the cops came busting in here. All the other customers scattered like scalded roaches. Mitzi was weeping and screeching."

"How long did it take to calm her down?" Helen asked.

"Hours," Vera said miserably. "There wasn't anything wrong with her dress, but Mitzi said she can't wear it now that it's been 'pawed' by strangers. She claimed she suffered irreparable emotional damage. Her husband is a lawyer. I'm looking at a new suit, all right—a lawsuit—thanks to that face-lifted freak.

"I'm the one who's had the irreparable damage. The cops confiscated three pairs of True Religion jeans and a Versace evening dress, all traced back to Roger. The burglary squad crawled over this place like ants on a candy bar. The cops wanted to know where I got every designer label in my shop—down to the last shirt and shoe. I had to close the store for the rest of the day while they examined my records. They didn't finish until two this morning. The store looked like a hurricane hit it. I was up all night trying to make it presentable."

"Ouch," Helen said.

"Double ouch," Vera said. "A major legal mess and more damage to my reputation. Now Snapdragon's Second Thoughts is linked to murder *and* burglary. I've lost stock and another day's sales."

"Are you in trouble for receiving stolen goods?" Helen asked.

"No, but it was close." Vera gnawed a ragged nail. Helen saw three were broken. "The cops tried to say I was Roger's partner and profited from his theft. They acted like I was some criminal mastermind directing that dimwit. If I was really going into a life of crime, I'd choose a smarter partner."

Vera was still angry, but calmed down as she told her story. "What saved my ass was I keep good records. I wrote down the date and time of everything I purchased, as well as the designer name, size and color. I also had a description of Roger, along with his right thumbprint and a signed statement that he'd purchased the items at garage and estate sales."

"You took his thumbprint?" Helen asked.

"I should have taken his right nut," Vera said. "But I'd followed the law to the letter. I didn't give Roger a better deal than any other source, no matter how much he flashed those blue eyes at me. I hope he'll be batting them at some biker in prison."

"So you're off the hook?" Helen said.

"Not quite," Vera said. "The cops are going through my records, seeing if they can match the dates of Roger's imaginary garage sales to his burglaries. If his case goes to trial, I'll have to testify for the prosecution. Otherwise, the police can get me for a second-degree felony."

"Do you really think they'd do that?"

"I can't afford to find out," Vera said. "This could ruin my business. In fact, it's hurt it already. Notice how we're brimming with customers?"

"Uh, no," Helen said. "I only saw two people in the store. They said they were just looking."

"That's our sum total for the day, and it's three o'clock. If you want bad news to spread quickly, try a crime connected to a hair salon. Every dye job between here and Palm Beach knows about Roger the thieving valet."

Vera's phone rang. She leaped on it like the instrument might escape.

"Hello?" she said warily.

Her face relaxed into a smile and her voice became syrupy

sweet. "Commissioner Stranahan—I mean Loretta—how nice to hear from you. You want another suit after all? Ah, you have a television interview."

There was a pause. Then Vera said, "No, I totally agree. We both know TV cameras are snobs. They make you look bad if you aren't well tailored, no matter how thin you are. But we'll fix that. I have killer suits in your size. When can you come by?"

Another pause, while Vera's smile grew wider. "Tomorrow afternoon? Excellent. Ask for me and I'll take care of you personally."

Vera hung up the phone with a sigh of relief. "The bad news hasn't reached Loretta Stranahan yet. She wants to shop for a new suit."

"I thought she had too many," Helen said.

"A working woman can never have too many suits. She's being interviewed on the *South Florida Sunshine* talk show. She needs to look successful, but not too successful."

"How do you do that?" Helen asked.

"The vision is all in her head," Vera said. "And I have to put it there." She was still smiling, though Helen thought it seemed slightly forced.

"Listen, this may be the wrong time to bring it up," Helen said, "but my friend Peggy has some barbecue aprons she wants to sell. She bought them herself, so I know she didn't steal them."

"Have her bring them by and I'll take a look," Vera said. "Cute barbecue items and cocktail napkins with clever sayings sell to well-heeled suburbanites." She was still smiling, but it wasn't quite as wide.

"Excuse me." An elderly woman with skin like old ivory held up a white jacket with gold buttons. "How much is this?"

Vera studied the tag. "Twenty-five dollars," she said. "It's a Gucci."

"It has a stain on the collar and there's a loose button."

"Yes," Vera said.

"Can't you lower the price?" the woman asked.

"I've already dropped it down from forty-five," Vera said. "It's a five-hundred-dollar jacket. It was new this season. I can't slash the price any more. But a nice pin would cover the stain. Michelle Obama made them fashionable."

"I don't want it." The woman dropped the jacket on the counter and slammed out the door.

"Why did she insult something and then try to buy it?" Helen asked.

Vera's smile had dimmed a few watts more. "It's a ritual. The idea is to convince me I'm selling something worthless so I'll give it away. I'm immune to that tactic. I'll hang this jacket back up. Watch the store, Helen. I need you to dust until more customers arrive."

Ugh. Dusting. Helen's least favorite chore. Vera liked to leave the front door open. She thought it invited in passersby. It definitely brought in dust. The front shelves had a thick coat. Helen tackled a lamp with crystal pendants, covered with lookie-loo fingerprints.

"Helen!" Vera screamed.

Helen went running to the back. Vera held up a black-and-white blouse on a hanger. "Is this yours?" she said. "It doesn't have a tag."

"No," Helen said. "I like it, though. I've seen a lot of black-and-white blouses this season. That's a nice one."

"It is not," Vera said. "It's a crappy polyester knockoff. I had a real silk St. John black-and-white blouse and it's gone. Some thief stole it and left this cheap imitation. I'm going to straighten the back room after the police wrecked it. Go back to your dusting and watch the store before they steal us blind."

Helen was glad to put down her dust rag and help a pert brunette in white cotton shorts who looked like Betty Rubble.

"You had a pair of black Manolos when I was in the other day," Betty said. "I can't find them. Do you still have them?"

"They may have been sold. Let me check."

"That's okay," the woman said. "I'm in a hurry. Do you have any polka-dot heels?"

"I thought we did, but I can ask the manager," Helen said.

"No, I don't want to wait." Brunette Betty was out the door before Vera came up front.

The shop owner was definitely not smiling.

"What did she want?" Vera asked.

"Shoes," Helen said. "Didn't we have a pair of polka-dot heels? You were going to freshen them and put them back out for sale."

"I stuck them on a shelf somewhere," Vera said. "They were too worn to sell. You could have shown that woman the Ferragamo slingbacks."

"She didn't want them. She asked about the size-eight Manolos, but I couldn't find them."

"This pair?" Vera typed on her computer and called up a photo on a designer-shoe Web site. The $845 heels, decorated with silver studs and metal buckles, were called Mary Jane.

Mary Jane must work in a torture chamber, Helen thought. There was nothing schoolgirlish about those shoes.

"We had that pair on display a few days ago." Vera started checking the shoe racks and shelves, then moved her search to the back room, furiously shifting boxes and bags.

Half an hour later Vera came charging out of the back. Anger seemed to stick out of her skin, like glass shards. "I can't find those shoes. Did you take them?" she demanded. "You're the only other person who goes in the back room."

"What would I do with size eights? I wear an eleven," Helen said. "The police have been all over this store. Maybe they misplaced them. The shoes will turn up."

"When they're out of style," Vera snapped. "Are you sure you didn't know Chrissy?"

"Never saw her except in this store," Helen said. "We didn't travel in the same circles. It wouldn't help Danny's career to socialize with a shopgirl and a private investigator."

"Too bad you didn't know her," Vera said. "You had the perfect opportunity to kill her."

"What?" Helen drew herself up to her full six feet. "First, you accuse me of stealing shoes. Now I'm murdering customers. If anyone had a motive to kill Chrissy, it was you, Vera."

"Me? Why would I kill my best source?"

"Because she knew you were buying stolen goods," Helen said. "Before Danny showed up, Chrissy asked you for more money. She said, 'I have the tags *and* the receipt. Unlike some of your sources, I don't steal.' I couldn't figure out why she'd say that. But now her argument makes sense. Chrissy knew some of your stock was stolen. We've already seen why that's bad for business."

There was an ominous silence. Something seemed to break in Vera, some last restraint on her patience. Her eyes were wild with rage. Her mouth seemed full of sharp teeth, outlined in red lipstick.

"Get out!" Vera screamed. "Get out now!"

"Am I fired?" Helen asked. She'd never seen this crazy-mad side of Vera before. The woman seemed capable of killing Chrissy, then machine-gunning every tourist on Las Olas.

"Yes. No. I don't know. Take tomorrow off," Vera said. "Then call me. I'll see if I can stand the sight of you."

CHAPTER 26

"Look! I'm legal at last!" Helen held her new driver's license over her head like an Olympic gold medal.

Peggy and Phil whistled and applauded. Phil jumped up from his poolside chair and said, "Let me see." He frowned at her license photo. "You look better than that."

"I should hope so," Helen said.

"That was fast," Peggy said. "Didn't you apply for your license today?"

"It's same-day service if you apply in person and have the right paperwork."

"What are you doing with that illegal license?" Peggy asked.

"I'm cutting it up," Helen said.

"You can use my special apron scissors," Peggy said. "They were free with my overpriced glue gun. I'll go get them."

She returned with a triumphant Pete riding on her shoulder. Peggy bowed and presented Helen with a foot-long pair of shears on a green velvet throw pillow. The little parrot clung to Peggy's shoulder when she bent forward, flapped his wings to keep his balance and squawked.

Helen snipped the old license in two and said, "Meet the new Helen, all legal, all the time."

"Thanks for removing one worry," Phil said. "Aren't you home early from work? It's only four thirty."

"I got fired—maybe," Helen said. "Vera blew up and ordered me out of the shop. She told me to take tomorrow off. Then I call the store to see if I still have a job."

"What happened?" Phil asked.

"Vera was upset because the police arrested Roger, her hot source. Turned out Roger was hot in more ways than one. He was stealing designer clothes. The police hassled Vera about her connection to Roger for hours. She was tired, worried about her business and on edge. She accused me of stealing shoes and murdering Chrissy, and that was the last straw. She had a better motive for killing Danny's wife, and I said so. Vera went ballistic and told me to leave."

"You don't really believe she's the killer?" Phil asked.

"I don't want to," Helen said. "But I've never seen Vera so angry. She sure seemed capable of killing. Vera was in the back of the store when Chrissy was murdered. Chrissy knew Vera bought stolen goods. Vera swore she wouldn't kill her best source. Now I don't know what to believe."

"She'll calm down," Phil said. "I'm glad you have tomorrow off. I've checked the property lists. Vera owns a four-room house near Snapdragon's. I drove by it today. The street has tiny one-bedroom cottages built in the nineteen twenties. Her home may have two toilets, max.

"Roger doesn't own any property. He's two months behind on

his rent. His motorcycle was repossessed, he owes three thousand dollars on his credit cards and his phone has been disconnected."

"No wonder he stepped up his stealing," Helen said.

"His financial trouble started when Roger lost his job at the Exceptional Pool Service."

"He's certainly hot enough to work there," Helen said.

"What's so exceptional about that pool service?" Peggy asked.

"They're sort of Chippendales with chemicals," Helen said.

"You seem to know a lot about hot pool boys," Phil teased. "Would you care to tell me how you acquired that knowledge?"

"Vera said Chrissy was one of their customers," Helen said. "Did she get Roger fired?"

"Technically, he wasn't fired," Phil said. "Roger was allowed to resign. A woman customer complained that Roger helped himself to a hundred dollars in her wallet. Roger said she gave him the money as a tip. The woman—who was married—refused to press charges. Roger resigned, but didn't get another job for six months. While he was out of work, his motorcycle was repossessed."

"Was this married woman Chrissy?" Helen asked.

"I didn't get her name," Phil said. "I had to pay my source plenty to get this dirt on Roger. Finding out more will cost me extra."

"How much?" Helen said.

"Five hundred dollars, minimum," Phil said.

"I can come up with the cash," Helen said. "It would be worth the investment if we could prove Roger killed Chrissy."

"Let's use our free option first," Phil said. "That's Commissioner Loretta Stranahan. She owns a condo in Broward County in her district. I checked the real estate listings for her building. She lives in the east wing. The units on that side have three baths. The real estate agent told me no unit in the building has more than three."

"I guess that rules her out," Helen said.

"Not quite," Phil said. "Loretta also owns two houses in Palm Beach County."

"Two Palm Beach houses," Peggy said. "That's a ritzy location."

"Palm Beach County likes you to think it's for the rich and glamorous, but not everyone has a mansion with live-in servants," Phil said. "Palm Beach has poor neighborhoods and modest homes. I'm guessing Stranahan's two houses fall into those categories. Both cost under two hundred thousand dollars."

"How many toilets?" Helen asked.

"They're listed as having one bathroom each—but that doesn't mean they do. Homeowners often add extra toilets without getting the permits. Want to drive with me tomorrow and see them?"

"How can I resist such a romantic date?" Helen said. "I'd love to see the toilets of Palm Beach County. I've been gone most of the day. How is Margery? I'm worried about her."

Peggy looked at Phil and lowered her voice. "With good reason," she said. "Margery has been holed up in her apartment since Phil told her the bad news."

"Which was?" Helen asked.

"I didn't find a Mark Smith in Chicago," Phil said. "Not one who could be the tenant in apartment 2C. I did find a Marco Rupert Gomez of Chicago with Mark Smith's same birth date. That Gomez is wanted for aggravated assault and the rape of a twenty-year-old college student."

"That's horrible," Helen said. "How do you know he's Mark in 2C?"

"The story ran in the Chicago paper. His victim was paying her way through college as a model. He beat her so badly she needed facial reconstruction. Even if Mark avoids being tried for Jordan's murder, he'll be extradited back to Illinois for that crime."

"Brilliant detective work," Helen said. "But you still didn't say how you know Mark Smith is really Marco Rupert Gomez of Chicago."

"'Gomez' is a common name, a sort of Latino 'Smith.' Mark used a version of his real first name," Phil said. "People often do that when they take an alias. They're likely to keep their same birth date, too. Makes them easier to trace. Here. Look at Marco's photo."

Helen studied the newspaper picture. "That's him, all right, but he looks more thuggish."

"It's a mug shot. Police stations aren't known for flattering lighting."

"I had no idea he was Latino," Peggy said. "Mark never spoke Spanish."

"He's third-generation," Phil said. "He was born in Illinois. His parents are schoolteachers. Helen's family is German-American and she doesn't know a word of German."

"I do, too," Helen said. "Strudel. Wiener schnitzel. Bratwurst. That's my complete German vocabulary."

"Point taken," Peggy said. "Do you think Jordan knew Mark had beaten and raped a young model?"

"I doubt it," Phil said. "Mark met her when she was waitressing at Beach Buns and they moved in together at the Coronado a month later. That's what he told me over brews by the pool, anyway."

"Is Margery still blaming herself for Jordan's murder?" Helen asked.

"Yes," Phil said. "Margery says she should have hired me to do a background check on the guy. Then she could have warned Jordan. She spent most of today in Mark and Jordan's apartment, doing heaven knows what."

"Brooding," Peggy said.

"Awk!" Pete said.

"Margery came hobbling down from 2C about three o'clock," Phil said. "She turned dead white when I told her about Mark's Illinois warrant. She shut herself in her apartment and hasn't said a word since."

"I'll go talk to her," Helen said.

"Good luck," Peggy said. "The door is locked. Neither of us can get through to her."

Helen knocked on Margery's jalousie door. No answer. She pounded on the door until the glass slats rattled. More silence.

"Margery, open this door or I'll break the glass," Helen said. "You know these slats are a pain in the neck to replace."

"Hold your horses, I'm coming," Margery said.

Helen could see her landlady's form against the frosted-glass slats. "What do you want?" Margery asked.

"I want to know if you're all right," Helen said.

"I'd be fine if you weren't butting in my business," Margery said. "Go away."

"We want to help you. You haven't been yourself."

"You want to help? Fine. Go pack Jordan's things in her apartment. Her parents are driving down from Orlando tonight to pick them up. I've piled her clothes and papers on the kitchen table. There are three suitcases in there that you can use. The cops have unsealed the apartment, so you can get in."

"What about the key?" Helen asked.

Margery's door opened a few inches. A liver-spotted hand slid out, holding a key. "Here. When the parents show up around six o'clock, come get me."

"We can handle it for you," Helen said.

"It's my apartment complex and my responsibility," Margery said. "Jordan's parents are Bud and Susan Drubb."

"Nobody's named Bud Drubb," Helen said.

"Do you want to help or yammer?" Margery slammed the door.

"What did she say?" Peggy asked when Helen returned to the umbrella table.

"She insulted me," Helen said. "That's a good sign. She wants us to pack up Jordan's things for her parents."

Apartment 2C stank. Helen opened the door and the unpleasant tang of rotted meat, old blood and Florida mold rushed out, along with top notes of floral air freshener. As she and Peggy walked into the living room, they heard the peculiar hollow deadness of an empty apartment.

Helen was relieved the couch where Jordan had been murdered had been taken away. She winced at the blood on the living room walls. The door to the bedroom where the drunken Mark had passed out was shut. His empty beer bottles were gone.

Peggy shivered. "This used to be such a cute apartment. Now it's horrible."

"I don't think Margery will be able to rent this for a long time," Helen said.

"Let's pack up and get out of here," Peggy said.

Helen recognized many of the dresses she folded into a black suitcase as Snapdragon's bargains. Peggy packed shoes, underwear and makeup into another suitcase, then started stacking photos, bills and papers into the third.

"This photo here must be her parents," Peggy said. A couple in their fifties smiled at the camera from a sunlit beach.

"The mom looks like Jordan with short hair," Helen said. "Jordan had her same green eyes. Her dad has a nice, craggy face. They seem too young to have a twenty-something daughter."

"Had," Peggy said. "I dread meeting them tonight. Looks like we're finished here. We can take these suitcases downstairs. Jordan's parents shouldn't see this apartment. Are we going to tell Margery when the Drubbs show up?"

"She wants us to, but let's let her sleep," Helen said.

The two women carried the suitcases out by the poolside table. Then Peggy brought out two glasses of cold wine, and Phil added a bag of cheddar-and-sour-cream potato chips.

"Ew," Peggy said. "They're orange."

"They're pretty good once you get past the first bite," Phil said.

Helen and Peggy stuck to the wine. Helen hoped one glass would be enough anesthesia to get her through the meeting with Jordan's parents.

The couple who came to the Coronado that evening could have been the grandparents of Bud and Susan in the photo. Bud's hair was nearly white. Susan's face was lined and sagging. They walked as if some monster had stripped off their skin and sucked out their souls.

"We came to get our daughter's things," Bud said. His dignity was heartrending. They refused any drinks, even water. They did not want to sit down. Phil helped Bud carry the suitcases to their white Buick.

"We want to get back on the road," Susan said. She seemed to be fighting back tears. "We knew our baby would get in trouble someday, but we hoped it wouldn't happen. Jordan always said she liked bad boys. She thought good men were dull."

"Did she know Mark was wanted for assault and rape?" Peggy asked.

"Oh, yes," Susan said. "She told us. We were so frightened for her. We sent her money so she could get a place of her own, but she said she wanted to stay with Mark. Mark told Jordan that he didn't really rape and beat that young woman. He said she'd liked rough sex—then afterward she'd changed her mind and cried rape. Jordan believed him. She said Mark was the kindest, gentlest man and deserved another chance. Well, look where his chance got my daughter."

Helen couldn't bear to see the pain in Susan's eyes.

She heard the rattle of glass and saw Margery in her doorway, standing straight and tall. She wore a violet caftan, dangling earrings and purple sandals with flowers on them. A cloud of cigarette smoke covered her face like a veil.

"Margery," Helen said. "You're back."

"You were supposed to tell me when Jordan's parents arrived," Margery said. She took Susan's hand in her own and said, "I'm so sorry about your daughter."

"Thank you," Susan said. "I was telling your friends that my little Jordan was too trusting. She knew Mark had a violent past, but she thought he'd reformed."

Bud came up to his wife and said, "We should leave now, sweetheart. We have a long drive ahead."

"Would you be my guests at a hotel for the night?" Margery asked.

"No, we want to leave this place," Bud said. "No offense."

"I understand," Margery said.

They watched the couple drive off.

"Margery, did you hear them?" Helen asked. "Jordan knew that Mark had raped and beaten a woman. You're not responsible."

"What the hell are you talking about?" Margery said.

"You've been punishing yourself for Jordan's death."

"Oh, now you're a psychologist as well as a sales clerk," Margery said. "I'm so relieved. When I need a psychiatric evaluation, I won't have to bother with a professional. I have an amateur on call to hand out half-baked diagnoses."

"You're angry," Helen said.

"No," Margery said. "I'm furious." Her voice was no longer a quaver. She thundered. "I asked you to tell me when the Drubbs arrived, but you didn't bother."

"You're wearing purple," Helen said.

"Well, alert the media," Margery said. "I always wear purple, you twit."

"You're cussing, too."

"Hell, yes. What's wrong with that?"

"Nothing," Helen said. "Everything is fine."

CHAPTER 27

Ameat market. A doctor's office. A tiny storefront church with a sparkling window framed by white curtains.

At least, Helen guessed that's what these businesses were. She translated the signs as Phil's black Jeep rolled down the street past a *carnicería*, a *médico*, an *iglesia*. They were on a potholed road near the Dixie Highway, literally on the wrong side of the tracks in Palm Beach County. The area between Dixie and I-95 was considered poor by Palm Beach standards.

"We're a long way from Worth Avenue," Helen said. "Tourists never see this."

"They're missing the interesting part," Phil said. "You can find Brooks Brothers, Neiman Marcus and Tiffany stores at any upscale mall. These shops are one of a kind. I bet that meat market has sensational hot sausage. And look how the congregation has fixed up that church. They painted red roses and a gold cross on the window."

"I didn't realize there were Latino neighborhoods here," Helen said.

"Who do you think works in the mansions?" Phil said. "I bet if I yelled 'green card,' I could make half the people on this street disappear."

"You wouldn't, would you?" Helen asked.

"Of course not," Phil said. "Then we'd never find Commissioner Stranahan's two houses."

He turned right, then left, then right again. "Be careful," Helen said. "If anything happens to you, I'll never find my way out."

"Your concern is touching," Phil said.

She yanked his ponytail playfully and said, "You know I can't live without you."

They were on a dusty sunbaked street lined with square cinderblock houses in faded tropical colors. The lawns were brown and dry. Most of the homes had chain-link fences and iron bars on the windows.

Phil stopped in front of a lime green house with its screen door hanging off the hinges.

"Shame on the commissioner," Phil said. "I see a dozen housing-code violations just standing here."

Helen and Phil walked carefully up the cracked concrete steps. Phil reached through the torn screen and knocked on the door.

After a long wait, a Latino built like a melting ice-cream cone answered. His eyes were frightened. "No spik English," he said.

"Do you know if—," Phil began.

The frightened man interrupted. "No. Go away. *Vete.*" He made shooing motions with his hands and slammed the door.

"Do you think he really doesn't speak English?" Helen asked when they were back in the Jeep.

"Who knows?" Phil said. "It's a good way to get rid of strangers. You speak Spanish, don't you?"

"Gringo Spanish," Helen said. "That's what my old Cuban

boss, Miguel Angel, called it. My Spanish is slow and my vocabulary is small. I couldn't help you if anyone started firing rapid Spanish."

"Let's drive to her other house," Phil said. "I don't want to attract more attention here."

Commissioner Stranahan's second house was almost a copy of the first, except it was sun-scorched turquoise and had a handmade *"se renta cuarto"* sign.

"I think that sign translates as 'room for rent,'" Helen said.

Phil coasted by the house and parked his battered Jeep half a block away, between a rusty pickup and a brown seventies beater with the trunk wired shut.

"I'll go to the front door and ask about renting the room," he said.

"You look too rich to rent here," Helen said. She took time to admire her fiancé's tight black T-shirt and jeans.

"It's not for me," Phil said. "It's for my imaginary construction manager, José. I'll stall whoever answers while you get a closer look at the place."

"Give me time to sneak around the side first," Helen said.

She crunched across the dead brown grass and looked in the garage window. Helen saw three mattresses on the concrete floor, two flat pillows and a tangle of gray white sheets. In one corner a white toilet squatted in the open. It looked oddly naked.

That's one, she thought.

A tiny back room had a pink sheet tacked over the window, but Helen could see scuffed turquoise walls, a sleeping bag and a mattress on a tile floor and a toilet in the corner.

Two toilets, she thought.

The third room was bigger, probably intended as the master bedroom. It had four mattresses, egg-yolk yellow walls and a toilet.

The long, narrow bathroom did not have curtains or frosted glass on its window. Helen looked into a shower black with mold. Through the parted plastic shower curtain, she could see a bedroll in one corner and a toilet in its proper place.

The kitchen had a toilet, too, opposite the stove and a fridge that hummed and groaned. The kitchen counter was cluttered with cans and boxes, most with Spanish labels. The sink overflowed with dirty dishes. Helen saw a huge roach on an open loaf of bread. A futon mattress and two sleeping bags were piled in a corner. A listing chrome-legged table with six mismatched chairs took up most of the room.

Helen hurried to the living room. The sliding doors also had sheet curtains, but she could peek inside. These walls were dark brown. A plaid couch sagged against the opposite wall. It looked like someone bunked on it. Helen counted five mattresses on the floor and more tattered sheets. A small brown TV was perched on a cinder block. Yet another toilet sat in the far corner. The count was up to six.

A sunporch had been converted into a room, thanks to unpainted plywood. Helen couldn't see in, but she bet this makeshift room had a toilet, too. She tugged on the door. Locked. Before she could explore further, she heard shouts from the front of the house.

Helen slipped around the side and ran for the Jeep. She was sitting sedately inside by the time Phil jumped in, started the engine and screeched toward I-95.

"Nice work," Helen said. "You kept him distracted while I looked. I could hear you didn't get along well with José's potential landlord."

"That slime," Phil said. "He told me the room would cost six hundred a month and José would have to share it with four people. He wanted three months' cash up front."

"Well, at least your imaginary supervisor would have his own in-room toilet," Helen said. "I think we've found the house of the seven toilets. I couldn't see into one room in the back, but all the others, even the kitchen and the garage, had toilets."

"The kitchen, too?" Phil asked. "That's disgusting."

"The house is a slum, Phil. Those poor people are sleeping on the floor. I counted maybe eighteen mattresses and sleeping bags. If Commissioner Stranahan is charging six hundred per person, she's raking in almost eleven thousand dollars a month from that house."

"Only if the renters are sleeping one person to a mattress," Phil said. "If they share, she's making even more."

"It's greedy and wicked," Helen said. "How does she get away with it?"

"She rents to illegal immigrants who don't dare complain," Phil said. "She may be paying off officials, too. Or the inspectors don't bother with poor neighborhoods. You can find houses like that throughout Florida. They're luxury accommodations. Some illegals send home most of their pay, or make so little they can't afford to rent. They camp in the woods and risk getting beaten and robbed."

"How do you think Chrissy found out about Commissioner Loretta Stranahan's house?" Helen said. "She'd never go to a Latino neighborhood. Chrissy thought visiting Snapdragon's was an adventure."

"Chrissy suspected her husband was cheating on her," Phil said. "Didn't she say Danny called Loretta a hundred times a day?"

"She did," Helen said. "I didn't understand that. Loretta is against Danny's Orchid House project. Why would Danny talk to her?"

"A man like Danny has business friends and business enemies," Phil said, "and he's smooth enough to keep in touch with all of them. In public, Danny would be polite, even friendly to his enemies. His type would hire investigators to look into the commissioners' lives."

"They can do that? Isn't it illegal?"

"It may be illegal and it's certainly unethical," Phil said. "But it happens."

"Who would take an investigation like that?" Helen asked.

"Some detective agency desperate for money, usually a small operation," Phil said. "The big agencies are taking over the lucrative national and international security and investigations. The small agencies live off the scraps, and some of them cross ethical lines to stay in business. If you're not burdened by ethics, looking for dirt on the commissioners would be a plum assignment with unlimited billable hours. It wouldn't be hard to get information about Loretta's houses. I found it in one day.

"Let's say Danny got the information on Commissioner Stranahan from a private investigator," Phil said. "Then Chrissy went through her husband's papers and found it. At Snapdragon's, she taunted Loretta with the house of the seven toilets."

"And wound up conveniently dead," Helen said. "Before she could ruin Loretta's career."

Phil expertly guided the Jeep through a construction lane change, then said, "Look, Helen, I wanted to have this conversation sooner, but your mother took a turn for the worse and we had to go to St. Louis. I may have to quit my job, possibly this afternoon."

"Oh, Phil. Why?" Helen asked.

"Last month, a multinational company, Mortmane, tried to hire the agency I work for to investigate ten state representatives. Mortmane wanted information about key committee members for an environmental issue. My section boss turned down the job. But now the economy is worse and jobs are fewer. He has a quota to make."

"Is Mortmane the big defense contractor?" Helen said.

"They do everything," Phil said. "What they don't do, they hire us to do for them. Office scuttlebutt is that two of our operatives will be sent to Mexico to bring home the Mortmane CFO's daughter. She ran off with a young man her father thinks is unsuitable. He wants her back in college. I won't do kidnapping. The woman is twenty-one, old enough to make decisions without a disapproving daddy dragging her home.

"I have to show up at four o'clock today to get my next assignment. I may come home without a job. I have some money saved, Helen. We can still get married."

"I have money, too," Helen said. "Remember my three hundred thousand dollars? The IRS may get a chunk of it later, but we can live on that until you find another job."

"Then let's get going," Phil said. "I researched marriage licenses online and brought the paperwork with me. It's in the folder in the backseat. I even filled out our online application."

"You expected me to say yes," Helen said, in mock anger. "We're not even married and you're already taking me for granted."

"I expected you to keep your promise to marry me," Phil said. "We have to apply in person to the Clerk of Court's office. We have five location choices, from the downtown county courthouse to Rick Case Honda."

"You're making that up," Helen said. "You can't get a marriage license at a Honda dealership."

"You can, too," Phil said. "It's called a One Stop Division and it's in the used-car building."

"Love the symbolism," Helen said. "Stop by for a used wife and a used car."

"Hey, I hear Rick gives one hell of an oil change," Phil said. "And he'll make your carburetor purr."

"I've got too much mileage on me for a used-car dealer," Helen said. "I want the downtown courthouse."

"Then let's go now." Phil took the downtown exit off I-95. "Do we want a civil marriage ceremony for thirty bucks?"

"Now that Margery is her old uncivil self, I'd rather she married us," Helen said.

"Me, too," Phil said. "Let's keep it in the family."

Phil parked in the courthouse garage. An hour later, they had their marriage license. "We can get married in three days," he said. "You'll really take me for better or worse, with no job and no prospects?"

"We'll live on love," Helen said, and kissed him.

"I still have forty bucks cash," Phil said. "There's a terrific lunch place called the Eleventh Street Annex. No booze, but delicious homemade desserts. I think they have mango cheesecake today."

"I'll postpone living on love for mango cheesecake," Helen said.

Phil threaded the maze of downtown streets.

"What kind of job will you look for if you quit?" Helen asked.

"I was thinking of starting my own agency," Phil said.

"Want to train a partner?" Helen asked.

"Seriously?" he said.

"Hey, it beats buttoning shirts at Snapdragon's. But I'm moving too fast. You haven't been fired."

"Yet," Phil said.

Phil parked the Jeep in front of an old-style Florida duplex, nearly hidden by a tropical garden.

"Let's continue this discussion after some food," Phil said.

The Annex was fragrant with coffee. The speckled terrazzo floor was dotted with stylish metal tables, funky chairs and a sofa. A cheerful jumble of teapots crowded the shelves.

Two women, one in a black-and-white blouse and the other in a red shirt, drank tea together.

The owners, Jonny and Penny, the self-named "Two Ugly Sisters," worked behind the counter. "The day's specials are shrimp ravioli, turkey and cheddar panini with a cranberry compote, and Mexican lasagna," Jonny said. "The Mexican lasagna is made with turkey. We've sold out of the other specials."

Phil wanted the panini and Helen had the shrimp. Both ordered the mango cheesecake. They ate in respectful silence until dessert.

"How did you find this place?" Helen asked. "The cheesecake is a religious experience."

"I'm a detective, remember? It's off the beaten path, but word is out among the foodies."

"Excuse me? Are you the man who eats orange potato chips?" Helen asked.

"And finds amazing cheesecake," Phil said, finishing the last forkful.

"Now that it can't ruin our appetite, can we go back to Chrissy's murder?" Helen asked. "We won't have much of a honeymoon with Detective McNally dogging me."

"Who do you think killed Chrissy?" Phil asked.

"Roger the smoking hot valet looks good, and I'm not talking about his handsome face. Chrissy indirectly threatened him when she tried to wheedle more money out of Vera for that pony-hair purse. She said, 'I have the tags *and* the receipt. Unlike some of your sources, I don't steal.'

"Roger was in the store then. If he thought Chrissy was onto him, he'd have a good reason to kill her."

"He'd commit murder to avoid a burglary charge?" Phil asked.

"Roger stood to lose everything if Chrissy ratted him out," Helen said. "Beautiful bored wives invited him into their beds. He made easy money stealing clothes. Parking cars has to be a softer job than working in the prison laundry."

"I can see where that beats sharing a cell and a toilet with some hairy con," Phil said.

"Danny the developer still makes the best killer," Helen said. "Too bad he has an airtight alibi. But why didn't Danny use his information about Loretta's Palm Beach house to blackmail her into voting for his Orchid House project?"

"Danny doesn't need Loretta right now," Phil said. "He has more than enough votes to get his project passed. Loretta is his long-term insurance. The Orchid House project will be a long, drawn-out battle. It may be another five years until they break ground for the new hotel. If Danny needs Loretta's vote for a future issue, he can ask for it."

"What happens if she refuses to vote Danny's way?" Helen asked.

"Danny tips off the authorities about the house of the seven toilets," Phil said.

"More speculation," Helen said. "But Loretta definitely had a good reason to murder Chrissy. The commissioner would lose a six-figure income if Danny's wife shot off her mouth about Loretta's Palm Beach rental scam."

"It would kill her political career," Phil said. "So how do we connect Loretta or Roger to the murder? There are no witnesses. The police don't seem to have any useful fibers, hair or fingerprints. Roger and Loretta were at the murder scene, right?"

"Wrong!" Helen said. "Vera let the commissioner out the back door before Chrissy was killed, giving her an alibi for the time of the murder. Vera showed Roger out that way, too."

"Couldn't they sneak back in the front door?" Phil asked.

"Not with those bells jingling," Helen said. "We'd have heard them return. But there are no bells on the back door. Vera doesn't lock it during the day."

Helen stared at her coffee cup, as if the answer were floating in it. "That's it!" she said. "Either Roger or Loretta could have slipped in the back door to kill Chrissy. We wouldn't have heard them."

"You still have no evidence," Phil said.

The tea drinker in the black-and-white shirt stood up to leave. Something clicked in Helen's mind.

"Yes, we do. We have shoes!" Helen said.

CHAPTER 28

Helen dragged a dazed Phil out of the restaurant. "What's the rush?" he asked. "I didn't finish my coffee. What are you doing?"

"Praying Vera will still talk to me after yesterday." Helen speed-dialed Snapdragon's Second Thoughts on her cell phone.

"Quick!" she said to Phil. "Drive me to Snapdragon's while I call her. It's an emergency."

"Yes, Your Majesty," Phil said. He was clearly put out by her curt command.

"Vera, it's Helen. Are you still mad?" she said into her phone.

"No. I was going to call you," Vera said. "I'm sorry I flew off the handle. You're a good employee. I don't want to lose you."

"You don't have to apologize," Helen said. "You've been under a lot of pressure. I bet you're swamped with customers."

"I wish," Vera said. "You could fire a shotgun through this store and not hit anyone. The bad publicity is killing me."

"I think I can help," Helen said. "Did you throw out those polka-dot heels?"

"What? That pair I decided not to sell?" Vera asked. "They're around here somewhere."

"Why couldn't you sell them?" Helen asked.

"They were too worn," Vera said. "They had stains on the bows."

"What kind?" Helen asked.

"Dark blotches," Vera said. "Could be paint or chocolate."

"What about blood?" Helen asked.

"I can't tell what the hell is on those shoes," Vera said. "All I know is I can't sell them. We're going to have to change our shoe policy. Some woman tried on those heels barefoot. She had something icky on her foot and got it on the shoes. Now they're ruined. I thought I'd get a box of those footies like they use in shoe stores."

"Forget the footies," Helen said. "Find the shoes as fast as you can."

"Why?" Vera said. "I'm going to throw them out. If you want them, take them."

"No!" Helen screeched. Phil slammed on the brakes, then realized she was yelling at Vera. He shook his head and kept driving.

"Vera," Helen said slowly. "You must find those shoes. Better yet, I'll come in and find them for you. I'm at Eighth and Las Olas. I should be at the store in less than ten minutes. For heaven's sake, don't throw out them out. Those polka-dot heels are our salvation."

"You're not making any sense," Vera said.

"I'll explain when I get there," Helen said. She shut her phone.

"Helen, what are you up to?" Phil said. He narrowly missed two tourists who wandered into the street to see a wild parrot. "Why are you in such a hurry to find shoes?"

"They're the key to Chrissy's murder," Helen said. "Loretta Stranahan wore those polka-dot heels the day Chrissy was murdered."

"How do you know?" Phil asked.

"I remember when she came in the store. I thought her shoes were cute. She hit Chrissy on the head with that stupid porcelain pineapple and knocked her out. That's why Loretta couldn't wear her own shoes. Chrissy's blood had dripped on them. After Loretta stunned Chrissy, she hanged the poor woman with a scarf.

"Loretta left her bloody shoes behind and wore other heels out of the store," Helen said. "It's a shoplifter's trick. Now we're missing an expensive pair of Manolos in Loretta's size. I remembered them when I saw the woman in the black-and-white blouse at the restaurant. It was shoplifted."

"The woman at the restaurant had a shoplifted blouse?" Phil asked.

"No, she wore a blouse like one that was shoplifted from our store," Helen said. "That's what jogged my memory."

"Do they give Olympic medals for jumping to conclusions?" Phil asked. "I think you've won the gold."

"You aren't listening," Helen said. "A couple of days after Chrissy's murder, a customer found polka-dot heels with no tag on them." Helen was talking too fast, hoping to convince Phil. They were only two blocks from the store. "Vera says they have dark stains on them. I think those stains are Chrissy's blood. The shoes are size eights. I'm sure those are the heels Loretta wore into the shop."

"And they're the only size eights in the whole store?" Phil didn't bother hiding his sarcasm.

"The only ones with dark stains on them," Helen said. "If the police find Loretta's DNA and Chrissy's blood, that will prove the commissioner murdered Chrissy."

"That will prove Loretta wore the shoes," Phil said. "That makes her guilty of shoplifting, not murder."

"Listen to me!" Helen said. "I've solved the murder. I have the motive: Loretta was renting that horrible Palm Beach house to illegal immigrants. I have the opportunity: Loretta was in the back where Chrissy was killed, looking at the scarves, and Chrissy was hanged with one. Chrissy taunted the commissioner with the house of the seven toilets. Vera showed Loretta out the back door after she fought with Chrissy. Loretta waited a bit, then sneaked back into the store through the same door and killed Chrissy while she was in the dressing room."

"I don't like you going to that store alone," Phil said. "I'll go with you. I'll help look for the shoes."

"No, you won't," Helen said. "It's almost three o'clock. You have to go to work and get fired. I'll be fine."

"Loretta could walk into Snapdragon's any moment," Phil said. "She's already killed once."

"So? What's she going to do? Attack me? I'm a foot taller than Loretta. The killer could be Roger, too, and he can't hurt me. He's in jail."

"This isn't a joke," Phil said. "We don't know who killed Chrissy. If it's Loretta, she's already killed once, boldly and in daylight. She can do it again, and this time she'll find it easier. Promise me you won't go after Loretta by yourself."

"Phil, there is no one in the store now except Vera. I'm not confronting a killer. All I'm doing is looking for a pair of shoes that may have potential evidence. When I find them, I'll call Detective McNally and he'll get them. This isn't remotely dangerous."

Phil stopped at a red light in front of the Floridian. Helen opened her door and started to hop out. Phil grabbed her arm. "You almost got killed in June trying to investigate a murder on your own."

"I did not," Helen said. "I was with someone and I got bonked on the head. It was no big deal."

"Don't be stupid, Helen," Phil said. "Police officers do not go in without backup, and they're armed. I am not letting you out of this car unless you swear you won't tackle a killer without calling the police."

"Okay," Helen said, and started to leave the Jeep.

But Phil hung on to her arm. "I said, swear to me."

Helen held up her free hand. "I solemnly swear," she said. "Now let go of me, or the wedding is off."

The light turned green, and an impatient driver honked at them. Helen jumped out of the Jeep, waved good-bye and ran toward Snapdragon's.

Vera was behind the counter, looking more like her old self. Her hair was chicly smooth and her outfit this side of outrageous. She had a warm smile for Helen.

"Did you find the shoes?" Helen said.

"Not yet," Vera said. "But I've already searched the front of the store. They aren't here. They have to be in the back room, probably where I keep the extra shoe stock on the bottom shelf. You still haven't told me why those shoes are so important."

"Phil and I have narrowed the murder suspects down to two: Roger, who's in jail, and Loretta Stranahan," Helen said.

"So how do you prove it, Sherlock?" Vera asked.

"With those polka-dot heels, we might be able to nail Loretta," Helen said. "Chrissy knew the commissioner was making a fortune renting to illegal aliens, and taunted her with 'the house of the seven toilets.' Phil and I found that house in Palm Beach County. Loretta killed Chrissy, got the victim's blood on her shoes and left them behind. Loretta wore those Manolos out of the store. As soon as I find the shoes, call the police."

"Quiet!" Vera said. "Keep your voice down. She's here."

"Who?" Helen asked.

"Loretta. The commissioner is trying on suits in the dressing room," Vera said. "She might hear you. You know how sound carries in here. I don't want to lose a good customer."

"You'll lose her anyway when she goes to jail," Helen said.

"I said shut up!" Vera looked frantic. The doorbells jingled and a tourist began trying on necklaces. Helen knew Vera would have to watch the woman. Necklaces were easy to shoplift.

"I'll wait on this customer," Vera said. "You go in the back and look for those shoes. If Loretta needs anything else, get it for her, please."

Helen dropped her voice and said, "Then do me a favor, too. Call Detective McNally."

"I'll do no such thing," Vera said. "Not till you find those shoes."

Helen made her way quietly to the back, passing the ridiculous monkey lamps, the Limoges china, the Blue Willow ginger jars and other breakable knickknacks, then the racks of designer clothes and shoes. The light was on in the front dressing room. Commissioner Stranahan must be trying on suits.

Helen parted the curtain to the back room. To the left was Vera's desk, a landfill with a phone. On the right were floor-to-ceiling shelves. The top two overflowed with shirts, skirts, jeans and sweaters in boxes and bags. The middle section was loaded with lamps, china and more monkey monstrosities, from bookends to fruit bowls. The bottom shelves were a hodgepodge of shoes, unsorted by size, color or style.

Might as well get to work, Helen thought, though she didn't want to kneel on that hard concrete floor. She unearthed a throw pillow still in its plastic bag, used it to cushion her knees and started at the lower shelf section closest to the curtained entry.

Helen moved a heap of designer heels, cleared away a flock of flats and shoved aside a swarm of suede boots. After ten minutes, her back hurt. Helen sat up, stretched, then went back to six lace-up leather shoes, tangled together by their shoestrings. Helen was struggling to separate them when she heard a slight noise, followed by a whoosh and a thundering crash. Shards of pottery flew across the hard floor like shrapnel. A green lamp had exploded near her head.

Helen was startled to see Loretta standing over her, wielding a plaster bookend. She ducked, and it narrowly missed her head. At least it's a monkey bookend, Helen thought. She shrieked like an air-raid siren and hoped Vera could hear her up front. Loud noise could save her life. Helen scrambled to her feet and screamed louder, all the while looking for a weapon.

She threw a Waterford vase at Loretta. The commissioner dodged it expertly, and the crystal vase broke into a shower of diamonds.

Loretta was barefoot. She carefully sidestepped the broken glass. A too-tight skirt and a crookedly buttoned shirt should have hampered Loretta's movements. But she reached effortlessly for a white porcelain pineapple on a middle shelf.

"Oh, no," Helen said. "That's how you killed Chrissy. I'm not going to die by a damned pineapple."

"Some people are too nosy to live," Loretta said, and hurled the pineapple at Helen's head. She ducked and the pineapple smashed into her elbow. Pain shot up Helen's arm and left her dazed and dizzy. Between flashes of bright light and threatening darkness, she searched frantically for something else to throw.

There it was—a lamp with a turbaned monkey holding a pineapple. That made it triple ugly. Helen reached for it.

Loretta moved faster. She clobbered Helen on the shoulder with a green marble paperweight. Helen punched Loretta in the mouth and the politician landed on her rump. A second punch laid Loretta out flat on the floor.

Helen shrieked once more. This time, Vera materialized in the dim back room, clutching a polka-dot heel. The store owner stood over Loretta, aimed the spike heel at her eye and said, "Move and I'll drive this right into your brain."

"No! Don't!" Helen said. "You'll mess up the DNA." She was still holding the turbaned-monkey lamp over Loretta.

A man's silhouette filled the doorway. He was holding a gun.

"Drop it," Detective Richard McNally said. "Put your hands up and drop it right now."

Helen let the monkey monstrosity fall to the floor with a re-sounding crash.

CHAPTER 29

"Officer, arrest these women," Commissioner Loretta Stranahan said. "They attacked me."

Loretta brushed herself off and stood up amid the wreckage, her shoeless feet crunching broken pottery and plaster bits. She seemed to gain height and authority as she spoke. She looked Detective Richard McNally right in the eye when she lied to him.

"We attacked her?" Helen didn't try to hide her outrage. "She tried to kill me with the same weapon she used to stun poor Chrissy."

"I never touched that pineapple," Loretta said. "I wouldn't have such a hackneyed ornament in my home. She's lying, Officer." She looked regal, even barefoot and with a blouse buttoned crooked.

"No!" Helen said. "It's she who's—"

"Quiet, ladies," McNally said. His command silenced them.

"It's Detective McNally, Ms. Stranahan," he said. "Delighted to see you here. It saves me a trip. I was on my way to your office when Ms. Vera Salinda called my cell phone and said you were trying to kill Ms. Hawthorne at her store. I'd like to continue our discussion, Commissioner Loretta Stranahan, at Hendin Island police headquarters. Among other things, we can talk about how you knew Mrs. Martlet was hit on the head with a porcelain pineapple."

"I read it in the paper," Commissioner Stranahan said.

"That information was never released to the media," McNally said.

"It was on television," Stranahan said, her voice growing shrill.

Detective McNally said, "You have the right to remain silent. . . ." He continued the chant familiar to crooks and cop-show buffs. Loretta Stranahan grew silent.

Helen felt dizzy. She leaned against the cluttered shelves.

"Helen, are you sick?" Vera asked.

"I don't feel well," Helen said. "I need some caffeine."

"Can I make a pot of coffee?" Vera asked.

"I need statements from you and Ms. Hawthorne," McNally said. "We have coffee at the station."

"I have to close my store again?" Vera asked. "I helped you and I have to suffer?"

"I hope this will be the last time, Ms. Salinda. As soon as the uniforms arrive, they'll take you in police cruisers."

"If I go out of here with the police, I'll look like I'm being arrested," Vera said. "This will ruin me."

"You are not under arrest, Ms. Salinda," McNally said.

"Can I call my fiancé?" Helen asked. "He's getting fired this afternoon. I want to make sure he's all right. If I don't come home at my usual time, Phil will worry about me."

"He should," McNally said. "You can make one call in my presence. I don't want you contacting the media."

Helen dialed Phil's cell and got his voice mail. "Hi, Phil, the police have Loretta. They caught her while she was trying to kill me."

"I did not!" Loretta yelled.

"I'm okay," Helen said, trying to reassure the machine. "Well, I guess I would be or I wouldn't be making this call. I mean I'm not hurt, just a few bumps and scratches. I kept my promise. I didn't confront Loretta Stranahan alone. She snuck up on me. Vera called the police, and Detective McNally arrived in time."

Might as well give McNally a verbal pat on the back, she thought. It couldn't hurt.

Helen continued her cell phone soliloquy. "Vera and I have to go to the Hendin Island police headquarters to give our statements. I don't know when I'll be home. I'll call you when I'm free. What happened at work—did you get fired? Did you quit? Are you still employed? I hope you're not upset. I'd better go. I love you." She shut her cell phone, and wondered if her rambling message would ease Phil's fears or worsen them.

It was after seven o'clock that evening when Helen emerged from the Hendin Island headquarters. The air was cooler and the station's walled garden was a tempting rest spot. She sat down on a concrete bench near a pink hibiscus bush. Helen had to admit, for a police station, this one was a beauty.

Her first act was to call Phil. This time, he answered his phone. "Helen, what happened? Where are you?"

"I'm sitting in the garden at the Hendin Island station," Helen said. "I'm fine. Can you pick me up? Did you get fired?"

"I'll be right there," Phil said. "No, I didn't get fired. I quit. They wanted me to go to Cancún to bring home that young woman and I walked out. We can talk about it when I see you. I'll be there in ten minutes." Helen shut her phone.

Vera staggered out of the station, looking ragged. The skin under her eyes seemed bruised and her face was pale. She sat down on
the concrete bench next to Helen.

"You arrived at the right time," Helen said. "Where did you get
that polka-dot heel?"

"In the section you were about to search," Vera said. "I think
they're going to book the commissioner. I heard someone in the
hall say Loretta won't talk until her lawyer arrives. He's on his way,
but he was over in Fort Myers."

"That's more than a hundred miles away," Helen said.

"Right. He's supposed to get here in another hour. It's going to
be a long night for Detective McNally. Serves him right for closing
my store. I was trying to be a good citizen."

"Do you want me at the store tomorrow, Citizen Salinda?"
Helen said.

Vera managed a grin. "No, I'm taking a couple days' vacation.
This week is wrecked. I need to decide if I want to save my business or sell it. Take some time off until I call you, Helen. I'll pay
you, if you want."

"No need," Helen said, and instantly regretted her grand ges-
ture. "I think I broke at least a week's pay in lamps and bookends."

"You definitely killed half that pair of monkey lamps," Vera said.

"I'm sorry," Helen said. "But it was the closest lamp. And it was
ugly."

"You're not sorry," Vera said. "You hated that lamp. And it's not
ugly. It's amusing. You don't seem to get that decorating concept.
But I forgive you. You solved the murder. Now the cops will leave
me alone and stay out of my store."

Vera stood up, shouldered her fashionably huge purse and said,
"I'm exhausted. Do you want a ride home?"

"Thanks," Helen said. "I've already called Phil. He should be picking me up any minute." Her cell phone rang, and she said, "That may be him now." She waved good-bye to Vera as she checked her phone's LCD display. It had a St. Louis area code.

"Helen! Helen!" Her sister was whispering into the phone. A shrieking whisper, if such a thing was possible. Kathy sounded terrified.

"What's wrong?" Helen asked. "Is it Tom? The kids?"

"It's Tommy Junior." Kathy started sobbing. "They found out. I—he—he's going to—"

"Kathy!" Helen said sharply. She went into older-sister mode. "Calm down. Take a deep breath, then tell me. I can't help if you don't tell me what happened. Where are you?"

"In my van, driving around," Kathy said. "I'm on Manchester Road."

"Pull into a parking lot. You shouldn't be driving when you're upset."

There was a short silence. Then Kathy said, "I'm parked in a supermarket lot. I have to get back soon. Tom took the kids to the library and they'll be home any minute."

"Why are you whispering if you're alone?" Helen asked.

"It sounds worse if I say it out loud," Kathy said. "I got that phone call, panicked and ran. I had to get out of the house. I felt like it was going to smother me."

"Tell me what's going on," Helen begged.

"Someone said I had to bring five thousand dollars in a plastic grocery bag and leave the money on the steps of the new church hall," Kathy said.

"And if you don't?" Helen asked.

"Then the new church hall will develop a sudden, terrible problem with its foundation," Kathy said. "The caller knew. He knew what we did."

Kathy sounded like she would start sobbing again.

"When do you have to have the money?" Helen asked, hoping to hear the whole story.

"He said I had two days. But where am I going to get that kind of money? I could have used the cash Mom left in the cookie jar, but I've already deposited it in the kids' college account. Tom will notice if it's missing."

"I have money," Helen said. "I still have that three hundred thousand. I'll get five thousand dollars and FedEx it to you."

"But if we pay him once, we'll have to pay him again," Kathy said.

"This will buy us some time," Helen said. "Some very expensive time, but Tommy is worth it. Give the blackmailer the money. The next time he calls and makes a demand, I'll fly to St. Louis and stake out the drop-off site."

"What reason will you have to come to St. Louis?" Kathy asked. "Won't Phil get suspicious if you suddenly want to come home?"

"I still have the IRS problem to straighten out," Helen said. "And I'll want to visit my family. What do we know about this blackmailer? What did he sound like?"

"I don't even know if it was a man. I just said 'he.' The person used one of those voice-changer thingies and sounded like Darth Vader," Kathy said. "He called our home, so he doesn't have my cell number. I tried to use the star sixty-nine function on our landline to see where the call originated, but the number was blocked. We don't know anything."

"Yes, we do," Helen said. "We know he wasn't an honest citizen, or he would have called the police when he saw us burying—"

She heard the station door slam. A uniformed officer ambled down the walk. Helen put on her best straight-arrow smile until he went to his car.

"Helen, are you there?" Kathy asked.

"Sorry, someone was going by," Helen said. "Your caller didn't tell the police when he saw us doing something he thought looked suspicious. Why didn't he? That tells us something. Also, he didn't call your cell. He called your home. He knows where you live, but he's not close enough to have your cell phone number. Maybe the blackmailer is that guy who was meeting his girlfriend on the church lot—what was his name?"

"Horndog Hal," Kathy said. "He needs money, all right. He has four kids, a wife and a mistress. I'd never give him my cell phone number. The caller could have been old Mrs. Kiley, my next-door neighbor, but she doesn't even have a computer. I can't see her getting a voice changer at RadioShack. The Kerchers in back of us were on vacation. And the Cooks on the other side—"

"Kathy, we'll worry about this later," Helen said. "I'll FedEx you the money tomorrow. And don't worry. I told you before: I'll go to jail before I let Tommy get dragged into this, and I mean it. Call me if you hear any more from the blackmailer."

"Thanks, Sis," Kathy said, and hung up.

The silence seemed shattering after her sister's emotional call. Helen cursed Rob and the day she'd met him. He couldn't die when she wanted him to. Now he couldn't even stay buried. That worthless twit was not going to ruin her nephew's life.

The sound of a vehicle interrupted her thoughts. It was Phil. Helen watched her fiancé leap out of the Jeep, his silver hair glowing in the setting sun. Her knight in blue denim.

"Helen," he said, folding her into his arms. "You're free."

She clung to him. "Right," Helen said. "I'm free."

CHAPTER 30

The black limo pulled up to the Coronado Tropic Apartments as night was falling. It was three days since Commissioner Stranahan was arrested for the murder of Christine Martlet. The limo was as long as the apartments' parking lot. A driver with bulging muscles and a baby face carried a vase of two dozen white roses and a gift basket the size of a shrub decked with white ribbons. He was nearly hidden behind the gifts.

Margery met the driver at the gate, her eggplant caftan a graceful sail in the evening breeze.

"I have a delivery for Miss Helen Hawthorne," the driver said.

"She's sitting out by the pool with her boy toy," Margery said. "Come in."

The driver carried his gifts to the umbrella table, where Helen and Phil were holding hands. Helen was drinking box wine. Phil had a beer and those orange chips. Peggy was stretched on a chaise with Pete the parrot on her shoulder and a glass of wine in one hand.

"Miss Hawthorne?" the driver asked.

"Here," Helen said.

The driver set the vase and the gift basket on the table, then stood before her like a high school student reciting a lesson. His dishwater blond hair stuck up in a cowlick. "Mr. Daniel Martlet presents his compliments and his thanks for your help in solving his wife's er . . ."

The driver skidded to a stop, backed up and tried again. "Mr. Daniel Martlet presents his compliments and thanks you for your help. He hopes you will enjoy these gifts as a token of his esteem." The driver bowed his way out of the backyard.

"This is so romantic," Peggy said. "It's like a prince sent you a gift."

"Good boy!" said Pete.

"Well, don't keep us commoners waiting," Margery said. "Open it."

Helen held the opulent bouquet of roses like a beauty queen and inhaled its scent. "Mmm," she said. "These smell like real flowers, not hothouse funeral roses."

"Take time to smell the flowers some other day," Margery said. "Show us your loot."

Helen winked at Phil, pleased that Margery was her sassy self again. She pulled the ribbons and cellophane off the basket. Inside were Krug Grand Cuvée champagne, pâté, Carr's water crackers, pistachios, clusters of tiny red grapes, apples, pears and cheddar.

"I'd say he was grateful," Margery said. "The man sent you almost two hundred bucks' worth of champagne. That's pretty high esteem."

"It's the thought that counts," Helen said.

"Then I like the way Danny the developer thinks," Phil said, abandoning his beer and orange chips.

"The envelope, please," Margery said, and handed it to Helen.

Helen opened the red wax seal on the envelope. The stationery was thick and expensive, suitable for edicts and declarations of war. Danny's writing was bold and black. " 'Thank you,' " Helen read. " 'I hope this will help compensate you for your trouble.' "

Helen's eyes widened in surprise and she nearly dropped the letter. "Phil! This is a check for ten thousand dollars."

"Let's break out the champagne and celebrate," Phil said.

"Let's save it for our wedding toast," Helen said.

"Let's do both," Phil said. "We can have the wedding toast tonight. It's been three days since we got our marriage license. We can get married now. That is, if Margery agrees. Madam Preacher, will you do the honors?"

"I thought you'd never ask," Margery said. "I'm not getting any younger, you know. Give me time to change into my minister's robe. A preacher of my standing deserves respect."

Margery had been ordained by mail for a dollar in the Universal Life Church. She could perform weddings in a slew of jurisdictions. Reverend Margery bought her purple robe on eBay. She claimed it had belonged to a Baptist choir singer, so at least her robe had been in a church.

"Wait! I don't have a dress," Helen said.

"What about your wedding dress?" Phil asked.

"I couldn't bear to look at it after that disaster in June," Helen said. "I sold it at Snapdragon's."

"You've already had two wedding dresses," Margery said. "And one and a half marriages. Isn't that enough?"

"Everyone ignores the groom's wishes in a wedding," Helen said. "What would you like me to wear? Name your favorite outfit."

"The tight black dress with the slit up the side," Phil said.

"Black isn't bridal," Helen said. "It might be bad luck."

"Oh, for heaven's sake," Peggy said. "After what happened at the last ceremony, you're worried about bad luck?"

"Hello!" Pete said.

"Black looks a lot sexier than white on a grown woman," Margery said. "You didn't wear the black dress to your mother's funeral, did you?"

"No," Helen said.

"Then wear it now. If that man offered to marry me, I'd grab him in a heartbeat."

"What about me?" Phil asked. "What should I wear? What's your favorite?"

Helen kissed him and said, "Wear your blue shirt with the sleeves rolled up and your blue jeans. Isn't that what you had on when I first met you?"

"As I recall, you were topless," Phil said.

That was not a moment Helen wanted to remember. "I was working on a case," she said. "And I held up two soda bottles, so I wasn't completely bare."

"They were liter bottles, too," Phil said.

"Quit talking about her jugs," Margery said.

"Nice talk from an ordained minister," Phil said.

"I meant her soda bottles. Are you two going to get married or talk all night?" Margery said. "It's going on nine o'clock."

"Wait! Where are you getting married?" Peggy asked.

"The beach!" Helen and Phil said together.

"Finally, you agree on something," Margery said.

Thunder rumbled in the distance. The sky was black and starless. Helen suddenly realized their wedding could be rained out.

"I don't want the word 'obey' in my wedding vows," Helen said. "Love and honor, definitely, but I'm not obeying."

"Me, either," Phil said. "This is a marriage of equals."

More thunder. Lightning flashed to the east. "We'd better hurry, before we're struck by lightning," Margery said.

"Can I be your bridesmaid again?" Peggy asked.

"As long as you bring Pete," Helen said. "I have to get dressed and Margery has to put on her robe."

"Hurry, will you?" Margery said. "A storm is coming in."

They heard a fluttery voice say, "Hello? Margery? Helen, dear, are you there?"

It was Elsie, Margery's friend. "I wanted to show you my new outfit," she said.

Elsie had the heart of a teenager trapped in the body of a seventy-eight-year-old woman. When it came to her clothes, she was all heart. The results were startling. Elsie was some sixty years older than the teen fashion models she admired and maybe a hundred pounds heavier. The rising wind blew her fluffy hair flat, but Helen could see it was dyed orange red.

"Plaid is very big this year," Elsie said. "What do you think?" She attempted a twirl. Elsie's outfit looked like a girls' school uniform gone wild: Red plaid leggings covered her saddlebag thighs and varicose veins. The buttons strained on a long-tailed white shirt. The short Black Watch plaid jacket looked more like shoulder pads with sleeves. High-heeled plaid booties completed the ensemble.

Phil gulped.

"Amazing," Helen said truthfully. "Phil and I are getting married on the beach tonight. We just decided. Would you like to join us?"

"How exciting," Elsie said. "It's like an elopement. I have something for you in my car. I'll be right back."

Elsie tottered back in her towering booties with a covered casserole and a Tupperware cake holder. "I heard about your mother's death, dear. I'm so sorry. I was taught to bring food to people in mourning. I hope you don't mind. This is beef bourguignonne and a coconut cake. It's chocolate with white icing."

"Our wedding feast," Phil said, and kissed Elsie's rouged cheek. "Thank you, darlin'."

Margery appeared in her purple satin minister's robe, puffing on a Marlboro. She looked more like the devil's familiar than a minister of God. Maybe it was the trail of smoke. Or the lightning and thunder flashing behind her.

"We're going to get drenched if we don't move," Margery said. "My one-buck ordination didn't include the power to stop thunderstorms."

Peggy, Phil and Helen hurried to their apartments to change.

Thumbs the cat met Helen at the door and demanded dinner. "Okay, buddy," she said. "I'll feed you now." She quickly poured dried food into his bowl, then pulled the tab on a can of tuna. "Your pal Phil is about to become a permanent member of the household," she said. "You can celebrate, too."

Thumbs ignored her while he gobbled his wedding feast.

Helen put on fresh makeup, smoothed her hair, then changed into her black dress and ankle-strap shoes. She stepped outside her apartment and shut the door.

Peggy handed Helen the fragrant white bouquet, lighter now by three roses. "I took out one for each bridesmaid and made a boutonniere for Phil," she said. "Let me take your picture. You look sensational. When these pictures get out, black-and-white weddings will be all the rage."

"They already are," Helen said.

"I mean the bride wearing black, not the bridesmaids."

"My sister and her family will love the photos," Helen said. "I wish they were here."

But then she remembered Rob, the ex-husband she'd tried so

hard to forget these last three days. She could almost see him grin-
ning at her, eerie and insolent in the oncoming storm.

"You make such a lovely bride," Elsie said, and sighed. She
clutched her single white rose.

Phil raised his eyebrows when he saw Helen with her black
dress and white roses. "Killer," he said. "I'm shot through the
heart."

She pinned his boutonniere on his shirt and kissed him.

Peggy came out wearing a fresh green blouse, with Pete on her
shoulder as a feathered accessory. The little bird tucked his head
down to keep from blowing away.

"I put the champagne on to chill," Peggy said, "and took the
food inside until we return. Where are we going?"

"The beach at the foot of Las Olas on A1A," Phil said. "There's
a public parking lot. We'll meet there and walk across the street to
the beach. Helen and I can go in my Jeep."

"Peggy, you and Elsie can ride with me," Margery said.

Las Olas was one long traffic jam filled with revelers. Drunks
staggered between the stopped cars. Couples kissed on street cor-
ners. When the Jeep passed Snapdragon's Second Thoughts, Helen
began to have second thoughts of her own. The traffic jam broke
up at the Hendin Island turnoff and Phil drove faster toward the
beach. Helen could see Margery's car behind them. Peggy waved
out the front window and Phil honked back. Thunder boomed.

Phil's Jeep reached the parking lot first. He found a spot near
the entrance. Margery circled, looking for a place to park.

More thunder. Lightning ripped across the sky. The clouds were
black and pregnant with rain. Helen felt a stab of fear. My marriage
to Rob was a mistake, she thought, and I was too dumb to know
it. Phil is a good man, but I'm dragging him into blackmail and a
possible murder trial. I could wind up in jail. Is that fair to him?

Should I say something? Yes. He needs to know. I have to tell Phil. I have to be an honest woman. If he doesn't want to marry me, so be it.

The wind slammed her sideways, blowing her dark hair across her face like a veil. More thunder. She saw jagged lightning strike the ocean.

"Phil," Helen said. "This wedding—"

"Is exactly the way to get married," Phil said. "We have our friends, we have food, we have flowers and champagne. What's the matter? Are you worried?"

"Yes," Helen said. "It's a big step. What if things go wrong? What if Rob comes back and causes trouble?"

"What if my ex returns?" Phil said. "Kendra has a genius for screwing things up."

He kissed Helen and said, "There are no guarantees. I know that. So do you. I want you for better or worse."

"But it could get bad," Helen said. "Chaos seems to follow me around. I could drag you into it."

"That's why I love you," Phil said. He kissed her harder, as if he could make her fear go away.

"Excuse me," Margery said. "May I marry you first before you consummate the wedding?"

The glow of Margery's cigarette was the beacon that guided the party to the beach. The women carefully picked their way across the sand in high heels.

Helen held on to Phil and her huge bridal bouquet as her heels sank into the sand. She could see the bright lights of a cruise ship on the black water, but the night seemed endlessly dark.

"Let's get started," Margery said. "Let me ask the question that caused so much trouble last time. Does anyone know any reason why this man and woman should not be joined in marriage?"

Smoke rose over Margery's gray hair and was carried away by the wind. They heard the soothing surf and the growl of thunder.

Margery cleared her throat and said, "Do you, Helen Hawthorne, take this man to be your lawfully wedded husband, for richer, for poorer, in sickness and in health, till death parts you?"

Helen felt the panic stab her heart. Do I? she thought. Do I want to tie the man I love to my troubles?

The moon slid out from behind the dark clouds, and the beach was flooded with light.

"Look," Elsie said. "You have a silver lining."

I have to believe that, Helen thought. I love him. I need him. I've been alone too long. And he loves and needs me. I hope we'll have some good times before everything crashes in on us.

"Helen?" Margery said. "Do you want to get married or not?"

"Yes!" Helen said. "I mean, I do. I really do."

"Me, too," Phil said.

"I now pronounce you man and wife," Margery said. "At last."

CHAPTER 31

The wedding reception was lit by moonglow and bug lights, with flashes of distant lightning.

There was no receiving line, no best man making tasteless toasts, no garter to throw or bouquet to toss. An intrusive videographer did not command the couple to pose. Peggy took photos for Helen and Phil, then put her camera away.

The wedding feast was on a long folding table by the pool. The bridal bouquet was once more in its vase, doing double duty as the centerpiece. The bride and groom held hands and kissed. The guests laughed often.

None of them paid lip service to their diets. Boring excuses such as, "I'd eat that, but it's so fattening," were forgotten. The pâté, crackers and fruit were quickly demolished. Even Pete was allowed a single cracker. The pudgy parrot's perpetual diet had a one-night reprieve.

Phil polished off the last of Elsie's beef bourguignonne. Helen cut the coconut cake and served her guests generous slices.

Phil refilled the wineglasses for yet another round of toasts.

They'd drunk the champagne and were now working on the box wine.

"These are two words I've wanted to say for a long time: my wife," Phil said. "I will love you forever. I'm so glad you finally said yes." He gave Helen a lingering kiss as the wedding party applauded.

"Only a man as good as Phil could persuade me to marry again," Helen said, raising her glass. "To my husband."

"That's so sweet," Elsie said, wiping her eyes.

"And this toast is for Elsie," Helen said. "A bridesmaid at last. It's never too late to get your wish."

They saluted Elsie.

"Thank you, dear," Elsie said, patting Helen's hand. "I had to wait sixty years to be a bridesmaid, but I must say, it was worth it. I married at eighteen and I was pregnant with my Milton the summer when my friends married. In those days you couldn't have a pregnant maid of honor. It wasn't done. We missed so much fun by worrying about what people thought and it was all so silly. I'm glad I'm free of those self-imposed rules now. Milton says my clothes aren't appropriate for my age, but I think age is all in your mind."

"You've made the world a more colorful place," Phil said, and raised his glass again.

"This last-minute wedding is the way to tie the knot," Peggy said. "I've been to too many where the bride is frazzled and the groom is hungover. The couple is so tired after months of planning their wedding, they don't enjoy it. You both look relaxed and happy."

"Why not?" Helen said. "Our friends did all the work." She helped herself to another piece of coconut cake. "Terrific cake, Elsie."

"Thank you, Helen, dear," Elsie said. "It's good to see a young woman with an appetite. Was that your name in a newspaper story about the arrest of that crooked county commissioner? The newspaper said she attacked you."

"It did," Helen said, "and she did."

"My wife forgot to mention that she found the evidence that will put Loretta behind bars," Phil said proudly. "There. I said it officially. My wife." He kissed Helen again.

"Loretta hasn't been convicted yet," Helen said. "And my husband left out his own part." It felt good to use the H-word without hating the man connected to it. "Phil tracked down the slum house where Loretta was renting rooms to illegal immigrants."

"Danny the developer's detective did that, too," Phil said.

"But Danny didn't use his knowledge for good," Helen said. "He blackmailed the commissioner."

"Whoa," Margery said. "You lost me. I thought Loretta Stranahan was against Danny's Orchid House development."

"She was," Phil said. "But once the police arrested her for murder, she couldn't wait to rat out Daniel Martlet. She said he was blackmailing her in case he needed her vote on future Orchid House changes."

"Did the commissioner give him money?" Peggy asked.

"No, Danny wasn't after money. He has enough votes to get the proposal passed. She could oppose him publicly until her reelection. Then, if Danny needed her vote, he had it. She was his insurance policy."

"Awk," Pete said.

"How could she do that?" Peggy asked.

"Happens all the time," Margery said. "I know I sound cynical, but for more than fifty years, I've been watching Florida politicians spin like weather vanes in a hurricane. First, they oppose all development as evil. That gets them elected. Once they safely have their seats, they have a sudden conversion. Now development is good. It will bring more tourists and more jobs. In these troubled times, they say, Florida can't afford to lose this opportunity. Trust me, the times are always troubled. Nothing has changed in half a century."

"And the politicians get away with it?" Peggy asked.

"Almost always," Margery said. "If the bums get thrown out of office, they find a safe, salaried berth with the developer or his friends. Either way, they win and we, the people, lose."

"Loretta will be the exception," Helen said. "She's been caught, thanks to Phil, who found the house of the seven toilets."

"I think I read that book when I was a little girl," Elsie said, slightly tipsy from so many toasts.

"Probably not," Phil said. "There was nothing charming about this house. Every room, even the garage, was rented to illegal immigrants for outrageous prices. Every room had a toilet. And it was my wife"—he stopped to savor that word—"who counted those toilets."

"We know she's a talented toilet counter," Margery said. "But can we get to the end of this story before your golden wedding anniversary? You and Helen can split the credit for finding the house of the seven toilets. What happened next?"

"Loretta got arrested," Helen said. "Should we tell you about that?"

"Yes, dear," Elsie said. Her voice was gentler than Margery's. "We're anxious to know, if you don't mind discussing murder at your wedding."

"Marriage and murder go hand in hand," Margery said. Cigarette smoke formed a crown around her head.

"A customer at Snapdragon's showed me a pair of polka-dot heels that didn't have a price tag," Helen said. "I put them aside so Vera, the owner, could see them. Vera said the shoes were too damaged to sell and forgot them. Three days ago, I had a brainstorm. I remembered Commissioner Stranahan was in the store when Chrissy was murdered—and she wore polka-dot heels.

"I called Vera and asked her why the shoes couldn't be sold. She said they had dark spots on the polka-dot bows. I ran over to the store—actually Phil drove me—and told Vera we had to find those shoes. Loretta was in the store and heard me. When I was searching shelves in the back room, she tried to kill me with a porcelain pineapple. I hate pineapples."

"For good reason," Phil said loyally.

"Vera called the police when Loretta attacked me," Helen said. "Detective McNally came in just in time, and stopped the fight. Loretta was arrested and the police took the polka-dot heels. They've already confirmed that it was Chrissy's blood type on the bows. The police lab is still running DNA tests to see if it's really Chrissy's blood and if Loretta actually wore the shoes, but they have backup evidence."

"If Loretta left her polka-dot heels behind at Snapdragon's," Peggy said, "did she walk out of the store barefoot?"

"No, she shoplifted a pair of eight-hundred-forty-five-dollar Manolos," Helen said. "We were selling them for about a quarter of that price. Vera noticed the shoes were missing later. I think the theft upset Vera more than Chrissy's murder. She'll never get the shoes back to sell, so Vera is out a couple hundred bucks. The police searched Loretta's home and found the shoplifted Manolos. The police are fairly sure Commissioner Stranahan wore them after she killed Chrissy, and they'll have proof soon. The stolen Manolos had blood on them, too, and it's Chrissy's type."

"I'm a little confused by all these shoes, dear," Elsie said. "Or maybe it's the champagne." Her kind eyes were slightly glazed.

"Chrissy had accused Loretta of having an affair with her husband, Danny the developer," Helen said, as if she were teaching a class. "Chrissy taunted Loretta and said she knew about the house of the seven toilets. Loretta panicked. Renting to illegal immigrants and owning slum property in Palm Beach County would kill her career."

"So she killed Chrissy instead," Elsie said, shaking her head. "So foolish and wasteful."

"She didn't think it through," Helen said. "Loretta slammed Chrissy on the head with that heavy pineapple knickknack. The blow stunned her and made her head bleed. Then Loretta hung poor Chrissy with a silk scarf. The commissioner noticed the blood on her polka-dot heels, stole the Manolos and wore them out. But Chrissy's blood dripped on the tile floor, and Loretta got blood on her sole."

"Blood on her soul," Peggy said. "That's very poetic."

"Awk!" Pete said.

"It was blood on her shoe sole," Helen said. "The left one. The police also have a usable fingerprint now. The forensics lab used Super Glue fuming and a dye stain to find a print Loretta left on the pineapple. The fingerprint was the size of a pinkie nail, but it's big enough to have seven points. That counts as a valid ID."

"Your prints were on that pineapple, too," Phil said.

"They were," Helen said. "But my prints were consistent with someone holding it for dusting. Loretta gripped it differently, the way you would to hit someone."

"What made you suddenly remember the shoes?" Peggy asked.

"I was in a restaurant and saw a woman wearing a blouse. It looked like one that had been shoplifted from our store. The thief left her cheap blouse behind and took the expensive one. That's when I realized Loretta had worn another pair of shoes out of Snapdragon's. It's an old shoplifter's technique. Too bad I told my boss while Loretta was in the store. She attacked me and broke a lot of merchandise."

"But you weren't hurt this time, were you?" Peggy asked.

"A few bruises," Helen said. She tried to shrug, but her shoulder still ached.

"I've never attended a wedding where the bride and groom talked about murder," Elsie said. "It's nice not to have to compare caterers and wedding presents."

"There's no chance Loretta will go free, is there?" Peggy said. "Could she buy a 'dream team' lawyer?"

"Can't afford one," Phil said. "Palm Beach County took her money machine. They made Loretta pay big-time for damaging the county's reputation. Palm Beach County did not appreciate a Broward County commissioner creating slum housing on their turf.

"Commentators made fun of Palm Beach County's motto, 'The best of everything,' when the story went nationwide. The county penalized her to the full extent of the law. The inspectors found twelve hundred seventeen code violations, then gave Loretta a week to fix them."

"That was impossible," Helen said. "I saw those houses. There's no way they could be fixed in a week. Or even a year."

"Exactly," Phil said. "Loretta was fined two hundred fifty dollars per violation. Don't ask me how much that came to."

"It's $304,250," Helen said, proud she could still multiply after uncounted drinks.

"Loretta could have appealed the decision," Phil said, "but by then she was charged with murder and denied bail."

"Will she fix up the properties while she's in jail?" Peggy asked.

"I doubt it," Phil said. "I think Palm Beach County will impose liens on the two properties, then foreclose and raze them."

"What happened to those poor illegals?" Peggy asked.

"They're in the wind," Phil said. "When the inspectors showed up, both houses were empty. Loretta's illegal fortune will be spent on legal fees. There's a certain justice in that."

"And Loretta will go to prison," Elsie said. "I like happy endings." Her smile had a tipsy sweetness.

Peggy stifled a small yawn. Pete was sleeping with his head tucked under his wing.

Margery yawned, too. "It's two in the morning," she said. "Isn't it time for you to start living happily ever after?"

CHAPTER 32

The storm clouds were long gone. The afternoon sun was beating down on the umbrella table when Helen and Phil strolled out of Phil's apartment, with the smiling, insufferable smugness of the sexually satisfied. Helen looked glowing, but slightly worn. Phil was whistling.

Margery sat at the table, smoking a cigarette and drinking coffee. She grinned at the newlyweds. "Good morning. Or should I say good afternoon? How's marriage?"

"Fine," Phil said.

Helen glared at her chipper husband and shaded her eyes from the brilliant sun. "If you loved me, you'd have a hangover, too," she said. Her voice was a groan from a distant tomb.

Helen sat down carefully, next to her bridal bouquet, which was still in the vase on the umbrella table. Those roses got around. Today, they were surrounded by a basket of muffins, butter, jam and a platter of fresh fruit. In the center was a giant pineapple.

Helen looked at the pineapple and winced.

"At least it's a real pineapple," she said, "and not one of those freaking porcelain things."

"My wife means thank you for the lovely breakfast, especially the fresh fruit," Phil said, picking up a blueberry muffin. "This breakfast is so thoughtful. You've also cleaned up after the wedding feast."

"Wasn't much left to clean up," Margery said. "We ate and drank everything. It took Elsie, Peggy and me maybe fifteen minutes. Have you two come to give notice on your rentals?"

Helen looked surprised. "No. We don't want to leave. The Coronado is our home. The tax lawyer says we shouldn't change our standard of living until my IRS problem is fixed, but we may not want to move away even then. We'd like to keep renting the way we always have, if that's okay with you."

"How are you going to pay the rent on two apartments?" Margery asked. "Phil's quit work and you're not sure you're going back to Snapdragon's. This is a bad time to be looking for one job, much less two."

"I don't want another job," Phil said. "I want to start my own detective agency. Helen can be my partner at the agency. Or she can type, file and answer phones."

"You want me to be your secretary?" Helen said. She managed to muster some outrage.

"You've got great legs," Phil said innocently.

Helen stared at him. "I was joking," he said. "Except about the legs.

"Margery, Helen and I talked about this. She hasn't made up her mind yet. She can work with me. Or for me. She can keep on working dead-end jobs. She can get a job as a CPA again. It's up to her. She can be anything she wants. Our legal problems are nearly solved. Rob is no longer a threat."

"I've made up my mind about one thing," Helen said. "I will never work as a corporate number cruncher again."

"You don't have to, sweetheart," Phil said. He kissed her. "Margery, we're not making any major decisions until after the honeymoon."

"And when is that?" Margery asked.

"It starts today," he said. "We'll be gone for a week. We'd like to leave for the Keys. Sorry for the short notice."

"Does that mean I'll have to watch that damned cat while you're gone?" Margery blew an angry cloud of smoke.

"Just for a week," Helen said. "Please?"

"I hate cats, but I'll do it. Where are you going for your honeymoon?"

"We want to go back to Key Largo," Phil said. "We got married on the spur of the moment and we need a little time before we have to make serious choices. Thanks to Danny the developer, we have a little money."

"We want to spend half of Danny's ten thousand on the honeymoon, and the rest on starting up Phil's detective agency," Helen said. She thought it fair to pay for their honeymoon, since Phil had paid for her mother's return home.

"Since I quit work and the agency didn't give me any separation money," Phil said, "I don't have to worry about a no-compete clause."

"Where are you going to have your office?" Margery asked.

"Fort Lauderdale," Phil said.

"Rent's expensive," Margery said. "Even in an economic downturn."

"I've got a little saved," Phil said.

"Apartment 2C is empty," Margery said. "You could rent it for your office."

"Could I afford the rent on a third apartment here?" Phil said.

"I don't know," Margery said. "Can you come up with a dollar a month?"

Phil was shocked into silence.

"You'd be doing me a favor if you rented 2C for your office," Margery said. "But that one-dollar rent is not forever. Once you start making money, you can expect a substantial increase."

"That's very generous," Phil said. "I can't guarantee I'll make a go of the agency."

"You'll be helping me, whether your business succeeds or not," Margery said. "I'll have a hard time renting that apartment now. By rights, I have to tell the next tenant what happened to Mark and Jordan and it's not a pretty story: A young woman was murdered there and a man went to prison for killing his lover."

Helen sat up, startled. Margery had finally accepted that Mark was guilty. The landlady's recovery was complete.

Margery was still talking about Phil's new office. "If I can say my last tenant was a detective agency—even a failed detective agency—well, that puts a different spin on things. So will you do it?"

"Are you kidding?" Phil said.

"You don't like the deal?" Margery said.

"No, no, it's a great apartment," Phil said. "It's very romantic-looking. I mean, despite what happened there. Apartment 2C has style. I can see Bogie sitting there in a sleeveless shirt, drinking bourbon out of a water glass, killing the big hurt."

"You got your movies mixed, sweetheart," Margery said. "But I get the picture. Do you want the deal or not?"

"Yes, yes. Of course." Phil pulled three dollars out of his wallet and slapped them on the table. "Here's your first and last month's rent, plus another month for a security deposit."

Margery raised her coffee cup. "To the new 2C. May this new venture break the curse."

They clinked coffee cups.

EPILOGUE

While Helen and Phil were on their honeymoon, Vera Salinda reopened Snapdragon's Second Thoughts. Now that Christine Martlet's murder was solved and the killer was caught, the store was flooded with people. Some were curious, but many were customers. Business was brisk. Vera asked her sister in Plantation to work there full-time.

Vera sent Helen and Phil a wedding present: a lamp with a turbaned monkey holding a pineapple.

Peggy sold all her rejected aprons at Vera's store and earned $250. That was one-quarter of what she'd spent on her ill-fated work-at-home venture. Vera asked Peggy to make more aprons, but Peggy politely refused. She was busy with her full-time job. She spent the $250 on lottery tickets.

Loretta Stranahan was forced to resign from the Broward County Board of County Commissioners. The other commissioners competed for media time to denounce Danny Martlet's behind-the-scenes manipulation of the Orchid House project. They unanimously voted down the Orchid House project. Martlet was forced to declare bankruptcy. The Fort Lauderdale beach was safe.

Until the next developer came along.

The trial of former commissioner Loretta Stranahan was a Court TV sensation. One commentator praised the defendant's suits as "sincere," but they failed to impress the judge or the jury. Nobody believed her lawyer's argument that some unknown person, for reasons unknown, slipped in and hanged Chrissy Martlet. Too much evidence said Loretta did it.

Loretta Stranahan was convicted of second-degree murder in the death of Christine Martlet. Under the tough Florida sentencing laws, she will serve at least twenty years in prison. She appealed the verdict, but her funds were limited after Palm Beach County seized her rental property and razed it.

But that was months in the future.

For the rest of August, Helen and Phil stayed in an ocean-view suite in a Key Largo hotel. The weather was unusually stormy, but the newlyweds didn't care. They lived off room service, made love and watched the black clouds rushing over the water. Lightning flashed and thunder rattled the windows. Helen and Phil thought the storms were created for their entertainment.

Some nights, the black clouds cleared and the moonglow lit the dark water. Then Helen would wake up, walk alone on the hotel balcony and try to believe in that silver lining.